TO OUR GRAVES

To Our Graves

A Novel

Paul Nicholas Mason

Library and Archives Canada Cataloguing in Publication

Title: To our graves : a novel / Paul Nicholas Mason.

Names: Mason, Paul Nicholas, author.

Identifiers: Canadiana (print) 20230577725 | Canadiana (ebook) 20230577733 |
ISBN 9781989689615 (softcover) | ISBN 9781989689653 (EPUB)

Subjects: LCGFT: Detective and mystery fiction. | LCGFT: Novels.

Classification: LCC PS8576.A85955 T62 2024 | DDC C813/.54—dc23

Printed and bound in Canada on 100% recycled paper.

Now Or Never Publishing
901, 163 Street
Surrey, British Columbia
Canada V4A 9T8

nonpublishing.com
Fighting Words.

We gratefully acknowledge the support of the Canada Council for the Arts
and the British Columbia Arts Council for our publishing program.

To Gillian Cortes Mason and William Brown

The fact that I taught at an independent school for some years may cause readers to look for connections between that school and the one I portrayed here, St. Cuthbert's. Apart from some similarities in geography and governing structure, any such connections or correspondences are accidental. In the same way, it would be a mistake to think that my characters represent real people. Except for my friend Steven Silver—who has appeared, with his blessing, in several of my novels—the characters here are either wholly imaginary, or composites of several people I have known over the years. In brief, while the book is true to the ethos of many residential private schools across Canada, it does not seek to capture a particular school.

Paul Nicholas Mason

CHARACTERS (IN ORDER OF APPEARANCE)

Luke Nash, school chaplain
Dave Sommer, deceased grade twelve student, Roper House
Glenda Harvey, headmaster's wife
Jim Harvey, headmaster
Dick Cargill, senior master
Diane Stewart, detective-sergeant, Kingston Police
Jiao Lee, residential don of Wilcox House
Karin Rogstad, faculty head of Wilcox House, French teacher
Lauren, student head of Wilcox House
Chad Lowell, constable, Kingston Police
Art McCue, constable, Kingston Police
Angus Graves, grade eleven student, Ingram House
Baz Van Herten, coroner, Kingston Coroner's Office
Rory, Ident officer, Kingston Police
Carol Winchester, receptionist
Debbie, secretary to the headmaster
Mike, food services manager (not seen)
Bob Hepburn, director of athletics
Maurice Kahn, coach, first soccer team
Heather Dijon, director of academics
Lydia Arthurs, academic tutor
Samantha, student, Wilcox House
Bonita, grade eleven student, Wilcox House
Krista, grade eleven student, Wilcox House, Bonita's roommate
Martha Ellis, head nurse, health centre
Jill Donahue, nurse, health centre
Peter Grose, grade eleven student
Orhan Arat, grade nine student
Stephen Bradley, student head of Roper House
Hasan Kasab, grade twelve student, Roper House
Marcus Bolduc, grade twelve student, Roper House, Hasan's roommate
Gary Trotter, grade nine student, Roper House
Gary Edwards, grade nine student, Roper House

Chris Wong, faculty head of Roper House, chemistry teacher
Paul Makepeace, English teacher
Justine Moore, French teacher
Laura Black, Spanish teacher
Mary Howden, German teacher
Julie Murdoch, faculty head of Scott House, outdoor education teacher
Dennis Murdoch, Julie's husband, outdoor education teacher
Barbara Meeks, residential don of Scott House
David Waters, faculty head of Ingram House, history teacher
Pablo, grade eleven student, Ingram House, Angus's roommate
Rafael, grade eleven student, Ingram House
Matt Butler, residential don of Ingram House
Tiffany Burgis, grief counsellor, Kingston Health Unit
Lolly Cole, grief counsellor, Kingston Health Unit
Riley Morrison, grade twelve student, Boone House
Conrad Jones, grade twelve student, Boone House
Jorge, grade twelve student, Boone House, Conrad's roommate
Callum Brezicki, detective-sergeant, Ontario Provincial Police
Alexis Wardle, grade twelve student, Bath Secondary School
Joanie Fletcher, grade eleven student, Bath Secondary School, Alexis's girlfriend
Peggy Lawrence, grade eleven student, Bath Secondary School
Trevor "Trev" Lockhart, grade twelve student, Kingston Secondary School, Peggy's boyfriend
Steven Silver, director, Steven E. Silver & Son Funeral Home
Ernie Silver, associate director, Steven E. Silver & Son Funeral Home
Jonathan Harker, journalist, *Whig Standard*
Chantal Foster, broadcast journalist, CKWS television
Garth Tremblay, videographer, CKWS
Phil Harris, maintenance worker
Alison Greer, performing arts director
Bill Closs, chief of police, Kingston Police
Tim Peet, detective, Kingston Police
Kevin Goulet, drama teacher, director of the school play
Poppy Lockhart, Trev Lockhart's twelve-year-old sister

Gran, Joanie Fletcher's grandmother
Larry, grade eleven student, St. Cuthbert's College
Meadow Strong, grade twelve student, stage manager of the school play
Patti Anderson, grade eleven student, Eaton House
Ben Hendricks, math teacher, Monday teacher-on-duty
Hughes, senior student
Pete Grose, grade twelve student
Leslie Ng, grade eleven student, Scott House
Trish, grade eleven student, Leslie's roommate
Leah Makepeace, Paul's wife
Molly Makepeace, Paul and Leah's daughter
Jason McArthur, grade twelve student
Henry Cundill, grade twelve student, Jason's roommate
Emily Hill, Diane's romantic partner
Crystal King, grade twelve student who delivers a chapel talk Tuesday morning
Candace, Dr Van Herten's anatomical pathology technologist
Tracey-Lee Goodman, grade twelve drama student
Leopold Sommer, Dave's father
Greta Sommer, Dave's mother
Struan Lynch, grade eleven day student
Lou Harper, residential don, Roper House
Jason Smith, student, Colgrave House, first team soccer player
Raj Doshi, constable, Kingston Police
Doris Brooks, cleaner, Wilcox House
Sasha, former student of Ben Hendricks, graduate of St. Cuthbert's
Malcolm Thatcher, chair, St. Cuthbert's College executive board
John Hawkins, vice-chair, St. Cuthbert's College executive board
Sarah Carson, director of admissions
Aaron Firth, one of the Kingston community volunteers
Arthur Graves, Angus's father
Jane Graves, Angus's mother
Simone Doherty, Marcus's mother
Daphne Morrows, student taken ill in the chapel

SEPTEMBER 20, 2004: MONDAY, 7:00 A.M.

THE DAY BEGAN much like any other.

School chaplain Luke Nash finished brushing his teeth, then checked his reflection in the bathroom mirror. A presentable young clergyman, he wasn't handsome exactly, but certainly not ugly: dark brown hair and eyebrows, bright green eyes in an honest face, average height, a physique kept trim from long walks. He was thirty-one, unmarried and, indeed, single, but not for lack of social graces: the woman he loved, and who loved him, Claire, had been killed in a traffic accident shortly after they became engaged; and though this was nearly two years ago, he'd not yet found the emotional fortitude to ask anyone out. Besides, his position at St. Cuthbert's College School left him little time for romance.

Luke's weekday duties began at 7:40 A.M. when he greeted students arriving at chapel for the brief daily morning service. Actually, "service" was something of a misnomer. In generations past, each day would have begun with Morning Prayer, but since the early 1990s the Anglican ritual had become less and less service and more and more school assembly. Generally it started with a hymn, and Luke was free to offer a few words, or a prayer, or a blessing, if he chose, but the focus was morning announcements—announcements about the team bus schedule for off-campus games (and scores from the previous day or weekend), special visitors and events, disciplinary proceedings, and the like. Serious about his faith, Luke was a bit dismayed that the school administration was not interested in having him exercise his priestly skills, but his bishop had told him to go along with the modern trend, and to do his evangelizing quietly with students who asked questions or who expressed a desire to be confirmed.

On Monday mornings, however, Luke did like to deliver a sermon, always limiting himself to five minutes. His remarks took the form of an email from an imaginary boarding student to his parents back home in Vancouver. (He had chosen Vancouver because it was far enough away from rural Kingston that the student couldn't see his parents on weekends; some St. Cuthbert's students travelled to Toronto twice a month.) The sermon usually related something that had happened at the school during the past week, giving Luke the opportunity to slip in a message about the importance of not rushing to judgement, of lending a hand, of being kind. Most older students, he knew, found these addresses simplistic and old-fashioned, but they were received better than would have been the case with a biblical story—and every now and then he seemed to strike a chord. On this particular morning Luke wanted to set up a slide projector to show some photos taken during the school's annual September trip to Algonquin Park, where students spent three days canoeing and portaging and camping. He had a good message, he reckoned, to go along with the pictures.

So 7:10 found him crossing the playing field situated between his campus home and the school chapel, the sun shining down on a landscape that still, after three years, left him a little awe-struck with its beauty; manicured grounds, towering oaks, and gracious nineteenth century architecture. Luke had not attended this kind of school himself: he had graduated from a rough-and-tumble public high school thrown up in the late 1960s. Attempts had been made, over the years, to plant trees around it, but a dispiriting number had died through lack of watering or aimless vandalism. Mornings there had begun with announcements over a squawking PA, to which many students paid no heed whatsoever. Seen from that perspective, then, the St. Cuthbert's morning assembly was at least orderly and focused: information was presented and mostly heard. The whole school gathered—teachers and students, anyway—and one had the sense of belonging to a community.

The chapel doors were unlocked—but that didn't particularly surprise Luke. The Sunday teacher on duty often headed home before the final private piano lesson, leaving the chapel open. This wasn't ideal, but there had never been a problem with vandalism or theft: it was one of many small breaches of good practice that the school administration chose to overlook. Yet when Luke entered the chapel, and just before he switched on the lights, he was conscious of a darkness that wasn't simply physical. He was heading to his office at the back of the chapel to ferret out the slide projector, when he glanced toward the altar. Someone was sprawled across the steps leading to the sanctuary.

Shocked, Luke ran toward the prostrate body, the head pointed away from the altar. He recognized the boy immediately: it was Dave Sommer, a grade twelve student. Luke knelt beside him, feeling for a pulse in his neck, but the boy's absolute stillness, the blue colour of his skin, and the large puddle of dried blood surrounding him, made it clear that this was useless. Dave Sommer was dead; he had probably been dead for hours. Luke had watched enough police procedural television shows to know not to move the body. He made the sign of the cross over the boy, muttered a quick prayer, checked behind the altar to see if there were any more bodies there—and there weren't—then ran out of the chapel and into the adjoining main building of the school. The headmaster's home was part of the complex, and in a matter of seconds Luke had passed through the sitting room to the headmaster's office and was knocking urgently at the door of his residence. Upon his second knock the door was opened by Glenda Harvey, the headmaster's wife, a tall and elegant blonde wrapped in an emerald green dressing gown. "Luke," she said, with admirable poise, "you look like you could use a coffee."

"Glenda, no. No, thank you—something serious has happened. Is Jim up?"

"Yes, yes, come in," she said, and as she turned to call her husband, the headmaster himself appeared.

"What's up, Luke?" he asked. Jim Harvey had played rugby for Team Canada in the Olympics twenty years before, and he still looked and moved like an athlete. He was a big man, but with a kind of lumbering grace about him. Luke's bishop had said of the headmaster, before he sent Luke to his job interview, that

"he's the kind of man you'd want on your side in a bar fight"—
a characterization that at the time had struck Luke as rather odd.
But it had the virtue of being true, and it didn't obviate the fact
that Jim Harvey was also quick-witted. Not an intellectual, in the
classic sense, perhaps, but a steady, firm hand, and a good judge
of character.

"Jim, there's a body in the chapel. A student. Dave Sommer."

"A body," said Jim. "Do you mean a dead body?"

"I do," said Luke. "There's no pulse. And there's a pool of
dried blood around him."

"Oh my God!" said Glenda, bringing her hand to her mouth
in horror.

"All right," said Jim. "Glenda, call Dick Cargill—and call the
police. Luke, let's go." The two men rushed back toward the
chapel.

NO ONE ELSE had come by the chapel in the brief time Luke had been away. He and the headmaster went directly to the sanctuary steps. "God damnit," said Jim, squatting down by the body.

"I know."

"How did Sommer get in? How did... *they* get in?" The headmaster looked around as if expecting to see a portal into some sinister dimension.

"The chapel doors were left unlocked," said Luke. "They often are Monday morning."

"And the cleaners wouldn't have been here since Saturday evening." Jim rose to his feet.

"No," said Luke. "And won't be here until mid-morning—after chapel."

"We can't have chapel today," said Jim, stating the obvious. "I'm going to have to cancel classes. Tell students to go back to their dorms."

"And there's the day-student bus," said Luke.

"Yeah. We'll just have to turn it around and send the kids home. "We want as few people buzzing around here as possible until the police have had a look at things."

Luke nodded and found himself staring at the boy's blue face. He'd presided at the funerals of several older folk since his ordination, but this was the first time he'd ever seen the body of someone who had died violently, as seemed almost certain. Claire's funeral had been closed-coffin.

"Who was his roommate? Do you know?" asked the headmaster.

"He didn't have one," said Luke. "You remember the trouble we had with him last year? We wanted to lessen his influence—"

"—Of course," said Jim. "So he's got the attic room in Roper House?"

"Yes."

"Well, the first thing we need—here's Dick."

Dick Cargill came huffing through the chapel doors. Now in his late-fifties, he was the school's senior master—a term that reflected his long years of service, and the fact that he was the headmaster's most trusted adviser. Like Jim, he had been an athlete in his youth and early manhood, but decades of smoking had taken their toll. Like Jim, too, he was nobody's fool: sharp-witted, keenly observant, a shrewd judge of character. His own path to a headmastership had been thwarted, however, by his explosive temper. On several occasions he had pushed students who had frustrated him into walls. The last time had required a pretrial negotiation and settlement to avoid legal action. "Jesus Christ!" said Dick as he took in the sight of the body. "Is that Sommer?"

"It is," said Jim. "The *late* Dave Sommer."

"Any idea…?" Dick looked from one to the other. "Glenda didn't tell me anything on the phone."

"We don't know anything," said Luke, "except that the chapel doors were unlocked this morning and the blood underneath him has been dry for some hours. At least, that's my guess."

"He's blue," said Dick.

"He is blue," said Luke.

Dick looked at Jim. "What do you want to do?"

"Glenda was calling the police," said Jim, "so they should be here in a few minutes. Could you activate the phone tree for the heads of houses and tell them to keep students in their dorms after breakfast? Chapel is cancelled. And could you wait for the day-student bus and have it turn around?"

"I can do that," said Dick, "but there may be an issue with sending some of the grade nines and tens back if there isn't a parent at home."

"Yeah, true," said Jim. "Could you also activate the phone tree for day-student parents and tell them we've got an emergency on campus?"

"Yup," said Dick. "Should Luke maybe set up on the driveway and redirect any kids who are dropped off or who drive themselves?"

"Sure—" Luke began, but Jim interrupted him.

"Luke was the one who found the body, so he should probably stay here and talk to the police," he said. "I don't really know how these things work, but that makes sense to me."

"How about one of the nurses, then?" Luke said. "One of them will have been on campus overnight, and it's just a few steps to the driveway."

"I'll call right now," said Dick, and he pulled his BlackBerry out of his pocket as he headed down the chapel's central aisle.

The senior master hadn't been gone four minutes before a police constable from the village of Bath arrived, and five minutes after that two constables from Kingston Police. The village constable asked a few questions, took some notes, then set about putting yellow tape across the sanctuary. One of the city constables surveyed the scene, then went off to the side of the chapel and began describing what he saw into his walkie-talkie. The other took out his notepad and proceeded to ask exactly the same questions as the village constable had.

"We just answered these questions," said the headmaster.

"You'll probably have to answer them again, sir," said the constable. "You've got two police forces here already, and the OPP may be here in a little while."

"Are you the investigating officer?" asked Luke.

"No, sir," said the constable. "A detective—Detective-Sergeant Stewart—will be leading the investigation for the Kingston Police. And the OPP will probably assign one of their detectives, too."

"I have a thousand telephone calls I need to make," said Jim. "Can I leave you in Luke's hands for now? I'll be in my office in this building."

"Your office is not far, sir?"

"It's thirty seconds away. Just around the corner from the room you came through."

"Were you in your office last night?"

"Yes, briefly," said Jim, sounding a bit exasperated. "But I was mostly in my home, with my family. It *was* Sunday night."

"And is your home far from here?"

"No. It's literally on the other side of my office. I live here on campus. This is a residential school. I'm the headmaster."

"I'm sure you're upset, sir. But there's been foul play here. It's my job to ask questions."

"I understand that," said Jim. "I do. But, yes, I am upset. This was one of our students. He was in our care. We are in *loco parentis*. I need to take steps to ensure that the other students are safe."

"I understand, sir," said the constable. "Sure, you can go. But I know that the detective will want to speak to you very soon."

"Luke will bring him to me," said Jim, turning to go.

"Her," said the constable. "Detective-Sergeant Diane Stewart. She's on her way."

Wilcox House was a girls' residence situated down the hill from the chapel, headmaster's home, classroom block, and several other residences. While Wilcox lacked the architectural grace of many of the other campus buildings, it was large and well-built. When you entered the residence it smelled, much of the time, of an array of perfumes, shampoo and hair spray. You would be greeted by a cacophony of sounds: upbeat music from a boom box, animated chatter, high-pitched laughter. But if you timed your visit for an hour after dinner, you might detect just the slightest echo of retching behind closed bathroom doors. Many of the girls of Wilcox House were very attractive—slender, well-groomed, expensively clothed, but the aspiration to stay, or to become, slender, led a few of them to stick their fingers down their throats from time to time. It was something that St. Cuthbert's, like every other private school, was scrambling to address.

Jiao Lee was the residential don of Wilcox House. A petite young woman fresh out of university with a B.A. in English literature and a B.Ed. for employment purposes, she made sure the girls signed in at breakfast, stayed out of their rooms if they should be in class, headed off to their practices or rehearsal on time, kept the music low during study period, and had their lights out at the required time, depending upon their grade. She served under Karin Rogstad, the staff head of house, a generously proportioned French teacher in her late thirties who, in the wake of a divorce, and with no other romantic interest in prospect, had signed up to serve as surrogate mother to twenty-five adolescent girls. Karin was permanently frazzled.

Upon hearing through the phone tree of the death in the chapel, Karin summoned Jiao by text message to her spacious apartment just down the hall from Jiao's single-bedroom-plus-tiny-bathroom. Jiao arrived to find her senior colleague in a terrible flap, and it took a couple of minutes for her to understand what had happened, and what Karin needed her to do. When she grasped what was required, however, she acted quickly, and went up and down the halls telling the girls that classes were suspended for the day, and that a House meeting was scheduled for 9:00 A.M. in the student common room. The news about no classes set off a tremendous buzz.

"Can we still go to breakfast?" asked one girl, tugging at her hair.

"You should have gone already," said Jiao.

"I slept in. I was going to go to chapel from the dining hall."

"Go and grab a bagel or something, but come right back here."

Jiao knocked at the door of one of the few students she hadn't encountered in the halls. Lauren was the student head of house, the third in the triumvirate headed by the staff head of house and supported by the residential don. The school leadership believed it was important to give some authority to responsible senior students, and one of the privileges of the student head was to sleep in one day a week and not have to sign into the dining hall that morning. Lauren, a particularly beautiful and poised brunette with a flawless complexion, was in the process of applying her make-up when Jiao knocked.

Jiao liked Lauren: they got along well. In some houses there was tension between the residential don and the student head, but in Wilcox the two young women had hit it off from early on. Part of it was that Lauren was more interested in her studies than in partying. Part of it too was that they shared a passion for classical music. And part of it was their mutual recognition, though unspoken, that Karin was not competent to run her house, and if there was to be any order at all, they would have to provide it.

"Morning, Lauren," said Jiao. "We have a situation, and Karin is asking that we join her for a quick meeting before a House meeting."

"Oh, no," said Lauren, putting down her eyebrow pencil. "Has one of our girls been caught doing something?"

"No," said Jiao. "There's been a murder—well, it's probably a murder. In the chapel last night."

"Oh my God!" said Lauren, gripping the arms of her chair. "Oh my God! Is it one of our girls?"

"No," said Jiao, and she explained what little she knew. A moment later, both were on their way to Karin's apartment, navigating past several other young women clamouring for an explanation on the spot.

If Jiao had hoped that a few moments of reflection might have calmed Karin, she would have been sorely disappointed. If anything, the head of house's stress level had escalated. "We have to tell the girls without getting them all worked up!" she said, flapping her arms in a way that showed just how worked up she was. "I don't know how to go about doing it—I know they're going to be so upset!"

"Why don't we make some tea?" said Jiao.

"Right now?" said Karin. "I'm all coffeed-out! I don't need any more caffeine!"

"Herbal tea," said Lauren. "For the meeting. We can make several pots and serve it in the common room after we've told the girls. Just serving the tea will calm things down."

"It's the ritual of it," said Jiao. "You have a big teapot, Karin, and I can get one from my room, and Lauren has one, too. And we can ask a few of the girls to bring theirs, and we have lots of kettles between us."

"But I don't know what I'm going to say!" said Karin. "I mean, how do you tell kids that their friend has been murdered? They're going to be devastated!"

"A few of them will be really upset," said Lauren, "but not all of them. Some of the girls didn't really know Dave. And others may not have liked him."

"I'm going to tell you the truth, Karin," said Jiao. "The dons didn't like him either. He treated us like garbage. I mean, I'm sad that he's dead, and I'm a bit agitated that he was murdered, but he wasn't a very nice person."

"I agree," said Lauren. "Sure, some girls will get a bit hysterical, but if we're on top of things, we can keep everything relatively calm."

"But there could be a murderer loose on campus!" said Karin.

"Karin, we can't say that," said Jiao. "We have to reassure them that the police will do their jobs. They're going to be all over this."

Diane Stewart had known from a young age that she wanted to be a police officer: when other little girls played with dolls and Fisher-Price ovens, she played Cops-and-Robbers with the boys. Later, in the pre-streaming 1980s, teenage Diane watched some of the more sophisticated police shows: Hill Street Blues, Cagney & Lacey, Jake and the Fatman—and, in the 1990s the Law & Order franchise. And books. No Harlequin Romances for Diane! Sherlock Holmes, Father Brown, Philip Marlowe, Hercule Poirot, Inspector Morse and Sam Spade were her companions. She pushed her high school to introduce a law course in grade eleven, and studied criminology at the University of Toronto before heading off for twelve weeks of training at the Ontario Police College, from which she graduated second in her class in 1990. (When it came to winning the respect of her mostly male colleagues, it didn't hurt that she had a black belt in karate.) Fourteen years later, at age thirty-six, Diane was made the first female detective-sergeant in the Kingston Police.

This was not Detective Stewart's first visit to the St. Cuthbert's campus. Twice in the previous few years, Kingston Police had come to the school during the summer to practise hostage situations. She had seen the grounds, then, but now, as before, she was impressed with the elegance and cultivated greenness of the place. She parked her Chevy Impala in the driveway between the chapel and the health centre, ignoring the "DROP-OFFS AND PICK-UPS ONLY" sign." This would not be a normal day, and she wanted her car as close as possible. As she climbed out, she automatically checked to make sure that the holster carrying her snub-nosed .38 was securely closed.

Approaching the chapel, she was greeted by one of the two city constables attending the scene. "Morning, ma'am."

"Morning, Chad. Are things secure?"

"Yes, ma'am. Art is in there with the 10-45 and the school priest—and the constable from the village police is inside the building at the set of doors leading into the church."

"Thank you. Probably best that you stay here for the next little while." The detective noticed a woman in a white medical coat farther along the driveway, apparently directing cars away. "Who's that? Do you know?"

"She works here," said Chad. "I think she's a nurse. Maybe the head nurse."

"Okay," said Diane. "The coroner should be here soon. Make sure she doesn't try to send him away."

"I'll see he gets in," said the constable. He gave a few seconds of his attention to the detective's receding figure as she disappeared into the chapel.

Upon entering, Diane greeted the second constable. "Second time this week, Art."

"This time is way more serious, ma'am."

"It is that," she said, approaching the body. Luke was standing over Sommer, rehearsing, in his mind, everything he knew about the boy, but he looked up as Diane drew near.

"Are you Detective Stewart?" he asked.

"I am," she said. "And you are the school priest?"

"In a way, yes. I'm the school *chaplain*: Luke Nash. I found the body this morning."

Diane took a notebook out of her pocket and flipped it open. "What precisely is your role at the school, Mr. Nash?" she asked.

"I lead the chapel service every weekday morning. I also do some counselling and help out, sometimes, with disciplinary actions. I'm a spiritual jack-of-all-trades."

"Okay. And when did you find the body?" She looked up from her notebook.

"It would have been roughly 7:15. I arrived a little earlier than usual, because I wanted to set up a slide projector for this morning's service."

"And when was that scheduled to begin?"

"7:45. The students begin arriving at 7:30—unless one of them is speaking or scheduled to do something special."

"And was this young man scheduled to do anything special this morning?"

"No. No, he wasn't."

"Can you tell me his name?"

"It's Dave—Dave Sommer. A grade twelve student from Roper House."

"Roper House?" Diane cocked her head.

"One of the school's residences. It's actually attached to this building—connected by a hall."

"I'll have a lot more questions for you, Mr. Nash," said Detective Stewart, "but I'm just going to ask one more this moment. Do you have any suspicions about who might be behind this foul play—if there has been foul play? Was he the sort of boy who had a lot of enemies?"

Luke hesitated briefly. "I wouldn't say he was a particularly popular young man," he said. "Dave was something of a bully. The headmaster and I had to address that with him last academic year. We suspended him for a couple of weeks for his behaviour toward a younger boy."

Diane raised an eyebrow. "Is that boy still at the school?"

"Yes."

"His name?"

"Angus. Angus Graves."

"And is he the only boy who might have a grudge against Dave Sommer?"

"I'd be surprised," said Luke. "But you know, I really don't want to point you toward the boy we *know* he bullied. The headmaster told Sommer, forcefully, that any further aggression against him would not be tolerated."

"We have to investigate all possibilities, Mr. Nash," said Diane. "Unless our focus swiftly narrows, we'll be talking to a lot of people in the community. I trust you will help me with that?"

"Of course," said Luke. "Of course."

"Good, said Detective Stewart. And at that moment the coroner arrived.

Baz Van Herten had never intended to become a coroner. He'd stumbled into the job thirty-two years before when he arrived from the Netherlands, a newly-graduated doctor with a desire to see Canada and no practice to join. He'd swiftly completed the various medical competency exams, and was waiting for something interesting to turn up, when a coroner's position came available in northern Ontario. Without any other immediate opportunities, he'd applied, landed the job, and spent the next decade travelling a large area—from Keewatin to Kenora, from Dryden to Whitefish Bay. The special challenges of that area, which saw a disproportionate number of alcohol-related murders and assaults, had taught him a certain roughness, a willingness to speak his mind without much of a filter.

"What the fuck have you got for me?" he bellowed as he marched up the aisle.

"Baz, this is the school chaplain, Luke," said Diane, her tone a muted reprimand.

"It's not him I've come to see," said Baz, getting down on his hands and knees and looking closely at the body. "Has the Ident officer come yet?"

"No."

"Then get on the phone and tell him to get a fucking move on!" said Baz, "I'm here and I want to do my damn job."

"You're going to have to wait a few minutes to do anything more than look at him," said Diane. "Rory will be here soon enough. Take a quick scan, then go find yourself a cup of coffee."

"Piss off," said Baz, though his tone was friendly, by his standards. "So, I'm guessing a seventeen-year-old male, although he's not far off his eighteenth birthday. Reasonable physical condition—as he should be at that age." He brought his nostrils close to Sommer's face and sniffed. "A smoker, or someone who hung around smokers. Dead, maybe, maybe—" he reached out and gently touched Sommer's forehead—"ten hours, give or take."

"That's more than I expected you to be able to tell me at this point," said Diane.

"Lots of blood," said Baz. "Can't tell if it's from a knife or a bullet without turning him over."

"You can't turn him over yet," said Diane firmly.

"I spend half my life waiting for other people to do their fucking jobs," said Baz.

"Where can Dr. Van Herten get a cup of coffee?" asked Diane, addressing Luke.

"There's usually a pot on in the staff common room," said Luke. "And if not, we could go to the dining hall. Do you want to come with me?" he said to Baz. "If that's all right with you," he added, turning to Diane.

"Please get him out of here," Diane said. But at that moment the Ident officer came in through the interior doors.

"Hey, Rory—did you have to finish jerking off before you left?" asked Baz.

"Baz," said Diane. "We're in a church. Okay? A church? And this is the school chaplain—and he knew the boy. A little professionalism here."

"I'm sorry, Father," said the coroner, not looking the least contrite.

"It's fine," said Luke. "And please call me Luke—I'm not Roman Catholic."

"Just as well," said Baz. "I've got no time for Papists."

The Ident officer began unpacking his gear. "How about I go and arrange for coffee all 'round?" said Luke. "I can ask the food services to send over a trolley with an urn and enough cups for everyone."

"That would be wonderful," said Diane. "Thank you. But we can't have any coffee in here. Please keep it outside."

"Tell them to send real cream," said Baz. "None of that powdered shit."

"I doubt they have powdered shit," said Luke, evenly. And off he went.

On the other side of the interior doors, he encountered the constable from the village. "I'm going for coffees," Luke told him. "Can I get a cup for you, too?"

"Please," said the constable.

"Have you had to turn anyone away?" Luke asked.

"Four young people. They didn't seem to know that the assembly had been cancelled."

"They probably didn't return to their residences after breakfast," said Luke. "Some students go directly to the library afterwards, and then come here."

"They seemed pretty confused."

Luke passed through the narthex—the lobby outside the chapel—then turned left into the receptionist's office. Carol Winchester, a friendly middle-aged lady, looked up at him round-eyed and said, "Oh, Luke, this is terrible."

"It is, but the police are dealing with it, and we'll find our way through. Could you phone the dining hall and ask Mike for a large urn of coffee, cream and sugar, and, say, eight cups, to be delivered to the narthex? Tell him to charge the chapel budget. It's for the police and the coroner."

"I will," said Carol, reaching for the phone.

Luke proceeded past reception and into the headmaster's outer office, where he approached Jim's secretary—a slim, attractive woman in a white blouse and blue pencil skirt. "Is he with anyone, Debbie?"

"He's on the phone, but he said you can go right in," she said. The door was part-way open, and Luke pushed in and paused briefly: Jim was indeed on the phone, and he waved Luke to a chair across from his own desk.

"I'm calling a school meeting for this afternoon," the headmaster was saying. "I'm going to call Sommer's parents as soon as I'm off the phone with you."

Luke glanced at the desk, and saw that Jim had had Debbie pull Dave Sommer's file. It was a thick folder, containing copies of the boy's academic reports, and, Luke suspected, copies of a great many letters to his parents over the years, outlining the various "difficulties" Dave had experienced: violations of school rules against drinking and smoking, academic offences like plagiarism, and, yes, several instances of bullying, culminating in a very serious incident the previous spring. The Sommer scion had not had a distinguished career at St. Cuthbert's, and there had been some question about whether to accept him back—a question laid to rest, he again suspected, when Mr. Sommer made a stunningly generous contribution to the school's endowment fund. Luke respected his employer, but he had no illusions: he knew that at St. Cuthbert's, as in the wider world, the wealthy were sometimes able to purchase forgiveness for transgressions that cost less wealthy folk both position and reputation.

Jim hung up the phone. "The chair of the executive board," he said, by way of explanation. "He'll be down with the vice-chair tomorrow afternoon. We have to strategize." He rubbed his chin with his right hand. "Any developments in the past few minutes?"

"The detective and the coroner are here," said Luke. "I'll warn you that the coroner is a character: he speaks his mind. I left to arrange for coffee, and the photographer had just arrived."

"The photographer?" said Jim, briefly puzzled. "—Oh, of course. The crime scene. I was thinking press. The chair is worried about press."

"It's going to come out," said Luke.

"I know. I know. Of course it is." Jim drummed his fingers on the desk. "Luke, do you think Angus could be involved in this?"

MONDAY, 8:30 A.M.

BY THIS POINT, most staff and faculty, including the heads of house, had assembled in the theatre. The Mark Danby Theatre was one of the school's crown jewels, its steeply raked seating looking down on, and half-surrounding, a thrust stage. There was a subdued hum of conversation in the auditorium as people exchanged the limited information they had, but the hum quieted as soon as the headmaster and the senior master entered, Dick guiding the detective to a seat in the front row while Jim went directly to the portable podium.

The headmaster gripped the stand for a moment as he surveyed his staff. In his decade at the school, he'd had to make a number of difficult announcements, but this topped them all. He recognized that the tone he set now would have a significant influence on how people dealt with the issue and moved forward, and for that reason he consciously released his hold on the stand and did his best, with voice and posture, to suggest a calm he did not altogether feel. "Colleagues," he began, "by now many of you will have heard that Dave Sommer died last night, apparently in the chapel, and there are pretty clear indications that he was in fact killed. At this point we don't know why, and we don't know who is responsible." He proceeded to outline the plan for the day—day students already sent back home, residential students confined to their houses (meals delivered to them), grief counsellors arriving from Kingston in the early afternoon for those who needed to talk. "Our plan is to carry on with organized sports and arts events at 3:15 P.M.," he said. "No games are scheduled for today, but there are some tomorrow, and we've decided that rigorous exercise is probably a good thing for students who have been kept inside for much of the day."

"Jim," called out Bob Hepburn, the director of athletics: "What about the day students on sports teams?"

"Fair question," said Jim. "Dick, what do you propose...?"

The senior master rose from his seat. "We can activate the phone tree and advise parents to drive their kids back to campus at, say, 3:20," he said. "I can't organize a bus to bring them here, but the bus will run as normal to take them home. I haven't got around to cancelling that."

"Good call," said Jim. "Now—"

"Some of the players may not be able to make it back," Bob said. "Some of their parents—"

"—Bob, I get that it's not ideal," said Jim, with some irritation. "We're doing what we can with a very difficult, an unprecedented, situation."

"Okay, I'm just concerned that our first teams should get all the practice—"

"I understand," said Jim. "We've never faced a challenge of this kind before."

"Maybe we could pull the kids out of class for special practices during the day tomorrow," said Maurice Kahn, the coach of the first soccer team.

"No," said Heather Dijon, the director of academics. "Students missing classes today was disruptive enough to the academic program—"

"It will be as I've outlined," said Jim, raising his voice more than was customary for him. "Sports practices today, to the extent that's possible; classes and games tomorrow as scheduled. I want to get back to something approaching normalcy as soon as possible. Okay. Now, I want to introduce Detective-Sergeant Stewart of the Kingston Police. Detective Stewart."

Diane rose and walked over to the podium. She looked confident. "Thank you, headmaster," she said. "I am, as Mr. Harvey said, a detective with the Kingston Police, and I'll be investigating the death of David Sommer with a detective from the Ontario Provincial Police: he's already on route from Toronto." A woman raised her hand. "Could I ask you to hold off any questions for a moment, please? It may be that what I say next will

address your concern. Thank you.... Your chaplain tells me that
your heads of house, and some other faculty, live on campus, and
I'm going to ask any of you who went outside after, say, 8:00 last
night to make sure that your name goes at the top of a list he's
putting together. If you took your dog for a walk, or went for a
jog, or hopped in the car to go to the convenience store, please
make sure we have your name."

"Does that mean we're all suspects?" called out the woman
who had raised her hand, Lydia Arthurs. She was an academic
tutor who lived in one of the grace-and-favour apartments on
campus—rent-free accommodation for a handful of staff who
provided services during evening hours.

"No, ma'am. It means that we want to know if you saw any
students out and about, or if you saw anyone you didn't recognize, or any unfamiliar cars—especially near the chapel. We're
trying to put together a picture of who may have been in the area
around the time that Mr. Sommer died." She paused. "My colleague and I will be conducting a number of interviews over the
next few hours. In some cases they may be *preliminary* interviews.
Now, there's a real danger, in a case like this, of gossip running
rampant. I'm going to ask, please, that you avoid speculating as
much as possible—unless you're talking to me and my colleague,
in which case we may ask you to speculate a little, because sometimes, *sometimes*, a pattern of speculation can point investigators
in the right direction. But we want to avoid any *co-ordinated* speculation, if you see the difference."

"*I* don't see the difference," said Lydia.

Jim stepped forward and stood beside the detective. "Lydia,
I'll explain it to you in a couple of minutes," he said, his impa-
tience with her absolutely transparent. "Now, any heads of house
who had students come back late to the residence should see
Dick immediately after this meeting—and then return to your
residence: I know you have house meetings at nine. All staff and
faculty not attached to residential houses should go to your offices
and work, so far as you're able. No classes today, so this is a good
opportunity to catch up with marking or lesson planning. At
some point either I, or Dick, or Luke, or possibly a detective will

see each of you individually to determine whether you have any information about Dave Sommer's relationships that might cast light on what he was doing in the chapel, who he might have been with, or, or—I don't know what else. So. Does anyone have a question that just *has* to be asked?" His tone made clear that he didn't want any more questions.

"Will you explain now—" Lydia began, but the headmaster cut her off.

"I'll explain to you personally, Lydia," he said. "Everyone else seems to understand perfectly. Okay, one more question. Yes, Karin?"

"My question is for the detective," said Karin. "Do you think this was done by someone from outside the school?"

"I honestly don't know," said Diane. "It's simply too early to tell. But I can tell you that we'll find the perpetrator, whoever it may be."

As with the other house meetings on campus, the Wilcox meeting began promptly at nine. Head of house Karin rose to the occasion by telling the twenty-five girls that they—Karin, Jiao and Lauren—had some sad news to share, and that it was very important that everyone stay calm… this injunction, of course, had precisely the opposite effect. Then Jiao took over, telling the girls that a dead body had been found in the chapel that morning, and that it was at least possible that he had been killed. "It's Dave Sommer," she said. "Some of you know him. A grade twelve student who's been here since grade nine. The police are here, and they're taking care of things. I expect they'll make an arrest quickly, but they may need to speak to some of us in the next few hours. And there are no classes today, and lunch won't be in the dining hall: we'll be having submarine sandwiches and chips down here, in the house. You can eat in your rooms if you like, or you can join Lauren and me here in the common room."

A few girls had cried out when Dave Sommer's name had been mentioned—though not, Jiao suspected, from any great grief, but from a recognition that it was someone known to them. One girl, Samantha, did burst into tears—and Lauren went to her immediately—and several others went white and silent. Surveying the room, Jiao was struck by the response of two girls in particular, roommates Bonita and Krista. Bonita was among those who looked most shocked, but she stayed quiet—and her roommate, Krista, reached out and took her by the hand. Jiao was surprised because she knew that Krista was not usually a demonstrative young woman, but, she reflected, this was far from being an ordinary day.

"We're going to make some tea now," said Lauren, still over at Samantha's side, "so if you have a teapot or a kettle in your room, go and grab it. And if you have a mug, bring that, too. But if you haven't, that's fine. I think we'll have enough to cover everyone." She had intended to take the lead in tea-making, but a fresh burst of tears from Samantha forced her to stay where she was, so it fell to Jiao to do much of the work of organizing the girls and, eventually, pouring the beverage.

The idea of a death in the community slowly settled in. Some girls drifted off to call their parents or friends in other school residences. Someone turned on the common room television and several girls began watching game shows. Lauren escorted Samantha back to her room: Jiao muttered a brief prayer of thanks that there was one other responsible adult in the residence. Karin had left shortly after the kettles were plugged in. She had, she said, some important following-up to do, but Jiao suspected that taking a lorazepam might be the real agenda.

Bonita and Krista had been among the first girls to leave, Jiao noticed, and she made a mental note to check in with them later. She wasn't aware of any special connection between either of them and Dave Sommer, but sometimes relationships could be kept hidden. Not for long, certainly, given the bush telegraph that operated at the school—but for a little while.

THE HEAD NURSE returned to the health centre from the staff meeting as soon as it was over. Martha Ellis hadn't been the nurse out on the school driveway earlier that morning: that was nurse Jill Donahue, who had stayed at the centre overnight. There was always a nurse in the centre while school was in session: you never knew when someone might start vomiting or have an asthmatic attack, and given the huge fees parents were paying, they expected someone more qualified than a teacher with a bottle of acetaminophen available to their children if they fell ill. A nurse was usually on hand at major sports events, too: there had been a sad occasion some years before when a lovely residential don had gone into anaphylactic shock during a regatta.

Martha had been a nurse for forty years and had little patience for meetings of any kind. In truth, she had little patience for anything—but she reserved her most withering judgements for students who showed up regularly at the centre. She had developed a keen sense for malingering—a sense heightened by an academic calendar in her office in which she entered the dates of particularly important evaluations, when teachers remembered to report them to her. Students who came to the centre on mornings when they had term tests or independent study presentations were subjected to strenuous interrogation. She knew all the tricks: drinking hot coffee to fool the thermometer—sometimes combined with slapping oneself in the face a few times to redden the complexion (boys), or the strategic application of make-up (girls); coughing hard to cause hoarseness; rubbing one's face on one of the campus cats to bring on nasal congestion and hives. She met most claims of nausea, headaches, diarrhea or period pain with a hard-edged skepticism.

"Who have we got in?" Martha asked Jill. Her colleague was sitting at her desk, preparing the early morning reports for the headmaster and head of academics.

"Pete Grose is in room three with an upset stomach," said Jill, "and Orhan Arat is in room four."

"Grose!" said Martha. "He's got a constitution like a horse. He must be shirking something. I haven't met Arat yet."

"He's a new boy," said Jill. "Roper House. He was shaking when he came in, but he's not running a temperature. His file says there have been some psychological issues in the past."

"I'll look in on both of them," said Martha. "But I can pretty well guarantee that young master Grose will be heading out the door in the next few minutes. An upset stomach!" She snorted eloquently.

"What happened at the meeting?" asked Jill.

"I'm going to call Dr. O'Brien right now to bring him up to date," said Martha. "Listen to what I tell him. I don't want to repeat everything. God, that Arthurs woman drives me up the wall. She asks the most inane questions!" She reached for the phone and stabbed out the number for the doctor who visited the school every lunch hour when students were kept overnight in the centre.

Shortly after Martha's conversation with Dr. O'Brien was over, two female students arrived at the health centre, both with red eyes, and each accompanied by a residential don. Jill took one and Martha the other, and both were eventually settled in separate rooms in the centre. "Should we put them in one of the double rooms?" Jill asked.

"No," said Martha. "They'll just wind each other up. Hysterical girls! The worst!" Jill had a somewhat different opinion, but she kept it to herself. Besides, she was soon preoccupied with a phone call from a day-student mother saying that her son hadn't come to school that morning because of stomach flu or, possibly, food poisoning—and what was this about a murder?

"A bad day to be a nurse," Martha observed grimly.

ROPER HOUSE, BUILT in the early 1880s, was the oldest residence at St. Cuthbert's. A never-ending series of renovations had connected it to the chapel, administrative offices, headmaster's house and classroom block, and its central location on campus made it highly desired by some, but by no means all, students. Stephen Bradley was the student head of house: as student head, he had the extraordinary luxury of a room to himself—though he didn't have the tiny three-piece private washroom enjoyed by the residential don whose quarters were on the floor below. Dave Sommer had also had a room to himself, but his was in the attic of Roper House, and it was both tiny and, in the late spring and early fall, unconscionably hot. The room had traditionally been assigned to that boy who absolutely no one else wanted to live with, though when no one had fit that description, in decades past, it had sometimes been given to a young man whose attendance at the school was possible only through complete bursary assistance. Jim Harvey had ended that practice in the second year of his headmastership, just a year before he turned the school co-ed.

A tall young man with a slight stoop and a serious mien, Stephen Bradley sat on his swivel office chair facing away from the desk and out towards his bed. His friend Hasan Kasab had seated himself on the bed, and Marcus Bolduc, another senior student, was leaning against the wall. The mood was not light.

"We'll have to come clean about what we were doing last night," said Stephen. "It's not like we can hide it."

"But is it relevant?" said Marcus. "I mean, seriously, we were just fucking around. It's not as though it had anything to do with him being killed."

"Man, it was freaky," said Hasan. "If my parents hear—"

"It was a *game*," said Stephen. "Just a game. If we try to keep it quiet and then it comes out... Well, it will look suspicious as hell. And it wasn't."

"I wish I'd never brought it from home," said Marcus. "I think I'll just throw it away."

"You can't do that now," said Stephen. "They're probably going to want to see it."

"I feel sick," said Hasan. The other two boys looked at him.

"What do you mean?" said Marcus. "Like, sick to your stomach?'

"You have no idea what my parents are gonna do," said Hasan. "They're strict Muslims. I mean, my mom not so much maybe, but my dad... he might just send me back to Pakistan."

"You're not serious," said Stephen.

"I *am* serious," said Hasan. "He's always saying to us, *Don't get too Westernized, don't forget where you came from.* He's going to want to send me to live with my uncle."

"No way, man," said Marcus.

"You don't know my family," said Hasan.

"Okay," said Stephen, "maybe if we go to Wong and tell him what we were doing and tell him what might happen to you, maybe he can keep it quiet so it doesn't get back to your parents. Maybe."

"It's worth a try," said Marcus.

"So let's go over it," said Stephen. "Let's get our story straight, so we don't get confused and fuck up the details. Okay?" The other two boys nodded. "So, we were here, after dinner, in my room, the three of us—"

"—And Sommer," said Hasan.

"And Sommer," said Stephen, "and the two juniors came by, and we were talking about the school, right? Telling them what to expect this year."

"Right," said Marcus.

"And Gary said—"

"Which Gary?" said Marcus.

"Gary Trotter," said Stephen. "The other guy's Edwards. Gary Edwards."

"Two fucking Garys," said Marcus.

"Yeah, right. Anyway. So Gary Trotter said, he said something like, *I wish we could see everything that's going to happen this year.*"

"Yeah," said Hasan. "Dumb thing to say."

"Well, harmless enough," said Stephen. "And then you, Marcus, you said, *Hey, I've got a Ouija board. Let's ask the Ouija board.*"

"Yeah, I was the asshole," said Marcus.

"Man, you didn't know," said Stephen. "You didn't know. So you went and got the board, and we played a bit, and it was stupid but kinda fun, and then Sommer asked if, if the board had a message for him."

"Yeah," said Hasan.

"Right," said Marcus.

"And the board," said Stephen, "spelled out the message *Watch your back.*"

There was a silence in the room.

"Fuck," said Marcus.

"And we all laughed," said Stephen, "because it was funny. Right? It was *funny. Sommer* laughed."

"Yeah," said Hasan. "He laughed all right. And now he's dead."

"But that's… I mean, that's not related, the two things aren't related," said Stephen. "It's a dumb coincidence. I mean, the board also said *Yes* when Trotter asked if he was going to get laid this year, and that kid's not going to get laid for the next decade!"

"Right," said Marcus.

"So that's what we tell Wong," said Stephen. "Simple as that. A game. A dumb game after dinner. And then you guys went off to your room, and Sommer went up to his room, and the two Garys went to study hall. And I was here."

There was a pause. "Yeah," said Marcus, "but at some point fuckin' Sommer went to the chapel, for some reason."

Stephen raised his hands and shoulders in a kind of shrug. "Well," he said, "that was after we were all here. I mean, none of you followed him, did you? *I* didn't."

"No," said Hasan.
"No," said Marcus.
"Well, there you are," said Stephen.

ENGLISH TEACHER PAUL Makepeace shared Humanities Office C with three other teachers—Justine Moore (French), Laura Black (Spanish) and Mary Howden (German). Paul and Laura had desks by the large windows, which afforded them excellent views of the forest beyond the academic block; much of their time, however, was spent staring into their computer screens, reading and responding to the scores of emails that came in every day from administrators, students and parents. Justine and Mary faced the same demands, without the distraction of the view. Like most of their colleagues, all four were compelled, by the sheer volume of electronic correspondence, to reserve their marking and lesson prep for the evening.

The four humans shared the office with a large photocopier, the fumes from which Paul was certain would eventually give him lung cancer; the science department didn't have a photocopier of its own, so it sent all its multiple-choice tests to the humanities office to be photocopied... page after page, copy after copy, frequently jamming the machine at particularly inconvenient moments. For all that, it was usually a happy office: the four colleagues enjoyed an easy camaraderie, regularly giving each other words of encouragement, and brightly wrapped chocolates or fresh-baked cookies.

On this day, all four teachers had been asked to attend the house meetings of the residences to which they were, in a sense, attached, by virtue of having student advisees living there. (Karin had not thought to extend a similar invitation to the teachers connected to Wilcox House.) They returned to the office one by one, within roughly the same five-minute frame, sobered by the circumstance that had summoned them, and needing to talk, even in the teeth of Detective Stewart's request that they not do so.

"I'm making tea," Laura announced as she came through the door. "Anyone else want some?"

"Please," said Paul—and Justine and Mary echoed him. Laura filled her kettle from a large carafe on her desk and plugged it in.

"Well, this is a first," said Justine, arranging her chair so she could see the other three. "We've seen some strange things, but this…"

"It's frightening," said Mary.

"No—," said Paul, in an attempt to reassure her. "Not frightening. *Shocking*, yes, but I certainly don't worry that anyone else is going to be killed."

"*I'm* frightened," said Mary.

"So am I," said Justine. "It's a terrible thing that someone was… *murdered* just a two-minute walk from here. In the chapel. The school chapel."

"No, I get it," said Paul. "It's—it's grotesque. But I think it's a one-off. And I think that the culprit will be caught."

"Did any of you know Sommer?" asked Laura.

"No," said Mary. "I'm not sure I'd even recognize him."

"I'd recognize him," said Justine, "but I don't think I've ever actually spoken to him. He didn't take French with me."

"I had him for grade eleven Spanish," said Laura.

"How was he?" asked Mary.

"Honestly? I didn't like him. He wasn't interested in the language, and he was disruptive. He could be cruel, too. If anyone showed an interest in doing well, he'd, you know, put them down."

"Did you know him, Paul?" asked Justine.

"Yeah," said Paul. "I never taught him, but I had to deal with him at a disciplinary level. Last year he bullied one of my advisees, Angus Graves. He's nearly two years younger than Sommer is. Than Sommer *was*."

"Was it a nasty case?" asked Mary.

"Truthfully, it was the worst I've ever dealt with. Sommer beat Angus up badly, then stuffed dogshit in his mouth. I didn't think we'd see him back again."

"Jesus!" said Laura.

"That's terrible! So why is he back?" asked Mary.

Paul made the thumb-rubbing-forefinger motion. "I suspect Daddy made a little donation," he said. "Or, more likely, a big donation. But I don't know that for a fact."

"That is *so* wrong," said Mary.

"I know," said Paul. "But private-school ethics. You know how it works. It's like the old indulgences. Pay your money, and you get your kid out of hell."

"It's *disgusting*," said Laura.

"Yup," said Paul. "But that's how they pay admin what they pay them. They're all corporate executives now: Chief executive officer. Chief financial officer. Chief fund-raising officer. Chair of the executive board."

"I don't know," said Justine. "I wouldn't want Jim's job. Not today."

"I would," said Paul. "Not particularly today, but I wouldn't mind making a quarter-million a year."

"Do you think it's really that much?" asked Mary.

"Oh, yes," said Paul. "I'm sure it is. And probably more."

THE HOUSE MEETING in Scott House, another girls' residence, was similar in format to the one in Wilcox House, except that several members of the teaching staff were on hand to assist with students who were upset. Julie Murdoch, head of house and an outdoor education teacher, spoke calmly and clearly, and most of the young women were left feeling that things were under control. The meeting ended around 9:25 A.M., and though several girls hung around to talk with their advisers or with Julie herself, most of the others drifted back to their rooms to talk, to sleep, or, in a few cases, to work: Scott House had a number of scholarship girls with their sights set on the Ivy Leagues.

At around 10:00, Julie's husband, Dennis, another outdoor education teacher, went door to door in the residence, checking to see that none of the students had become distressed after the meeting. He paused to chat, pleasantly, with several girls. He was popular in the house: he had an easy manner and was perfectly happy to play second fiddle to his wife when it came to house management.

Coming to the end of the upper hallway, Dennis paused, then rapped softly on the door of the residential don, Barbara Meeks. At twenty-two, Barbara was a biology grad from Western: she was hired on the strength of that degree, and because she had been, for many years, a provincially ranked gymnast who had almost made it to the national Olympic team. She was petite, blonde, beautiful—and the girls idolized her. "Come in," she called.

Dennis entered, then did something he would never do if it were just a solitary student in the room: he closed the door behind him. "Hi," he said. "Weird day. How you doing?"

Barbara was stretched out on the bed and did not get up. "I'm okay," she said. "A little freaked out, but okay. The girls seem fine. Mostly."

"Yeah, I've just been checking on them."

"I'll check again in about an hour," said Barbara. "I think some of them will take a nap. Catch up on sleep after their weekend shenanigans."

"Yep, you're probably right," said Dennis. And then, wistfully: "I wouldn't mind taking a nap with *you*."

"I don't think we'd get much sleep." Barbara smiled.

"I'm getting out of here before I jump you." Dennis opened the door and left quickly.

CHRIS WONG HAD been head of Roper House for only a year. He hadn't really wanted the job, but the headmaster had signalled that his candidacy for a chemistry position would be that much stronger if he were prepared to take on house mastering responsibilities as well. In his more cynical moments, Chris suspected that this was because the school had no heads of house who weren't white, and that the governors desperately wanted to show off at least one ethnic minority. He and his wife, Xiu, had risen to the challenge, however, and he had found himself adapting to his duties more easily than he had imagined. He'd had a good student head of house in his first year, and he had handpicked Stephen Bradley, his new one, in the spring.

So he was taken aback when the sober-faced trio of Stephen, Hasan and Marcus came to see him about half an hour after the house meeting had ended. The boys in the residence had taken the news well, he thought, although the murder—if that's what it was—had happened closer to their House than any other, and that they had all known Sommer. Or perhaps, he wondered, was it *because* they knew Sommer: he was aware that the boy hadn't been particularly popular. He was reflecting on this when the knock came at his door.

Xiu was a legal secretary in Kingston and had left for work around 8:00, so Chris had the large apartment to himself. He escorted the boys into the living room, waved them into chairs, then sat down himself. "What's up?" he asked.

Stephen Bradley leaned forward, his elbows on his knees: "Sir, there's something we have to tell you about last night. It involves Dave Sommer."

"Yes," said Chris, his nerves jangling suddenly. "Well? Tell me."

"Can I first ask you to keep this as quiet as you can?" said Stephen. "We're going to tell you everything, but we're worried that Hasan's parents will be really angry with *him* if they hear about it. Because they're Muslim."

"I have no idea what you're going to tell me," said Chris, "so I can't make you any promises. I can tell you that I have no desire to see Hasan in trouble *unnecessarily*. If he's done nothing wrong, he has nothing to fear from me."

"Thank you, sir," said Hasan.

"But I can't speak for the headmaster or for the police," said Chris. "Please understand that. I'm just telling you what *my* position is. Now go on."

"Okay," said Stephen. "Last night we three guys and Sommer and two boys in grade nine—the Garys—were in my room and we played around with a Ouija board."

"You played around with a Ouija board," said Chris. "Is that it? Is that everything?"

"No," said Hasan, one of his knees bouncing.

"Well, not quite," said Stephen. "You see, the last thing that happened was—was that Sommer asked it, the board, if it had any message for him."

"And?"

"And the board spelled out the message, *Watch your back*," said Marcus.

"Watch your back?" repeated Chris.

"Yes," said Stephen.

There was a pause. "Fuck," said Chris.

"Yes, sir," said Stephen.

Chris thought about this for a moment or two. "So who did it?"

"Sir?" said Stephen.

"Which of you did it?"

"The murder?" Hasan said, incredulous.

"Not the murder—the message. The *message*. *Watch your back*."

"The board did, sir," said Marcus. "The Ouija board."

"Oh, come on," said Chris. "You're not fools. The board doesn't have a mind of its own. One of you spelled that out!"

"I don't think so, sir," said Stephen, looking from one to the other of his friends. "At least, I didn't. Did one of you guys?"

"No!" said Hasan. "No. Of course not."

"Not me," said Marcus. "I wouldn't know how to. I mean, we've all got our fingers on the wood thing—the pointer. We're all *looking* at it. I don't know *how* I'd have done it."

"One of you did it," said Chris. "Or if not you, one of the Garys—but much more likely one of you older boys. I'm going to ask again: which one of you?"

"None of us, sir," said Stephen, again scanning the faces of his friends.

"All right," said Chris. "I'll have to pass this on to the headmaster—or maybe to the chaplain. He seems to be involved in this up to his neck." He stood up.

"You will remember to tell them about Hasan's parents, sir?" said Stephen.

"Yes, I'll remember," said Chris "—although honestly, I'd like to throttle you three."

"Yes, sir," said Marcus.

"Sorry, sir—thank you, sir," said Hasan.

"See you later today," said Chris. "I'm sure there'll be some follow-up."

★

On their way back to their rooms, the three senior boys ran into the two Garys on the staircase. "Stephen," said Gary Trotter, "should we tell Wong about last night?"

"We've just told him," said Stephen.

"Oh," said Trotter. "Are we all going to get into trouble?"

"No. But we may be questioned at some point by the chaplain or the headmaster. So be ready for that."

"What should we say?" asked Gary Edwards.

"Just tell the truth," said Stephen. "Just tell the truth."

DAVID WATERS, A history teacher and Head of Ingram House, had been at St. Cuthbert's twenty years, in the process becoming something of an institution himself. A tall and angular figure in his early fifties, David was widely admired for his decency and discretion—and though his wife had very little daily contact with the boys in the house, Maureen had won their hearts, over the years, by cooking every single one of them a chocolate cake on his birthday. Ingram House was one of the newer residences on campus, and while this meant a long walk to the classroom block and dining hall on cold winter days, the compensation was a glorious view of Lake Ontario.

The meeting at Ingram House had gone quickly. David had quietly shared what facts he knew, fielded a couple of questions, then served tea and cookies. Maureen did shift work at Kingston General Hospital, and wasn't working that morning, so she had thrown herself into baking cookies. Their fresh-from-the-oven aroma was particularly reassuring for the six grade nine boys and the two grade tens who were new to the school. Three teacher-advisers were on hand for the meeting, too—as well as the residential don—but things seemed so settled by 9:25 A.M. that David quietly told the teachers he could handle things from there, and they slipped away. The don, Matt Butler, stuck around a while longer, but by 10:00 he had returned to his room: he was juggling a course at Queen's with his don responsibilities, and the two hours before his lunch duties began were precious to him.

David paused at the door to Angus Graves's room, then knocked quietly. Angus called, "Come in," and David entered.

Angus Graves had suffered terribly at Dave Sommer's hands the previous spring. Sommer had threatened him for weeks, then, seizing his opportunity one evening, had waylaid Angus on his way back to Eaton House, knocked him to the ground, kicked him in the ribs and head, then stuffed dog shit into his mouth. He had been stopped, eventually, by two other older boys who had pulled him off Angus, then escorted Angus to his head of house. The boy's parents had taken him home for two weeks, and had only with great difficulty been persuaded not to press assault charges against Sommer. They had initially thought that Sommer would be expelled, but the school had simply suspended him for a month, allowing him to return to write his exams on the clear understanding that he should go nowhere near Angus.

Many another boy might have been broken by this assault. Angus hadn't been. Once his ribs had healed, he set about transforming himself from a thin and rather frail young man, into something quite different. His parents had bought him a set of weights, and he had enrolled in a ninjitsu training program at a dojo in Ottawa. The Angus who returned to campus in September was a much stronger and more confident boy than the Angus who had left in June. Stronger, yes, but still, of course, nearly two years younger than Sommer, who had done some karate in his elementary school years, and who was a wiry defenceman on the St. Cuthbert's hockey team.

"Hi, Angus," said David. "Do you mind if I sit down?"

Angus had stood when his head of house came into the room, but he sat back down on his bed once David had settled himself in his desk chair.

"Where's Pablo?" David asked, referring to Angus's room-mate.

"He's down the hall visiting Rafael," said Angus.

"Well, I'm glad I have a few minutes alone with you," said David. "I have to ask you where you were last night. We're asking a lot of people this question, but I think you'll understand why we have to ask you. We know there were bad feelings between you and Dave Sommer, and so naturally the question comes up."

"I don't mind you asking," said Angus. "I was here. In the house. I was working here in my room for a while, and after study period I watched TV in the common room with some of the other guys."

"Okay, that's good," said David. "And honestly, that's what I expected. You didn't go to the library at all?"

"Not last night," said Angus. "I was here."

"In this room, then, until you went up to the common room?"

"Yup."

"And was Pablo here all that time, too?

"No. He was in Rafael's room for most of study period. I think they're working on a project together."

David nodded, but looked pensive.

"Mr. Waters, I hated the guy," said Angus, "and one day I hoped I would get the chance to take a swing at him, but I didn't kill him."

"No, I really didn't think so."

"But I'm glad he's dead," Angus continued. "I'm not going to pretend otherwise. I think he was a lousy human being. I'm glad he's gone. I'm not going to his funeral if they hold it here."

"No one would make you do that," said David. "I certainly wouldn't."

"My parents were really angry when they heard he was back at the school," said Angus. "I wasn't too thrilled, either."

"I understand why you'd feel that way." Privately, David felt precisely the same way, but he couldn't say so for fear of being seen to question the headmaster's judgement.

"I think my parents would have sent me to Lakefield or Trinity if they'd known he was coming back," said Angus. "Of course, it's too late now."

"Yes. Okay," said David, rising. "Thank you. I'll let you get back to your studies, then."

"I'm reading a book for English," said Angus, holding up his copy of *The Night Drummer*. "It's really good."

David nodded. "I'll see you later, Angus. Please tell Pablo I came by."

"I will. Good-bye, Mr. Waters."

"Good-bye for now." David left the room.

★

Proceeding along the hall, David decided to knock on the residential don's door, but there was no answer. He was just moving on when Matt Butler came down the stairs in his bathrobe, his hair wet from the shower. His room wasn't equipped with a bathroom.

"You looking for me, Mr. Waters?"

"I just wanted to check in with you, Matt."

"Come in," said Matt. He opened his door and David followed him into the tiny apartment.

"I've just spoken with Angus," David said. "The chaplain asked me to have a preliminary chat with him."

"I'm not surprised."

"I'm pretty well convinced he had nothing to do with it. He says he was here all last night—working in his room during study period and watching television in the common room afterwards. I'm going to suggest that the police don't need to interview him."

"Watching TV in *our* common room?" said Matt.

"Yes. With some other boys."

"He wasn't there when I went by after study period," said Matt. "The guys were watching *Law and Order*, and I sat down with them for about ten minutes."

"Oh," said David. "Well. That puts a different spin on things." The two men studied each other.

THE SCHOOL'S RECEPTIONIST, Carol Winchester, ushered the chaplain and the detective into the school's executive board room—a beautifully appointed space just around the corner from the headmaster's office. Diane adjusted her holster, sat down at the table, and removed a notebook from her breast pocket.

"So the first boy we're speaking to is Stephen Bradley," said Luke. "He's the student head of Roper House, the same residence Dave Sommer lived in. The house itself is just twenty yards away: you can get in through the foyer we crossed through to come in here."

"What do you mean by a student head?" asked Diane.

"He's the senior student chosen to lead a particular residence," said Luke. "He is, roughly speaking, the equivalent of the faculty head of house. He—or *she*, in the girls' houses—represents the students in the house to the faculty head of house. The faculty head of house consults him or her before making major decisions. Usually. And the don is part of the decision-making and supervisory mix, too."

"Okay," said Diane. "I think I get it. And do you know this young man?"

"Yes, to some degree," said Luke. "Stephen's a bright fellow. Serious. Mostly good-hearted, I think. But he's still a boy, in many ways. Seventeen. Quite capable of making bad decisions, as we all are at that age. I made some lousy decisions when I was seventeen."

"So did I," said Diane. "Let's bring him in."

"Is there anything special you want me to do?"

"Yes. I'll ask the first few questions, but feel free to jump in. Sometimes I just like to look and listen."

Luke went to the door that opened into a comfortable lounge where the admissions department often met with parents and children considering enrolment. He opened it, stepped out, and saw Stephen Bradley sitting with his friends Hasan and Marcus. "Come in, Stephen," he said. When he and Stephen were both seated at the board table, Luke made a quick introduction: "Stephen, this is Detective-Sergeant Stewart of the Kingston Police. She's leading the investigation into the death of Dave Sommer. Detective-Sergeant Stewart, this is Stephen Bradley, student head of Roper House."

"Hi, Stephen," said Detective Stewart. "Thank you for talking to us. Your head of house says that you came to him with some information about Dave Sommer on the night of his death." There was no inflection at the end of the sentence.

"Yes," said Stephen, shifting a little uneasily in his chair. "He was with me and some of my friends for part of the evening. The early evening."

"Can you tell us what you told your head of house?"

"Yeah," said Stephen. "Last night, Marcus and Hasan and Sommer and me, and two boys in grade nine, were in my room and we played around with a Ouija board. This was after dinner, but still early. And we played around, you know, and the Ouija told us things— it said that one of the grade nines was going to, going to have sex this year—and then Sommer asked if it had a message for him."

Stephen looked at the chaplain and the detective, as if expecting them to say something. Neither spoke, however.

"So, yeah, the pointer spelled out the message, *Watch your back*, and we all laughed about it, and then we decided that was enough of that, and the grade nines left, and Sommer left and then Marcus and Hasan.... And we said this to Wong already, but please don't tell Hasan's parents about it because they're strict Muslims and they might send him to Pakistan. Don't tell them about the Ouija board, I mean."

There was a brief silence. "Watch your back," said the detective thoughtfully.

"Yeah, that's what the board said."

"And who do you think might want to send that message to Dave Sommer?" She looked intently at the young man across the table from her.

"That's the question Wong asked—Mr. Wong—but I mean, I don't know. *I* didn't send it, and I don't think Marcus or Hasan did, or the two grade nines. I mean, everyone can see the pointer. We've all got our fingers on it. If someone was... *controlling* it, we could all tell."

Detective Stewart leaned back in her chair and looked at the ceiling. Luke took his cue.

"Was this your Ouija board, Stephen?"

"No, it was Marcus's board. He got it from his room."

"And you all had your fingers on the pointer?"

"Well, not all of the time. Not for every question, no."

"And for this one?" Luke pressed.

"I think it was me, and Marcus, and Hasan, and Sommer."

"So what's your explanation for what happened? Luke continued.

"I don't know. I really don't know. I don't have an explanation. It was so weird that I think, maybe, there was something supernatural about it..."

"No, Stephen," said Detective Stewart, jumping back in. "I don't think so. I think that one of you boys somehow manipulated the pointer. You are saying, though, that it wasn't you?"

"It wasn't me," said Stephen. "It definitely wasn't me."

"And how did *you* feel about Dave Sommer?" The detective asked, again looking intently at the boy.

"I didn't like him. But I wouldn't want to *kill* him."

"What was he doing in your room?"

"He just came by. I was talking with Marcus and Hasan and the door was open."

"And why didn't you like him?"

Stephen hesitated. "I didn't like what he did to Angus Graves last year. And he's done some other things to people that I don't like. He can be a bully."

Luke cleared his throat before picking up the questioning. "How do you think Marcus and Hasan feel about him?"

"I don't think they like him much either. Not many people in our grade do."

"Would either of them dislike him even more than you?"

Stephen hesitated again. Then: "*None* of us liked him. No one wanted to room with him."

"And when was the last time you saw him?" Luke again.

"He left a few minutes after we did the Ouija board thing. He said he was going back to his room."

"And did he go alone?"

"Yeah. I think so. Study period was starting. He went up to his room, and Marcus and Hasan went to theirs."

"And absolutely no contact after that?" Luke asked.

"No. None."

"Okay," said the detective. "Thank you. That's all for now."

"That's it?" said Stephen, surprised. Luke looked surprised, too.

"That's it for now," said the detective. "But could I ask you to go straight back to your room? Please don't speak with your two friends."

"Okay," said Stephen, getting up. Luke rose, too. "Um, thank you."

"Thank you," said Detective Stewart. Luke followed Stephen to the door, opened it into the waiting area, and watched Stephen pass his friends and begin to cross the foyer toward Roper House.

"We'll be with one of you in a moment," Luke said to Marcus and Hasan, then returned to the table. "What did you think?"

"You may have missed your vocation," said Diane, smiling.

"Sorry?"

"You're good at questioning. You asked the right things."

"Oh. Thank you. I often sit in on discipline meetings here. We have something called the discipline committee. Students call it the Star Chamber."

Diane nodded. "Do you think Stephen really believes there is something supernatural about the Ouija board?'

Luke thought for a moment. "No, but I hesitated because residence is a hot house atmosphere and strange ideas can sometimes take hold. He's a particularly bright boy."

"Bright people can believe some crazy things."

Luke nodded. "Whatever he believes about that, though, I don't think he hated Sommer enough to want to kill him."

"You don't suppose Sommer could have made a play for some girl he's in love with? That can wind people up a lot."

"News like that would spread like wildfire on this campus," said Luke. "So, no, I don't think so."

"One final thing before we call in one of the other boys. Would there be a good reason for students to go into the chapel in the later evening? A legitimate reason?"

"Not the later evening. Private piano lessons take place throughout the day and into the evening—when there aren't chapel services, of course—but the last one would end at around 8:30, 9:00 P.M. I checked earlier, and there weren't any scheduled past 7:00 last night. Now, sometimes our more serious musicians do go in there to play after the lessons—we've got a baby grand in there. But the doors are usually locked by the teacher-on-duty at 10:00."

"Usually?" Diane arched an eyebrow.

"Not on Sundays. Sometimes—but not always."

"And would students ever go in there after 10:00—if they could?"

"On two occasions last year we found used condoms behind the altar," Luke said. "It has been a trysting place for couples."

"So he could have been meeting a girl there?"

"Yes."

"Or, I guess, another boy," said Diane.

NOT LONG AFTER Martha and Jill had settled the two upset female students in separate rooms in the health centre, and just twenty minutes after Martha had dispatched a robustly healthy Peter Grose back to his residence, a couple of bright-faced, well-dressed women in their mid- to late-thirties presented themselves at the front desk. "Hello," said Jill. "What can I do for you?"

"We're the grief counselors," said the taller of the two. "I'm Tiffany Burgis, and this is Lolly Cole."

"The grief counselors," Jill repeated. "Were you told to come here?"

"Yes," said Lolly. "We're from the Health Unit. We understand there's been a death, and we were sent here to help out."

"Oh," said Jill, "well, this is the health centre, not the main office—"

"Hold on," said Martha, coming to the desk from her little office behind the reception area. "I've just got an email about these ladies. You're here to counsel the kids about the death of the Sommer boy, is that right? To talk to anyone who's having problems?"

"That's right, yes," said Lolly.

"The email said you'd be here in the *afternoon*," said Martha, in a mildly accusatory tone.

"Our supervisor said that the sooner we got here the better," said Tiffany. She picked a small white thread off her purple blouse.

"Well, we've got two girls in here now, and you're welcome to speak to them," said Martha. "They didn't really know the boy, so I've no idea why they're so upset."

"Adolescents feel things very keenly," said Lolly.

"No, I don't think that's it. Not with these two. They're just caught up in the drama of it all. Girls love drama."

"I think it may be a bit more complicated than that," said Tiffany.

"I don't. Jill, can you take these ladies to the girls' rooms? They might as well speak with them there." Jill rose, went around the glass partition, and led Tiffany and Lolly down the hall to the rooms where the girls were resting. "Any problems?" asked Martha, upon her return.

"Not really," said Jill. "One of the girls began crying again when we went in."

"Of course, she did," said Martha. "Drama. They both think they're the main character in some epic movie." She snorted. "And if those two women were men, I'd have taken them for Mormon missionaries."

"Please come in, Hasan," Luke said, and ushered Hasan into the board room, gesturing him to a seat across the table from himself and Detective-Sergeant Stewart. Hasan sat down.

"Thank you for your patience, Hasan," said the detective. "We'd like to go over a few details about yesterday evening with you."

"Sure." Hasan's face was composed, but he kept rubbing his right thumb with his left thumb and index finger.

"Can you tell us what happened in Stephen Bradley's room after dinner?"

"Yeah. Um, me and Marcus were in there talking with Stephen, just hanging out, and two new boys went by and Stephen called them in—"

"Why?" Detective Stewart interjected.

"Pardon?"

"Why did he call them in?"

"He was just being friendly. He's the student head of Roper, and… and he takes it seriously. He asked if they were doing okay." He looked from the chaplain to the detective, as if expecting another question.

"Go on, Hasan," said Luke.

"Well, we were talking, and then Sommer came by, and he came in, too, and the new boys, the grade nines, said they were a bit nervous about the year, wished they knew what was going to happen, and Marcus said we should ask the Ouija board."

"Was this Stephen's Ouija board?" asked the detective.

"No, no—this was Marcus's. He went to get it from his room. And he brought it back, and we fooled around with it for a while."

"Sommer was a willing participant in this?"

"Yeah. Oh, yeah."

"And then?"

"Well, the grade nines asked questions, and Marcus asked a question, and I think Stephen maybe asked a question, and then Sommer."

"You didn't ask the board anything?" Luke asked.

"No. No. I'm Muslim. We're not really supposed to go near that sort of thing."

The detective leaned forward a little. "But you *did* participate? You put your hand on the pointer."

"My finger. Yes, I did. It was dumb." Hasan began massaging his whole right hand with his left.

"It may have been dumb, Hasan," said Luke gently, "but it wasn't *criminal*. We're not really concerned about the fact that you guys were using a Ouija board. We just want to know what happened next."

"Well, Sommer asked if the board had any information for him."

"*Information?*" Detective Stewart pressed.

"Message. I think he said *message*."

"And what did the board spell out?" The detective again.

"Watch your back. It said *Watch your back*."

"And how did you all respond?" Luke asked.

"We sort of laughed. You know, it was a joke kind of thing. No one took it seriously."

"Sommer included?"

"Yeah. I mean, he accused Marcus of moving the pointer, but he wasn't being serious."

"Why do you think he accused Marcus?" the detective asked.

"I don't know. Probably because it was his board," said Hasan, shrugging.

"And did you move the pointer, Hasan?"

"No. No, I didn't. I had a finger on it, but I didn't try to move it. The thing just moved. It seemed to move by itself. It was a bit freaky."

"How do you feel about Sommer, Hasan?" asked Luke.

Hasan was silent for a moment. "He's not my most favourite person."

"Why?" Luke again.

"I think he's gross. I don't like the way he talks about girls. And he has these magazines that I... I think are weird."

"What kind of magazines?" asked the detective.

"Photos of women tied up and getting, you know, whipped and... and stuff. Porno stuff. It's too much."

"Are you glad he's dead?" the detective again.

"No," said Hasan, looking her in the eyes. "People can change. I've seen people change. Maybe he could have got better."

"When was the last time you saw him?"

"In Stephen's room. He left just before Marcus and I did."

"And you didn't see him at all after that? You didn't bump into him in the bathroom, or see him in the common room?" Luke asked.

"No. None of us did. So far as I knew, he went up to his room to study. Or to look at his magazines."

"Anything else you want to tell us, Hasan?" Detective Stewart asked.

"Yes." Hasan looked at Luke. "Please don't tell my parents I touched a Ouija board."

"I cannot make you any promises," said the detective gently, "but if the board turns out to be irrelevant to his death, I wouldn't myself be interested in saying to anyone, look, that young Hasan Kasab was playing with it. That's as far as I can go."

"And I don't personally plan on reporting to your parents," Luke said. "What they may hear, possibly, is that you spent some time with him early in the evening, but maybe no more than that. But again, I can't make any guarantees. It depends where Detective Stewart's investigation takes her."

"Okay," said Hasan. "Can I go?"

Luke looked at Diane. She nodded. "You can go," Luke said. "But please don't speak with Marcus on the way out."

"I won't," said Hasan. He got up and went to the door. "Sommer didn't have many friends here, but I think he just got himself a girlfriend. You should probably speak to her."

"Wait—what?" said Luke. "Who is she?"

"I don't know her name. I think they just got together a couple of days ago. He told Marcus, not me."

"Thank you," said Detective Stewart. "We'll ask Marcus about her."

Boone House was one of the newest residences at St. Cuthbert's. Named for an alumnus who made a fortune in retail sales, the building went right up to the edge of the woods. It was a boys' house, and many of the young inhabitants on the ground floor slipped out of their bedroom windows and into the woods for a smoke once night fell.

It was not dark at nearly 11:00 in the morning, but nicotine is a demanding mistress. So it was that Riley Morrison left his room with a couple of cigarettes in his shirt pocket, stopping by the room of his friend, Conrad Jones. Conrad was stretched out on his bed, while his roommate, Jorge, was at his desk, headphones on, watching a movie.

"Wanna go for a dig?" Riley asked Conrad.

"Is it safe? Isn't Boomer around?"

"I think he's gone into town. I saw his car pull out a couple minutes ago."

"Sure, then." Conrad scrambled off the bed.

"Should we ask Jorge?"

"Nah, he's trying to quit. He promised his mother, or something." Conrad went over to Jorge, tapped his shoulder, mimed smoking a cigarette. Jorge waved his understanding, and the two other boys exited the room, went to the main door, glanced back down the hall, stepped through the doors, quickly scanned what they could see of the campus, then ducked around the residence and into the woods.

"So why'd Jorge promise his mom not to smoke?" asked Riley. "It's a bit of a weenie thing to do."

"I think she's got cancer."

"Oh, man, that sucks," said Riley, his sympathy aroused. "I take the weenie thing back."

"Yeah. It's a close family," Conrad said. They reached a nicely sheltered area and well-worn spot among the trees. "Oh, Christ, I forgot my digs."

"Don't worry. I brought two," said Riley, producing them. "Ya mooch."

The boys lit their cigarettes, drew the smoke in their lungs, looked around at the trees. "So. Sommer," said Conrad. "Holy shit."

"Holy shit is right."

"Do you think the 'vampires' could have done it?" Conrad drew exaggerated air quotes in the air around *vampires*.

"I don't know. I've been wondering about that. Some of those village kids are crazy."

Conrad spat out a small shred of tobacco. "I hung around with them for a weekend last year. That was enough for me."

"Sommer liked them," said Riley.

"They were nice to him—or nicer than anyone else, anyway. He had money. He bought them booze."

Riley took a deep drag on his cigarette. "That dude Alexis really thinks he's a vampire. And he makes some of the girls believe it, too."

"Some good-looking girls in that group," said Conrad. "If you don't mind Goth."

"Did you get some?"

"Nope. I'm saving myself." Riley was poker-faced for a moment, then they both laughed. "No, man, that's more crazy than I can handle. I don't mind the make-up and the hair, but the little, what do you call them, *vials* of blood and the candles and shit... No."

"But Sommer liked it."

"Yeah. Yeah, he did."

"As you know, Marcus, Detective Stewart and I have already talked with Stephen and Hasan," said Luke, seating himself as Marcus settled into a chair at the board room table. "We're hoping you can clear up some minor inconsistencies in what they said."

"What were the inconsistencies?" asked Marcus.

Detective Stewart opened her notebook. "What we'd like to do is have you tell us what happened last night, and we suspect the inconsistencies will be resolved as we go along. As the chaplain says, these are not major things."

"Okay," said Marcus.

"So," said Luke, spreading his hands. "We're all ears."

"Yeah, so we were in Stephen's room, and some grade nines came along, and they were feeling nervous about the year, because, because they're new, and I suggested we use the Ouija board. My Ouija board."

"When you say *we*," said Luke, "you mean…"

"Right. I mean Stephen, me, Hasan, Sommer. And the grade nines. Gary and Gary. We call them the two Garys."

"And everyone was up for that?"

"Yeah."

"So you got the board, and you asked it some questions…?"

"Yeah, the grade nines asked if they would, like, make a hockey team, pass the year—that sort of thing. One of them asked if he would have sex with anyone this year."

"Go on," said Luke.

"The board said yes, and we all laughed, because it's not going to happen. Not to this kid. He's covered in acne and he's, you know, not very—"

"—Thank you," said Luke, "but I really meant, move on to the question Sommer asked."

"Yeah. Okay. He asked if the board had anything to tell him. And it said, *Yes. Watch your back.*"

"It said *Yes* before *Watch your back*?" Detective Stewart asked, leaning forward.

"No, I guess I was—no, it just said *Watch your back.* Just that. No *yes*."

"And what was Sommer's response?"

"He laughed. We all laughed."

"He didn't accuse you of manipulating the pointer?"

"He didn't *accuse* me, no. I mean, he *said* it—but he was joking. It was a joke. We were friends."

"Friends," said Luke. "Good friends?"

"No," said Marcus. "Not like Stephen and Hasan and me. But we talked, you know. We hung out sometimes."

"So you liked him a bit?" Luke again.

"Yeah. I mean, we weren't close, but we got along. If he'd asked for help with his math, or something, I'd have helped him."

"And what about Stephen and Hasan?" the detective asked. "Did they like him a bit, too?"

"I don't think they liked him all that much. But he was in the house, you know, so they had to get along with him. There's always drama in the girls' houses, but the guys mostly just chill. And if we don't get along with someone, we have a fight—in the basement, or wherever—and then it's over."

"So a fight sort of clears the air?" said Detective Stewart.

"Yeah. In a way. Usually. We put on hockey helmets and gloves and just go at it."

There was a knock on the door, and Carol Winchester entered with a tray of soft drinks and glasses. She put them on the table.

The detective looked surprised. "For us?" she said.

"Yes," said Carol. "The headmaster asked me to bring them in." She smiled and exited.

"We don't get that kind of service at the police station," Detective Stewart said.

"Can I pour you a drink?" Luke asked.

"No, not now, thanks." said Diane. She shook her head slightly. "Marcus? Would you like a Coke or something?"

"No. Thank you."

Luke took a can of apple juice from the tray and caressed it in his hands for a moment. "Did Sommer confide anything to you in the past few days?"

Marcus thought for a moment. "How do you mean, *confide*? He showed me his stash of porno magazines just after we got back from the park. I guess he doesn't show those to everyone."

"Maybe something more personal," said Luke.

"Well, I guess he jacks off with them," said Marcus. "That's pretty personal. He didn't say that, but..."

"Let me be a little more specific," said Detective Stewart. "Did he mention a girlfriend?"

"Oh! Yeah! Yes, he did," said Marcus. "He said he just landed himself a... well, he didn't say *girlfriend*, exactly."

"What word did he use?" asked Luke.

Marcus screwed up his face. "I don't really want to say the word he used."

"Let me help you out," said the detective. "Fuckbuddy?"

Marcus looked even more uncomfortable. "No. It was sort of worse than that."

"I'm not squeamish. I'm a cop. We see—and hear—everything."

Marcus looked at Luke. "Go ahead, Marcus," Luke said.

"He said he'd got himself a whore."

There was a pause. "And by that did you understand that he'd hired a prostitute?" Detective Stewart said.

"No," said Marcus. "I got the impression that it was a student."

"A St. Cuthbert's student?" asked Luke, a note of incredulity in his voice.

"Yeah. That was the impression he gave me."

"And did you believe him?" Luke again.

Marcus shrugged. "I don't know. I thought he called her a whore because he wanted to, you know, sound like a big man—a hot shot. And some guys just call women *whores*, so... I mean,

I know that's not right, and I don't do it, but some guys just do. I didn't think much about it. The magazines distracted me."

"Because they were so explicit?" asked Luke.

"Yeah, but they were also weird. And sick. I've seen porno magazines before, but these were a whole different thing."

"And did he give you the name of his... partner?" asked the detective.

"Nope. I asked him, and he said he might tell me later. I didn't push it."

"I'm curious why not?"

"Because, as I said, I didn't know if I should believe him," said Marcus. "It may have been true, but... Most of the girls here don't like him."

"Anything else you think we should know?"

"I don't think so....Who's going to tell his parents?"

"The local police will already have sent someone," said Detective Stewart. "His parents will have been informed by now."

DICK CARGILL LOWERED himself into an armchair in the headmaster's office, breathing heavily. He had been preoccupied, in the time since the faculty meeting, with debriefing heads of house and drawing up names of staff and students who should probably be interviewed, either by the headmaster and himself, or by Luke and the detective, or perhaps by other police officers. Dick did not enjoy talking on the phone: it was a necessary evil in his administrative position, but he felt most fulfilled and happy in the music room or onstage directing the school band—and he'd had to surrender the latter role upon becoming senior master.

"Any leads, Dick?" Jim asked.

"One, maybe. I had a talk with David at Ingram House. He spoke with Angus Graves a little while ago and came away thinking he probably wasn't involved."

"Well, that's a relief."

"Yeah, *but.*" Dick raised a finger. "Angus said he was in the common room watching television yesterday evening, and David believed him. But then he spoke with Matt Butler—"

"—*David* spoke with Butler?"

"Yeah, *David* spoke with Butler, and Butler said that he spent some time in the common room and Angus *wasn't* there. So…"

"So it's possible that Angus is implicated somehow." Jim blew his breath through his teeth. "Jesus."

"Otherwise, no real news. None of the heads saw or heard anything at the house meetings that struck them as suspicious. I haven't yet spoken with any of the dons, though, and sometimes they have their ears a little closer to the ground."

"Okay." Jim drummed his meaty fingers on his desk. "I spoke with Sommer's father."

"How did that go?"

"The police had just left, so maybe he was in shock. I don't know. He sounded flat."

"Flat?"

"Detached. As if he had something else on his mind. It must have been shock. They're coming here tomorrow to talk about funeral arrangements."

"Will the funeral happen here?"

"I think so. That was my impression. And they don't have a family minister, so Luke will probably be doing it."

"Has he done any funerals since his fiancée died?"

"I don't know. Not here, obviously, but the bishop sometimes has him step in when another priest is sick. He hasn't mentioned funerals, but I just don't know." Jim got up and looked out the large window behind him: his view was of a grove of soaring oaks, with, incongruously, in the centre, a small circular pond and modest fountain — the gift of a donor whose generosity had built the school's new dining hall. Jim's predecessor had tried to tell her that the intake valve of the fountain would regularly become clogged with leaves, but she had insisted that St. Cuthbert's accept the gift.

"Have you been in touch with the board chair?" asked Dick.

"We've spoken three times in the past three hours. He and John Hill are coming down tomorrow morning. They want to meet with me and Sarah."

"I'm guessing that Sarah is freaked out?"

"She says that we can expect applications to dry up completely once word gets out. It's already a brutal market." The headmaster turned away from the window. "This could sink us."

Detective-Sergeant Stewart put down her can of club soda, jotted a brief note into her notebook, then stared off into space. Neither she nor Luke felt they could fully exculpate any of the Roper House seniors, but both thought, on balance, that none of them had discernible motive to kill Sommer. They also felt that Steven's glibness told against him, at least to some degree.

"I still think," said Luke, picking up the thread of that conversation, "that of the three, Stephen was the one most likely to manipulate the pointer."

"I agree," said Diane, "but why—to what end—if he wasn't involved in the killing?"

"Embarrassment? Or maybe he wanted to avoid any focus on himself? And if he said he had guided the thing, we would be paying more attention to him."

"I'm not sure I would," said Diane. "If he came clean and said he did it because he didn't like the guy, that he just wanted to scare him, I might buy that."

"It would be a pretty weird coincidence, though."

"That's one reason we can't rule it out." Diane's BlackBerry rang, a loud jangling noise that made Luke jump. "Hello?" she said. A brief conversation followed, ending with "see you in five."

"Another police officer?" asked Luke.

"Callum Brezicki, a detective-sergeant from the OPP," said Diane. "My inspector called the OPP for support as soon as he heard that Sommer is from Toronto. Plus we've got a murder investigation going in Joyceville right now, so our resources are stretched pretty thin."

"He must have set out right away if he came down from Toronto."

"Three hours," said Diane. "He'd have set out at 8:15, or thereabouts. Very doable, with the right weather conditions. More difficult if he'd been going the other way." She closed her notebook. "I'll take him to the crime scene, then he and I should go somewhere private so I can bring him up to speed. Do you mind if I use this room?"

"I'm sure that's okay," said Luke. "Do you want some lunch brought here?"

"Can you arrange for that?" asked Diane, still startled by the hospitality.

"Sure," said Luke. "I'll ask Carol to put in a call to the food services staff. I need to go and speak to the headmaster, so I'll do that on the way."

"Great, thank you," said Diane, getting to her feet. "The driveway's through that door, correct?" She pointed.

"Yes," said Luke. "I'll catch up with you later."

Bath Secondary School, some kilometres west of Kingston, was one of many rural Ontario high schools struggling to stay open in 2004. Even with students bussed in from a large area, the population in grades nine through twelve only just stayed above four hundred. A wealthy independent residential school like St. Cuthbert's could flourish with three hundred and fifty, but public-school trustees had warned that if BSS's enrollment fell below four hundred, the school would be closed and students bussed into Kingston, or, worse still, out to Ernestown.

Bath Secondary was essentially a concrete block, two stories high, with a gym, a cafeteria, a small library, and one playing field. It had no air-conditioning, and the heating ceased working several times each winter. The teachers were mostly hard-working and conscientious, but the knowledge that the school could close at any time, and that they might be deployed to any of eleven other schools over a large area, discouraged them from putting down roots in the community.

Alexis Wardle was skipping gym class. There was nothing unusual about his skipping gym class—or any class, for that matter. Alexis had no interest in school. A tall and slender young man of seventeen, dark hair to his shoulders, gold earring in his right earlobe, a braided gold chain around his neck, trench-coated even in warm fall weather, Alexis cut a striking figure in the school and in the village. On this particular late morning he was sitting in the cafeteria drinking a coffee with his girlfriend Joanie, also seventeen, also tall and slender, also dark-haired, with a ring in her lower lip and—though this was new—another in her right nipple. The nipple-ring was hurting her, and she kept rubbing it.

"Do you want me to lick that better?" Alexis asked. "I'll use my tongue on you any time." He stuck his tongue out at her and wiggled it provocatively.

"Later," she said, pain warring with desire. "I think I should get some cream for it."

"I'll get you some," he said. "Tell me what you need, I'll buy it."

"You'll *boost* it, you mean," she said. She examined her black nail polish critically. It needed touching up.

"Nah, I'll buy it. I've got some cash." He took her hands in his and brought them to his lips. Her heart beat a little faster. She liked it when he was romantic.

"Where'd you get cash from?"

"Dave fronted me some for some weed."

"Dave Sommer?"

"Yup."

"How much?"

"Two hundred."

"Two hundred!"

"Aw, it's a drop in the bucket for a rich kid. I'll get him a baggie for one hundred and keep the rest as a broker's fee. And you and me can do something together in Kingston later this week."

"Will he be okay with that?"

"He'll be happy as a little puppy dog with the pot, and he'll cream his jeans if he can smoke it with you and Peggy."

"He's a bit gross, you know. I don't like the way he looks at me. And Peggy and Trev hate him."

"Why do they hate him?"

"I think he made a pass at Peggy's little sister. And she's like twelve. She hasn't got her period yet."

"That's so not cool," said Alexis, his voice hardening.

"I know. Trev wanted to go out to the school and rough him up last night."

"Did he go?"

"I don't know." She shrugged. "I can ask Peggy."

Detective-Sergeant Callum Brezicki pulled his Ford Crown Victoria into St. Cuthbert's long, tree-lined driveway with mixed feelings. He was glad to be working: he always felt most fully alive when dealing with death. Two lost marriages testified to the obsessive nature of his focus when working a case. On the other hand, he had a deep-rooted hatred of wealth and privilege, and to him St. Cuthbert's embodied both things. He grudgingly admired the beauty of the grounds and the judicious way that the school's buildings had been nestled into the landscape, but he felt strongly that properties like this one should be in public hands. He'd been affectionately nicknamed "Bolshie Brezicki" by an English-born detective, a former partner, and while, in truth, he was no fan of communism, he wore the label with a little pride.

Callum and Diane had never met, but his detective inspector had shown him a photograph of her, raising his eyebrows and muttering "Affirmative action bullshit" as he did so. Callum was less disposed to judge: he had a couple of adult daughters—daughters who had worked hard right through school and university, and were now trying to make their own way in the world. From what he'd seen of their male peers over the years, he was perfectly prepared to believe that a woman might sometimes do a better job, faster, than a man... but, yes, he too had encountered cases when hiring or promotion had been based more on sex or race than competence. In any event, he would have recognized Diane as a policewoman even if she'd been part of a crowd of people waiting for him on the driveway: there's something about the way an officer stands that allows another officer to recognize a kindred spirit. "Detective-Sergeant

Stewart?" he asked, pulling up beside her and rolling down his window.

"Yes. Good to meet you, Detective-Sergeant Brezicki," she replied. "Please call me Diane."

"Callum—please. Where do you recommend I park?" Diane pointed him to the parking-lot near the health centre, and a minute later the two of them were striding towards the chapel. "Has the coroner come?" Callum asked.

"Come and gone. He suspects that the murder—and it was a murder—took place between 9:00 and 12:00 last night. Two stab wounds: the first, probably, to the belly and another to the neck. Both were delivered with great force, so he thinks the assailant was probably male."

"Is the body still here?" They were drawing near the chapel, and Constable Chad Lowell retreated a few steps to open the doors for them. "Thank you, constable."

"Sir. Ma'am."

"Yes," said Diane as they entered. "The body is still here— though the funeral home team will arrive any moment to pick it up." They proceeded up the central aisle. Constable Art McCue was standing a few feet from the body, and he stiffened and stood up straighter in a rough approximation of coming to attention. There were two other police constables in the chapel, both combing the place for anything the killer might have dropped or discarded, and there were several lights on tripods scattered here and there, though only one was still on.

"Skeleton crew," said Callum.

"We have a big case in Joyceville right now. We're stretched thin."

"So I've heard."

"Detective Brezicki, this is Constable Art McCue," Diane said. "Detective-Sergeant Brezicki is helping us with our inquiries, Art."

"Sergeant," said Art.

Callum nodded, then squatted down next to the body. "Major bleed-out. And significant lividity."

"Someone was really angry," said Art.

"It looks that way," said Callum. "And it looks as though he was on his way out of the chancel, but didn't get far. I wonder if he was behind the altar when he was stabbed."

"There is a spray of blood on the carpet back there," said Diane. "And on the back of the altar. I think you're almost certainly right." She had reached the same conclusion herself.

Callum went behind the altar to confirm this. While the great mass of blood was under the body, there was indeed some on the blue carpet behind the altar, and on the great grey carved rock itself. "Has this whole area been dusted for prints?"

"Yes," responded one of the other constables from half-way down the nave.

"All right," said Callum. "Good." And to Diane: "Is there somewhere we can go and have a chat?

Back on the school driveway, a black Dodge van with chrome landau bars on the rear side panels arrived, *Steven E. Silver & Son* stencilled on the side window. The van drove just past the pathway leading to the chapel, then backed up so it parked as close as possible without trespassing onto the grass. Two black-suited, gloved men in sunglasses climbed out, one fifty-five and greying at the temples, the other in his mid-twenties—both on the heavy side but impeccably dressed. "Good morning, constable," the older man said to the officer standing outside the chapel.

"Morning, Mr. Silver," said Constable Chad. "Hi, Ernie."

"Chad," said the younger man. He went around to the back of the vehicle, opened the doors, and pulled out a collapsed stretcher on wheels, which he and his father then raised to a proper height and began wheeling toward the chapel: there was a body bag on top of the stretcher. The constable opened the doors for them.

"Thank you, constable," said the older Silver, and the two men proceeded into the chapel—meeting Detective-Sergeants Stewart and Brezicki as they came down the aisle on their way to the board room.

"Mr. Steven Silver and Mr. Ernie Silver," said Diane. "May I introduce my colleague from the OPP, Detective-Sergeant Brezicki? He's just come down from Toronto to help us with our investigation."

Callum would probably have been content with a nod, but the older Silver was a more formal fellow: he removed his right glove and extended his hand, obliging the detective to shake it. "Always glad to meet a police officer," Mr. Silver said. "The thin blue line is an important thing to us. Isn't it, Ernie?"

"It certainly is," said the younger man.

"Uh, thank you," said Callum. "We cops aren't used to hearing that in Toronto."

"Welcome to the heart of Loyalist Ontario," said Mr. Silver. "We're church-going, law-abiding, patriotic Canadians down here."

Callum looked a little stunned by this declaration, but he managed to smile: "I'm glad to be here."

"Yes, sir," said Mr. Silver. "It's just a shame it's such a sad event that brings you down here." He shook his head thoughtfully a few times. "Well, Diane, I guess we'd better attend to the deceased."

"Forensics are finished, Steven, so we've done all we need to do here," said Diane. "You are good to go."

"Ernie," said Steven, indicating that they should move forward. Ernie pushed the stretcher up close to the body, then took the body bag and set it down next to Sommer's corpse. "Do you need a hand?" asked Art.

"No, thank you, constable," said the older Mr. Silver. "We've got this. The boy and I have done this a few times before, haven't we, Ernie?"

"A thousand times, Dad," said Ernie.

"Give or take a couple," said the older Mr. Silver. "Give or take." Ernie opened the bag as wide as it would go, then the two men expertly lifted the body into the bag. Mr. Silver senior zipped it up, while his son lowered the stretcher to make the second lift easier. This done, the two men lifted the bag onto the stretcher, then secured it with two straps. They stood up, took identical linen handkerchiefs from their pockets and mopped their brows, then Ernie raised the stretcher again and began pushing it back down the aisle.

"So young," said the older Mr. Silver to Art. "So very young. He should be outside kicking a ball, not inside a body bag heading for the mortuary slab. This kind of work gives me no joy, Art."

"I guess it wouldn't, Mr. Silver," said Constable Art.

"What man can live and not see death?" said Mr. Silver. "That's from a psalm—Psalm eighty-nine. A lot of wisdom in the psalms, constable."

"Yes, Mr. Silver," said Art.

Mr. Silver senior rocked back and forth a couple of times, then followed his son out of the back doors of the church.

When the van left the school a few minutes later, it was closely followed by a police car. Rules respecting the continuity of evidence required it.

Whig-Standard JOURNALIST Jonathan Harker, forty-eight, married but childless, pulled into the St. Cuthbert's driveway, steering cautiously for fear of having students suddenly dart out from either side of the road. His editor had been very direct: "Get out to the school—something's going on. Drive carefully when you hit the grounds. Those little fuckers have more money than God, and their parents will sue our asses to hell and back if you hit one of them." Jonathan had visited the school twice before in his three years at the *Whig*—both times to attend concerts in the theatre. He had a fondness for choral music, and a cultural group in Bath sometimes rented the facility to showcase choirs from all over Canada and the United States.

He had a eureka moment when he drew near to the chapel: the sight of Silver Funeral Home's black van told him that there had been a death, and the presence of Detective-Sergeant Stewart's Chevy Impala, and of two squad cars, signalled that the death was almost certainly suspicious. He parked his 1997 Mazda2 in the lot near the health centre, turned off his police scanner, and unfurled himself from the driver's seat. The vehicle was too small for his six-foot frame, but it was all he could afford.

As he crossed the driveway heading toward the chapel and the reception office in the main building, he saw a skinny young woman in a very short blue school skirt heading toward the health centre. "Hey," he called, "do you know why the police are on campus?"

"There's been a murder," she replied. "Dave Sommer was killed."

"Is Dave Sommer a student?"

"Yes, he's in grade twelve," she said. "Do you have a kid here?"

"No," he replied. "I'm on my way to see the principal."

Reassured that this man must be legitimate, she nodded. "I've gotta go. I have an allergy shot."

"Sorry to have detained you," said Jonathan. The girl moved on, her skirt not far below her buttocks. He reflected that had she been a student at the Catholic school he himself attended, she would have been sent home for the day: his principal had been obsessed with skirt length. Apparently Anglican schools were a little more relaxed about these matters. He moved on, nodding to the constable standing outside the chapel—who eyed him with mild suspicion—and passing through the large door into the main building. He turned left toward the reception area, noting that there was another police constable in the narthex, standing in front of what he assumed to be the inside entrance to the chapel.

"Good morning," said Carol Winchester, her receptionist cheer doing battle with a general air of anxiety and distress.

"Good morning," said Jonathan, unleashing his most winning smile. "I'm from the *Whig*. I wonder if I could speak to the principal?"

"I think the headmaster is going to be busy all day," said Carol, "but I can pass you through to his secretary. She's through there." She gestured to another door, through which Jonathan passed before she could change her mind. Debbie was behind her desk, and the headmaster, Jonathan saw, was behind his, on the phone. His door was open, and no one else appeared to be in the room with him.

"May I help you?" asked Debbie.

"I'm Jonathan Harker from the *Whig*. I'm just hoping I can have a quick word with the *headmaster*." He'd got it right this time.

"May I ask what this is about?" Debbie's tone was lukewarm.

Jonathan decided to go for broke. "It's about the murder of one of your grade twelve students," he said. "I'm sure Mr. Harvey would like to get out ahead of this one."

"I'm afraid Mr. Harvey is going to be busy all—" but at the moment the headmaster emerged from his office, looking like a disgruntled bear.

"It's all right, Debbie," he said. "I'll speak with Mr. Harker. Come in." He turned and headed back into his office, gesturing at one of the chairs that sat across from his desk. Jonathan took the seat, very much aware that the headmaster would sooner punch him than answer his questions, but that he did indeed recognize the desirability of 'getting out ahead' of the story.

"So," Jim growled. "What do you know, and how did you hear?"

IN THE BOARD room, Diane briefed Callum on everything she had gleaned to that point. They were interrupted early on by the arrival of lunch—sub-sandwiches, potato chips, a side of vegetable soup, and a carafe of coffee—which surprised the Toronto detective-sergeant as much as the offer had surprised Diane. "For us?" he said to the young woman who wheeled in the tray.

"Yes, sir," she said. "Courtesy of the chaplain."

"Please thank the chaplain," said Callum, as she headed out the door.

"You'll be able to thank him in person soon," said Diane. "He's been very helpful."

"Okay, look," said Callum, biting into his sandwich. "I'm glad he's been helpful. But I have reservations about someone who isn't police sitting in when we question people who could be suspects."

"I understand that," said Diane. "But these people—these teachers and heads of house and the chaplain—are *in loco parentis.* They serve in place of the parents of the kids who live in residence: they're their legal guardians while they're at school. It was the chaplain's presence that made it possible for me to question the boys without their parents' consent."

Callum chewed thoughtfully. "All right. That makes sense."

"As it happens," said Diane, "he also asks good questions. I think I got more from the kids with him there than I would have otherwise."

"Have you considered the possibility that *he* might have committed the murder?"

"Yes."

"And?"

"It seems to me so unlikely that I've set it aside—at least for the moment. My instinct is that we'll solve this one fairly quickly. If I'm wrong, we can look seriously at unlikely suspects. But I don't think I'm wrong."

"So you've questioned three students to this point?"

"Yes. The chaplain and I questioned them separately. We intend questioning all three of them, side by side, this afternoon." Diane poured herself a coffee, then raised the carafe at Callum to ask if he wanted one, too.

"Yes, please…. And you're doing this because you think there are some discrepancies in what they've said?"

"Yeah. But also because I think it may reveal more about who else we should be questioning."

"Okay. I think I'd like to be there for that session."

"By all means. That meeting is here at 4:15 P.M. There's also a session with students and grief counsellors in the chapel at 1:30. I think one of us should—"

"Grief counsellors!" said Callum. "Oh, God, *those* vultures!"

Diane smiled. "Still, I think one of us should be there for that. You never know what might shake loose from the trees."

"Okay," said Callum. "You go with that. I'm going to spend a few hours today focusing on whether the killer might have come from outside the school. I'll whip away for now—but be back at 4:15. I should also check into a hotel."

"The Holiday Inn is just a stone's throw from the station," Diane said. "And I'll call ahead to 11 Queen to tell them you can use my office, if you need it."

"Thank you. I'll take the rest of my sandwich to go," said Callum, taking a good slurp of coffee before he got up, grabbed the remains of his sub and a packet of chips, and made a quick exit.

JUST AS THE meal trolleys were beginning to be returned from the residences to the school dining hall, carrying the largely untouched tureens of vegetable soup that had accompanied the subs and chips, a crew of two arrived on campus from CKWS television in Kingston. The journalist, Chantal Foster, tall, blonde, lithe, and heavily made-up, stepped out from the SUV's passenger seat, followed rather more slowly by her balding driver, Garth Tremblay, who also served as her videographer. Garth lumbered round to the side of the vehicle and pulled out his camera, while Chantal rummaged for her microphone.

"Right," said Chantal: "Let's see who we can find." She headed to the school driveway, her high heels clicking aggressively on the asphalt, while Garth wrestled with his equipment behind her, swearing under his breath at a station management that still declined to invest in less bulky digital gear.

The first person they saw was one of the school's maintenance workers on his way from the maintenance building to one of the residences, a toolbox in his right hand. Phil Harris was a short man, grey-haired, ex-military—still lean and spry at fifty.

"Excuse me," said Chantal, advancing toward Phil like a cat approaching an unwary chipmunk. "Can you spare us a minute?"

Phil stopped and gazed at Chantal as if mesmerized. He was used to seeing beautiful young women on campus, but they rarely paid any attention to him.

"What can you tell us about the murder here at St. Cuthbert's College?" Chantal thrust her microphone towards him.

"It was a student," said Phil. "I don't know his name."

"Are the other students upset?"

"I guess they are. I mean, who wouldn't be? Everyone's upset. It's a… it's a terrible thing."

"Did you know the deceased?"

"No. I work for the maintenance. We don't talk much with the students unless they want something."

"And where did the murder take place?"

"In the chapel." Phil gestured toward the building. "I guess it was right in there. They took the body away about an hour ago. I don't know much more than that."

"And your name, sir?"

"Phil Harris. I work for the maintenance," he repeated. "I used to be in the Forces. Twenty-five years."

"Thank you, Mr. Harris," said Chantal, disengaging from Phil as swiftly as she had swooped down on him. "Garth, follow me. I want some shots of the chapel. I'm gonna talk with the cop."

Jim Harvey hadn't been wildly enthusiastic about inviting grief counsellors to the school. He shared some of his head nurse's skepticism about group therapy, and his own reservations were fuelled by the fear that therapists might be indiscreet about what they heard at St. Cuthbert's. He'd dated a psych major, a terrible gossip, in his undergraduate years at Western, and a headmaster always has to worry about his school's reputation in the community. Still, the Canadian Association of Independent Schools, of which the school was a charter member, had a playbook for crises of every kind, and a violent death in the community apparently called for grief counsellors. So here they were—though the headmaster himself was not in attendance.

The chapel would normally have been the venue for any sensitive meeting with a large group, but the chapel, of course, was a crime scene, and would remain under police guard for at least another twenty-four hours... and after that it would require a thorough cleaning. So as was done for the morning staff meeting, the meeting was called for the theatre. At 1:30 p.m., counsellors Tiffany Burgis and Lolly Cole were escorted by Dick Cargill to chairs on the thrust stage. They sat watching as about thirty students and six teachers straggled in, finding places in the first three or four rows of raked seating. Detective-Sergeant Stewart slipped in shortly before the meeting began and took a seat some rows above everyone else. A moment later, the chaplain sat down beside her.

The senior master introduced the two counsellors, doing his best to sound sympathetic and warm—two qualities with which he was not normally associated. He then took a seat in the front row and sat breathing noisily from the exertion required.

"We're so glad you've come," said Tiffany—she of the purple blouse. "Lolly and I have a lot of experience with helping people come to terms with their grief, and we know that the first step to processing it is to speak it out loud. So, please, feel free to share with us anything you're thinking or feeling. Nothing is inappropriate here. Nothing is off-limits. If you feel it, speak it."

A brief silence followed this declaration. The truth is that several of the students—and a couple of the teachers—had come out of curiosity more than anything else. Yes, a few students were genuinely distressed and had cried real tears, but most of them were more upset by the *idea* of a violent death here, among them, than by any grief over who had died.

But Lydia Arthurs did have a question, and she raised her hand. Dick cursed under his breath when she stood up. "How are we supposed to feel safe?" she asked. "How can we feel confident that one of *us* won't be murdered? I mean, there could be a killer loose on the campus right this instant!" That created a stir.

"I don't think we're really able to address—" Tiffany began, but at that moment Diane Stewart rose.

"You may remember that I am the Kingston detective-sergeant assigned to this case," she said. "While I cannot give an absolute guarantee that there are no persons-of-interest on campus, I can tell you that we have no reason to believe that anyone else is in danger. The police presence alone should discourage any further violence. But more than that, it's our experience that killings of this sort are very personal, very specific. If we suspected otherwise, we would have asked the headmaster to send everyone home." Some of the tension went out of the room.

Lydia began to speak again, but the senior master was already on his feet. "Thank you, Detective Stewart, for those words," Dick said, "and may I just say that this forum is really for *students* to talk about their... their grief and insecurity. We will gladly provide another time and place for staff to speak out."

"No one said that staff weren't supposed—" Lydia began, but Dick cut in again.

"Thank you for respecting that, Ms. Arthurs," he said. "The headmaster and I will gladly discuss this with you further." Lydia Arthurs took the point.

An older student put her hand up. "I didn't really know Dave," she said, "but I know some of his friends, and they're really upset. What can I do to offer them support?"

"Good question!" said Tiffany—and Lolly Cole nodded her head enthusiastically. "Are they here now?"

The young woman quickly surveyed the audience. "No."

"Well," said Tiffany, "then a good place to start would be to encourage them to come and talk with Lolly and me privately. Because obviously they were too upset to come to this meeting."

"I think one of them's in the health centre," said the young woman.

"Oh, then we spoke to her," Lolly piped up. "We were at the health centre this morning. We had a good talk."

And that, essentially, was that. There were a few more desultory questions, but it quickly became clear that no one in the room was experiencing any great trauma. And so things wrapped up, and people left fairly quickly. Luke and Diane stayed where they were for a moment or two longer.

"What did you make of that?" Luke asked.

"I think we've just seen confirmation that Dave Sommer didn't have many real friends," said Diane. "And that's interesting."

"Does it lead you to any conclusions?"

"*Conclusions* would be too strong a word. But it suggests, a little more strongly, that the perpetrator could be another student." She took out her notebook. "Do you know the names of the girls in the health centre?"

"No, but I can get them for you."

"I'd appreciate that." She closed her notebook again. "I'm going back to the chapel for one last look before the clean-up crew arrives."

Joanie Fletcher—"Vampiress Beach Babe" as she was quietly called in the village's tiny heavy-metal circles—entered the girls' bathroom in the basement of BSS at 1:32 p.m. for her pre-arranged smoke break with best pal Peggy Lawrence. Peggy had already lit up and was leaning back against a sink.

"Hey, bitch!" said Joanie, cheerfully.

"Hey, tart!" said Peggy, exhaling a stream of tobacco smoke tinged with just a hint of hash.

"Have you got a snake there?"

"Nah, I had a crumb of hash and I just poked it in the top. Want a draw?"

"Is there any left?"

"I dunno. Try." She extended the cigarette.

Joanie drew in deeply, held her breath, exhaled, coughed. "No, I don't think so. Maybe a little. Thanks."

"You're welcome. What's up?"

"My nipple hurts."

"From the pin? Is it infected?"

Joanie pulled up her shirt and pulled down the right cup of her bra. "Maybe. Alexis is getting me some cream this afternoon."

"It doesn't look too bad. You're getting me all hot and bothered."

"Lesbo. You're so weird." She re-cupped her breast and pulled down her shirt. "So how's Trev?"

"We just had a quick phone call at lunch. He's in a funky mood."

"Why?" Joanie took out her own pack of cigarettes and offered one to her friend. Peggy shook her head no.

"I don't know. He didn't want to talk about it."

"Did he see Sommer last night?"

"I think he went out there, but he was in such a strange space I didn't want to push it."

"Maybe you're not putting out enough."

"Maybe you're a big slut."

Both girls rocked with laughter, and after another couple of minutes, headed back to their separate classes.

YET ANOTHER MEETING in the theatre—this time for all students, with teachers welcome but enjoined by email not to speak unless called upon. Lydia Arthurs had also been sent a personal email from the headmaster's secretary inviting her to a one-on-one meeting with Jim Harvey just before the assembly. She had emerged from his office in tears, heading straight back to her grace-and-favour apartment on campus.

The headmaster and senior master talked quietly together on the stage as students filed in. Usually at school assemblies, Jim liked to wait until all students were seated before making a grand entrance—an entrance that required students to stand until he invited them to sit. But on this occasion, he had decided on a lighter, less formal approach. At a minute or two after 3:00, Dick took a seat in the first row of the theatre, and Jim moved to centre stage.

"We've had a very difficult few hours," he began. "Very sad, very challenging. I want to assure you that the police are confident of solving this crime—and yes, there was a crime—quickly. I also want to tell you that they don't believe anyone else here is in any danger." This went just a little further than what Diane had told him, but Jim saw reassurance and confidence-building as an important part of his role. He didn't want parents summoning their children home, and that was already beginning to happen.

"There will be a limited sports program immediately after this assembly," he continued. "No games—but all teams will be expected to practise. Also yoga, I guess, and tai chi. Oh, and are there any rehearsals scheduled?" he asked, suddenly remembering that the school did have an arts program.

"There are auditions for the fall play," Alison Greer, the performing arts director, called out. "And for the jazz band, I think. Is that right, Corey? Yes, that's right."

"Okay," said Jim. "Well, then, all sports will practise, and all auditions will proceed as planned.... But I also need to tell you that we may be pulling some students out of whatever they're doing, to talk with the chaplain, with Dick Cargill, with myself, or even with the police. Because we're trying, we're trying to put together a picture of where everyone was last night. Now, I want to make clear that just because you're invited to a meeting doesn't mean you're in any kind of trouble. Okay? We're just trying to get a 360 on things. That's all. So, no cause for panic. We're going to get through this....Anything else, Dick?"

The senior master rose from his seat. "Just one thing, Jim. If anyone here has anything they think might—just might—be significant, come and see me, or Luke, after this meeting. It may seem small to you, but if you think it might have the slightest bearing, we'd like to talk to you."

"Yes, good," said the headmaster. "Thank you, Dick. Now, I think that's all. Oh, Heather?"

Heather Dijon, the director of academics, rose from her seat in the third row. "Classes carry on as normal tomorrow," she said. "Day 3A, just as it appears in the published calendar. So it's back to class on Tuesday."

"Thank you, Heather," said Jim. "Okay, everyone. Dismissed."

"Jim," said Dick, approaching the headmaster at centre stage. "I've just remembered something. I've got a bit of a concern about the school play."

"Why's that?"

"It's called *Murder in the Cathedral*," said Dick. "Maybe not the best choice in light of recent events."

After leaving the school campus, OPP Detective-Sergeant Callum Brezicki had gone by the Holiday Inn on the Kingston waterfront and lined up a room. He'd left his suitcase behind the desk, and walked to the nearby Tim Hortons, grabbed a grilled-cheese sandwich and coffee, then crossed the road to the Kingston Police headquarters at 11 Queen Street. The station covered a whole city block, and his inspector had told him to enter by what was called the west door, where on-duty officers rendezvoused with their partners. He'd held up his warrant card and badge to the camera and been buzzed through, and a young constable had directed him to Detective-Sergeant Stewart's office on the second floor. A quick call to Diane secured him her computer password, and he'd logged on to the Canadian Police Information Centre and spent two hours reviewing knife crimes in Kingston, Belleville, Gananoque, Smith Falls, and Brockville. Knife crimes were not uncommon, but knife murders were: the most recent one in Kingston had been two years before, in 2002, but the details of that one, still unsolved, did not resonate at all with the situation at St. Cuthbert's.

Shortly after 3:00 p.m., Callum pushed away from Diane's desk and made his way down to the first floor, where there was a small room set aside for making tea and coffee. He poured one, and nodded to the relatively short gentleman who came in after him—before doing a double-take upon realizing that it was the chief of police. "Sir," he said.

"Detective-Sergeant," said the gentleman in question. "I'm Bill Closs. I'm guessing you're here in connection with the stabbing at St. Cuthbert's."

"I am, sir, yes," said Callum.

"If there's anything you need, don't hesitate to ask. We want this one solved quickly."

"Thank you, sir. I've just been looking at knife crime in the area."

"Good place to start. And you're working with a fine detective. Diane Stewart is very sharp."

"Yes, sir. I'm heading back to the school in a few minutes to meet up with her again."

"Good." Closs nodded. "Good." He picked up his black coffee and headed back to his office.

Callum stirred sugar into this own mug and wandered to the window to look out at the parking lot behind the station. He was standing there when a voice hailed him from behind.

"Oh my God, the competition is in town." The speaker was another detective with the Kingston Police, Tim Peet. Callum had been on a couple of courses with him over the years.

"Hi, Tim," said Callum. "How you doing?"

"I'm well." The two men shook hands. "You're down for the St. Cuthbert's case?"

"I am. No secrets here, clearly."

"Aw, you can't keep secrets from real police. We're always a step or two ahead of you guys."

"Odd that I was called in, then."

"Yeah, well." Tim laughed. "We have to tread carefully when the victim's parents are big honchos in the Big Smoke."

"Have you any thoughts about the whole business? Any advice?"

Tim suddenly got serious. "It's a damnable business. Not simply because it's a kid, and because a knife wound is a brutal way to go, but also because of the ripple effect. This will make the provincial news, and all sorts of other crazies will feel it's time to make their own little statements. And we're already stretched thin here."

"So I gather."

"This Joyceville murder. Man. It looks as though there may be gang involvement. We were throwing everything we had at that, and then this comes along."

"Yeah, I was a little surprised Diane is the only detective working it from Kingston."

"Unless you have a real break in the next twenty-four hours, that could change tomorrow. But with the Joyceville thing, I think Closs had difficulty springing five constables to go to Bath."

Callum nodded. "I get it. Cutbacks everywhere."

"Yup." Tim shook his head. "I've got to get back to my desk: I'm coordinating a little operation. One thought: Bath is a sleepy place, but we arrested a kid from there a couple of weeks back who said he was a vampire. Crazy, I know. But apart from drunk driving, break-ins, and two cases of downloading kiddie-porn, that's all I've seen from there recently."

"Thank you for that," Callum said. "Crazy, but you never know."

"Yup. Take care, bud. Good to see you." Tim left.

Callum thought for a moment, chugged the rest of his coffee, placed his mug in the sink, then headed back to his car in the Holiday Inn parking lot.

Dick Cargill hailed the performing arts director as she was heading down the stairs outside the theatre. "A word, Alison."

Alison looked up and, seeing it was Dick, and in deference to his breathing challenges, came back up nearly to the top. "What's up, Dick?"

"We've got a problem. With the school play."

She allowed herself a small smile. "I know. I sent Kevin an email about it a few hours ago."

"Has he got back to you?"

"Yes. We are… negotiating."

"I wouldn't have thought there was anything to negotiate. He clearly can't direct a play called *Murder in the Cathedral*. Not after these events."

"I mostly agree," said Alison, "but I try not to be too dictatorial about these things."

"Well, feel free to dictate away," said Dick irritably. "Jim and I say it cannot go ahead. He'll have to do something else. Or maybe we'll just scrap the play this year and he can coach volleyball, or something."

Alison did her best to keep her voice level. "Dick, he worked hard over the summer preparing for this. He studied the text carefully. He ordered copies of the script. He did a set design. He did a lighting design. He's had Vanessa design costumes. I don't feel right about just issuing an order."

"He can't direct that play," said Dick. "That's final. No negotiations. Tell him to do a goddamn comedy instead. Or a musical. The parents like musicals."

The two stood looking at each other for a moment, Alison four steps below the senior master. "I'll handle this my way," she said. "Kevin will not be directing *Murder in the Cathedral*, but I'm going to let him feel that he has contributed to the decision. And I'm not going to dictate what he does instead." And having said that, she turned and continued on her way downstairs.

Trevor Lockhart—"Trev" to his friends—sat hunched on his bed in the basement of his mother's north end Kingston townhouse. He had ventured out the previous evening, but things had not gone as he'd expected. He'd come home late, showered, put the clothes he'd been wearing in the laundry, and been in a funk ever since. A half-drunk mickey of vodka sat on the milk crate beside his bed, and he'd taken several belts over the course of the late morning and early afternoon. They hadn't improved his mood.

A timid knock sounded on his door. "Trev." His little sister, Poppy.

"What?"

"Can I come in?"

"No."

"Please."

Trevor thought for a moment, then grabbed the bottle of vodka and hid it under his pillow. "All right."

Twelve years old, Poppy looked at least two years younger: Peggy had once described her as "boob-less and with a figure like a boy." She had said it affectionately—Trev's girlfriend and his sister got along well—but it was true.

"What do you want?" Trev asked.

"Just to talk."

"What about?"

"What's wrong?" She climbed up on his bed and sat facing him.

"What do you mean, *What's wrong*?"

"Something's wrong."

"Yeah, the world's gone to shit."

"No, it hasn't." Poppy made a fist with her little right hand and gave him a gentle punch on his knee.

"It feels that way right now."

"I think things are pretty good for you."

"Oh, you do, do you? How's that?"

"Well—" Poppy raised her fist to her eye level, then uncurled one finger. "I love you."

"Yeah, I love you, too, kid."

She uncurled another finger. "Doing one finger at a time is hard... Mom loves you."

"Yeah, I know."

"Peggy loves you." Another finger.

"Yeah." Trev stared at the coverlet in front of him.

"You love them, don't you?"

"Yeah. I do." But he wouldn't look at her.

Detective-Sergeant Stewart looked at the three young men across the board room table and smiled disarmingly. "Boys, I'm sorry to have taken you away from your practices, but I wanted you to talk with my colleague here, Callum Brezicki of the Ontario Provincial Police. He's very experienced with investigations of this kind, and the chaplain and I are hoping he can prompt you to remember any little details that escaped you when we spoke this morning." Detective-Sergeant Brezicki nodded his support for this. Luke, now sitting behind the two detectives, closed his eyes as if meditating on the importance of review and clarity.

Stephen Bradley cleared his throat. "That's fine."

"Good," said Detective Brezicki. "Now, Detective-Sergeant Stewart did note a couple of inconsistencies that cropped up when she and the chaplain interviewed you separately, and I want to touch lightly on those. She said"—he consulted a page of notes—"she said there was some disagreement among you as to who manipulated the pointer."

"We all did," Stephen said quickly. "I mean, we all had our fingers on it. Didn't we?" He looked to the others for support.

"Yeah, we all had *a* finger on it," said Hasan. "I mean, I had one. I think, maybe, both of you guys had two. And I didn't have my finger on it all the time. I took it off to scratch a mosquito bite or something."

"Yes," said the detective, seeing his opening, "yes, there was a suggestion that maybe one of you had exercised *more* control over the pointer."

"Wait a minute," said Marcus. "Maybe I did have two fingers on it, but *I* wasn't moving it. The thing moved itself."

"Yeah," said Stephen. "It's not like any of us was making it move. It just moved."

Detective Brezicki allowed a silence to settle on the room.

"I mean," Marcus said, "I don't believe in occult stuff… but it *felt* like it moved itself. *I* didn't move it. I kept my fingers on it and I could feel it moving. I swear to God. Really."

Again, Brezicki said nothing. Detective Stewart studied her fingernails. Luke opened his eyes and gazed at the ceiling.

"Stephen, you had two fingers on it, too," Marcus said. "We both had two fingers on it. Hasan maybe only one. I don't know."

Detective Brezicki looked from Stephen to Marcus, then back to Stephen. Stephen bit his lip. The silence was palpable.

Stephen gave a sort of half-sigh. "Look," he said, leaning forward, "okay, I may have helped it spell out *Watch*. I may have done that. I was thinking it would be cool if it said something—said something like a warning, to Sommer. Because he was such a jerk last year. But if I had, I don't know, carried through, I would have made it say something—something more like, just *Watch out*, or *Watch that you don't pick on people*. I wouldn't have made it say *Watch your back* because I, I don't believe in threatening people unless you're going to do something. And *I* wasn't going to do anything to Sommer."

The detective nodded. "Okay, I get that. It makes sense. And I'm grateful that you shared that with us, because it helps. It helps when someone tells the truth. And the truth doesn't necessarily lead us to a conclusion, it doesn't necessarily point us toward a crime, but it helps us rule certain things out." He paused. "So, Hasan."

"What?" said Hasan.

"One finger on the pointer?"

"Yeah. Yeah, most of the time."

"Because you're Muslim, and you're uncomfortable with something that smacks of black magic."

"That's right."

"And some of the time you just had one finger on the pointer?"

"Just one, yeah."

"But some of the time, two?"

"Maybe at the beginning."

"Okay. Marcus."

Marcus looked up.

"You did have two fingers on it all the time?"

"Yeah, probably. I don't have any mosquito bites." He threw an angry glance at Hasan.

"Yeah, well, that's the way the game's played," said Detective Brezicki. "And it is just a game."

"Yup. Just a game."

"I mean, you didn't buy it thinking, *Hey, I'm going to let this thing guide my future.*" He gave a little laugh.

"I didn't buy it."

"It was a gift?"

"Yeah."

"But it's just a game, as you said. An entertainment."

"That's how I saw it," said Marcus.

"And you're a modern young man. You're all modern young men. You don't believe in magic."

"I don't," said Marcus.

"Of course, you don't. Of course not," said Detective Brezicki. "And you didn't think much of Dave's magazines."

"Pardon? I beg your pardon?" Marcus was thrown by the switch in focus.

"You didn't like his collection of magazines." Brezicki let the statement hang there.

"No." Marcus grimaced.

"I understand," said the detective. "I really do. Something disgusts you, you want to do something. You want to show that you don't like it. But it's hard to say something directly without sounding like a, like a…"

"Prude," said Detective-Sergeant Stewart. "No one wants to sound like a prude."

"Like a prude," said Brezicki, nodding. "I was going to say *douche!*" he added, laughing suddenly. The boys laughed too, grateful for the tension-breaker.

Detective Stewart didn't laugh. She smiled, dangerously, and looked directly at Marcus. "*Your back,*" she said. "You contributed *your back.*"

Marcus was silent for a moment, then his whole body sagged. "Yeah," he said. "Maybe. I don't know. When it spelled out the word *Watch*, I thought, I thought, Well, why not? Why not just finish it? But I didn't kill him. I didn't kill him."

"This is good," said Detective Brezicki, rubbing his hands together. "No, really, this is good. Because when we clear away the, the *confusion* we get closer to the truth. We really do. It means we can focus in on what's important. And I want to say right now, very clearly, that I don't think any of you is a bad person. I really don't."

"Thank you," said Stephen.

"No need to thank me," said the detective. "No need at all. That's simply an objective truth. I mean, all of us have little, what shall I say, *kinks* in our character, but let's be honest—Dave Sommer was a whole other ball of wax. I mean, I've seen those magazines. Jesus."

Hasan nodded vigorously. "Yeah."

"Yeah," said Detective Brezicki. "Sick shit. Choking. Vomit. And Detective Sergeant Stewart tells me he called his 'girlfriend' a *whore*. Isn't that right, detective?"

"Yes. Marcus told us that."

"That's no way to speak about a classmate," Brezicki said. "That's just wrong."

All three boys nodded.

"So to sum up," the detective said, "you're all modern young men, you don't believe in black magic, you don't like really *twisted* sex—nothing wrong with *healthy* sex, but none of this torture garbage."

The boys nodded again.

"Let's be honest: Dave Sommer wasn't a very nice young man. Right?"

"Right," said Stephen.

"Good," said Brezicki. "So we're going to talk with you separately again. We'll begin with Marcus. Stephen and Hasan, you can wait outside."

ANGUS HAD RETURNED from his audition for the jazz band to find a note on his door from the residential don, Matt Butler: *Angus, can you come down to my room when you get back? Mr. W. and I need to have a chat with you.* He'd done as he'd been asked, and Matt took him directly to David Waters' large family apartment, where they'd found Paul Makepeace, Angus's faculty advisor, and David himself in the living room.

"Thanks for coming, Angus," David said, waving him toward a comfortable armchair. "Would you like a coffee?"

"No, thank you, sir."

"A soft drink? Coke? Ginger-ale?"

"No, thank you, sir. I'm trying not to drink too much sugar."

"Just a water, then? I think we have some mineral water."

"No. Thank you."

"Okay," said David. "I've invited Mr. Makepeace to join us because he's your faculty adviser and I know you have a good relationship with him. I think he was very supportive of you last spring at that difficult time."

"Yes, sir," said Angus. "He was."

David put down his coffee mug and leaned forward, his hands on his knees. "Angus, we need to talk some more about last night."

"I thought we covered that this morning," said Angus.

"We did," said David, "but some more information has come to light since then."

"What new information?" said Angus.

"Well, you told me that you were watching television in the common room last night."

"I was. After study period."

"And do you remember what television show you were watching?"

Angus paused, thought for a moment. "I think it was *Law & Order*."

"And did you watch the whole episode?"

'Pretty much all of it. Why are you asking?"

"I'm asking because Matt tells me that he was in the common room for a while, and that you weren't there."

Angus shot Matt a look whose hostility could not be doubted. "I was there," he said.

"Do you remember the plot of the episode?" David asked.

"They're all the same," said Angus, with apparent exasperation. "There was a murder, and the cops thought one guy did it, but it was another guy."

Matt Butler cleared his throat. "It was a rape."

"Oh, yeah. There was a rape, and the cops thought one guy did it, but it was another guy. And they nailed him in the end."

David looked at his hands. "Big difference between a murder and a rape, Angus."

"Well, maybe I wasn't concentrating too hard," said Angus. "Sometimes I just sort of space out when I'm watching T.V."

"Angus, we have to take this very seriously," said David. "A student has been killed. You had reason—good reason—to dislike that student a great deal."

"I hated him," said Angus.

"You had good reason to hate him," said David. "But that becomes an, an issue, when he's found dead. And it's even more of an issue when we find out you must have been somewhere other than where you told us you were."

"I was in the common room," said Angus. "Maybe I went to the bathroom while Matt was there. I don't remember. But I watched *Law & Order* last night."

"A couple of the boys who were there say they don't remember you being there," said Matt, quietly. Angus began to say something, but then went silent.

Paul spoke up. "We're honestly not trying to catch you out, Angus," he said. "We're just doing our due diligence. We have to solve this—or help solve this. Can you tell us anything—anything—that could help us feel better about where you were last night?"

The three men looked at Angus. Angus looked down at the floor. "No," he said. "I was here at Boone. And I didn't kill fucking Sommer."

THERE WERE WEALTHY neighbourhoods in Bath—places where people had sold up in Toronto and travelled east along the 401 to buy brand new homes with four bedrooms and four bathrooms and manicured yards; and there were some older neighbourhoods, where the houses mostly had two bedrooms, one bathroom, and a patch of asphalt to park on. Joanie Fletcher lived in one of those houses.

She walked home from school, having exchanged a long, lingering kiss with Alexis first—and after making plans to see him later that evening—and unlocked the front door. "Hey, Gran!" she called out. "I'm home!"

Joanie's grandmother had one of the two bedrooms upstairs: at seventy-six, she was bedridden with, as she called it, "the cancer." It wasn't her only affliction. She had been diagnosed with adult-onset diabetes in her fifties and had now largely lost the use of her legs. Her son, who was probably Joanie's father—in his cups, he sometimes wondered whether his wife might have strayed—had invited her to move in with them some years before. He worked in the kitchen in one of the nearby prisons and wouldn't get home until after nine. His wife, indisputably Joanie's mother, had left for parts unknown when her daughter was four. There had been birthday letters (without return addresses) for Joanie for a few years, but they'd heard nothing now for half a decade.

"Would you like a cup of tea, Gran?" Joanie shouted from the bottom of the stairs. She knew what the answer would be. Tea with her granddaughter was the highlight of the old lady's day.

"Yes, please, dear,"—a croaking voice from upstairs. Joanie put the kettle on, dropped two teabags into a pot, and while it steeped made herself a small peanut-butter sandwich. Gran would not want to eat anything: getting her to swallow more than a few bites of supper would be challenge enough. Sandwich in one hand, Joanie went into the tiny living-room and collected the mug her father had left beside the sofa, bringing it back into the kitchen and putting it beside the sink. Her father slept in the living room. He'd insisted that Joanie keep her bedroom upstairs, and surrendered his own bedroom to his mother when she moved in.

And then up the stairs, the teapot on a tray with two cups, a small jug of milk, and a sugar bowl, because Gran liked to see the tea poured piping hot, and liked to make sure she got two lumps of sugar and just the right amount of milk. And she was old, and she wasn't well, and she liked to hear Joanie's stories about school, and talk about the soaps she'd watched on T.V. that afternoon; and she loved Joanie, and Joanie loved her, and sometimes, sometimes, lives have shapes and textures very different from the ones we might expect.

THE HEADMASTER LOOKED up from the documents on his desk, pushed back his chair, and massaged his hips. As he moved into his late forties, some of his old rugby injuries were beginning to announce that they hadn't altogether gone away. Weekly trips to a chiropractor in Kingston were now necessary, and Jim wondered sometimes whether he shouldn't line himself up with a physiotherapist. His oldest friend swore by his.

His secretary appeared at his door. "Do you need me to stay later tonight?" Debbie asked.

"No, thank you, Deb, no need today. It may be necessary tomorrow, with the board chair coming down."

"Okay. I'm just finishing up a letter, then I'll head out. I've got some mail to register at the post office."

"Have a good night." He forced a smile. Important to keep morale high in challenging times.

"You, too." Debbie returned to her computer. Jim rose, looked out the window at the towering oaks, stretched, then took the private door out of his office into his home and headed to the kitchen.

Glenda was sitting at the kitchen table reading a magazine, a cup of coffee at her elbow. There was, as always, a pot of coffee on the stove, and Jim helped himself to a mug.

"How you doing, Jimbo?"

"Not a good day, darlin'. Not a good day." He fished a piece of shortbread out of the cookie cannister on the counter.

Glenda pushed her magazine away and looked at him with some concern. "Do you think they'll find him quickly?"

"I don't know. The detective seems confident, but she hasn't made any guarantees." He sat down at the kitchen table across from his wife.

"It freaks me out that someone was killed in the same building we live in. While the kids were getting ready for bed."

"Yeah. It's too close to home."

"I'm trying not to focus on it." She drew a series of invisible spirals on the table with her index finger—a nervous habit since her teenage years. "Jim, do you think we're in any danger?"

"No. Absolutely not."

"I was thinking maybe we should send the kids to my parents."

"No. Absolutely no need."

"Do you have any suspicions about who it might be?"

Jim wrapped his large hands around his mug. "I'm trying not to leap to assumptions. I know that the detective is interviewing three boys from Roper House—Stephen Bradley and two of his friends. And I believe that they'll be talking to Angus Graves later today."

"Is he the one that Sommer beat up so badly?"

"Yep. And shoved dog dirt in his mouth."

"I thought we weren't going to have him back."

Jim pushed down a feeling of irritation—recognizing, as he did so, that that irritation was mingled with, and maybe fueled by, a large serving of self-reproach. "These things aren't simple," he said. "His dad offered to make a... generous gift, and Bart asked me to reconsider the expulsion. I have to balance all kinds of considerations, Misky."

"I know. I know."

"And there's always the possibility that it was someone from outside—some madman who came in off the highway, stumbled into the chapel, and left as soon as he did what he did. We can't rule that out. And what that means is that we need to hire a night watchman."

"Do we know what Sommer would have been doing in the chapel?"

"That," said Jim, "is the sixty-four-thousand-dollar question."

"HERE'S THE THING, Marcus," said Detective-Sergeant Brezicki, looking at a spot just above young man's head, "I don't think you killed Dave Sommer."

"I'm not so sure," said Detective-Sergeant Stewart. "I need a little more persuading before I'm comfortable ruling Marcus out."

"Well, let me ask this," Brezicki said. "Let me ask you this, Marcus. Between Hasan and Stephen, who do you think hated Sommer more?"

Marcus thought about that for a moment. He was no fool, and he recognized he was being played, but he was also frightened that his confession about manipulating the pointer might make him vulnerable to—well, to what? He didn't know, and that was the problem. Had he broken the law in initially denying his actions? Did he need to redeem himself somehow? Was it possible that either Hasan or Stephen had killed Sommer?

"I don't know that *hated* is the right word," he said eventually. "I mean, neither of them *liked* him, and I didn't like him that much, but there's a big difference between *hate* and *dislike*."

"Hasan's a Muslim," said Detective Brezicki. "We all know that Muslims tend to be… judgmental. And we've certainly seen recent examples of Muslim males killing people. And in this case, in this case, it would almost be understandable."

"Hasan's not like that," said Marcus. "He's a pretty gentle guy. He's not the kind of guy who would behead or bomb people. Seriously."

"So you would tend to suspect Stephen more?" said Detective Stewart.

"I didn't say that!" said Marcus.

"Have you ever seen Stephen lose his temper?" she persisted

"Not really."

"Hasan? Have you seen him lose his temper?"

"Once. In a rugby game. A long time ago." A reluctant admission.

"What happened?"

"He got into it with some guy from the local high school."

"Why?"

"I don't know. I guess the guy called him a name. Some of the locals are real skids."

"Skids?" Detective Stewart raised an eyebrow.

"It's an abusive term for small-town people," said Luke quietly. "We try to discourage its use."

"Ah. So the local called him, what, a *raghead*?"

"A sand-nigger," said Marcus.

"That's nasty," said Detective Stewart. "And Hasan laid into him?"

"He had it coming."

"Yes, he did. You won't get any disagreement from me on that."

"And if there's no one around to calm us down, any one of us might fly off the handle," said Detective Brezicki.

"I guess," said Marcus.

"So," said Brezicki. "I don't think it's impossible to believe that a guy who would stuff dog shit into a smaller boy's mouth might, just might, call a dark-skinned person a sand-nigger. And that a dark-skinned young man might take exception to that. That's all I'm saying."

Marcus said nothing. He just looked confused.

Alexis liked to have a coffee after school at the Tim Horton's in Bath. On this occasion he went by the pharmacy on his way there to pick up a tube of anti-biotic ointment for Joanie. There had certainly been occasions in the past when he'd shoplifted something he'd wanted, slipping whatever it might be into a pocket of his trench coat and paying just for gum or a chocolate bar at the cash. Alexis didn't have any moral qualms about this. He figured the pharmacy was part of a huge, impossibly wealthy chain, and that his modest thefts were withdrawals from a kind of cosmic credit union. He knew Joanie didn't approve, and he'd been trying to cut down a bit on his "boosts," but it was hard when he was short of cash.

But he wasn't short of cash now, and he paid for his coffee, and splurged on a bagel with cream cheese, with a twenty-dollar bill. It felt good to have money. He planned to drop by a friend's place on his way home to pick up some weed for Sommer, but he'd have enough left after that to treat Joanie to a movie and a pizza in Kingston. A broker's fee, yeah? Because he was taking the risk of buying the weed and holding it. That's how free enterprise worked.

He was drinking his coffee and waiting for his bagel to cool when a St. Cuthbert's student he'd chatted with once or twice approached him: Larry something—he didn't know his full name. "Hey," said Larry.

"Hey," said Alexis. "They let you out of there this afternoon?"

"I'm skipping practice," said Larry. "They're not going to notice today."

"How come?" Alexis unwrapped his bagel. "I thought they were anal about keeping track of you guys."

"Not today," said Larry. "We had a murder up on campus."

"You had *what*?" said Alexis, forgetting his bagel.

"A murder. In the chapel. Blood fucking everywhere."

"Jesus!" said Alexis, genuinely shocked. "Was it a student?"

"Oh, yeah," said Larry. "Guy called Dave Sommer. You know him? Medium height, sort of reddish-brown hair. Bit of a chip on his shoulder."

Alexis's hands involuntarily jerked, and he did something he'd only ever seen in the movies: he knocked his coffee mug onto the floor, where it shattered.

"So, Stephen," said Detective-Sergeant Brezicki, surveying a page of notes. "We've just had a very illuminating conversation with your friend Marcus." He looked up at Stephen.

"Okay," said Stephen.

"Let me cut to the chase and say that I don't think you killed Sommer."

"I didn't."

"But," the detective continued, "I think it's possible that you know, or suspect, something about who *did* kill him. Though perhaps you don't know that you know it."

"I really don't think I do."

"Well, let's talk about that, shall we? Let's explore that. The chaplain tells me that you are the student head of house at... is it Roper House?"

"Yes."

"And he also tells me that it was an honour for you to have been chosen for that position, and that you take your role seriously."

"I do. That's true." Stephen straightened his back a little.

"Good. Excellent. He also tells me that as student head of house, you will sometimes be called on to help faculty make decisions about disciplinary matters concerning boys in your house."

"Yeah. It hasn't happened yet, but it probably will."

"So. Between Marcus and Hasan, who do you think is more likely to fly off the handle if provoked?"

Stephen frowned and didn't respond immediately. After a moment, however: "I don't think either of them has a really bad temper."

"Are you a rugby player, Stephen?"

"A rugby—oh, I see where you're going with this. No. No, I don't play rugby. But Hasan didn't *kill* that guy. He just punched him. It's not like he pulled a knife."

"Well, there were other people there," said the detective. "Who knows what he would have done if he'd been alone."

"No," said Stephen. "No. I just don't see it. I don't think Hasan is that kind of guy."

"Can you think of anyone who might be?" asked Detective Stewart quietly.

"From Roper House?"

"Anyone you know well at the school. Anyone who is known to push things to an extreme."

"Yeah," said Stephen. "I do."

"Who?"

"Sommer. He was the one guy I could see pulling a knife on someone."

Detective Stewart held Stephen's gaze for a moment, then turned to Detective Brezicki and gave the slightest of nods.

"Okay, Stephen. Thank you," said Brezicki.

"Can I go?"

"You can go."

Stephen left.

Luke, sitting behind the other two, leaned forward: "Are you two suspecting Hasan?"

"No," said Callum. "Of the three boys, I think he's the least likely to have done it."

"We were trying to make the other two feel comfortable that we don't suspect them," said Diane. "Sometimes, when a suspect feels safe, he lets his guard down."

"So you suspect one of them?"

"We suspect everyone," said Callum. "At this point, we have no choice. "But," and he closed his notebook, "I'm not feeling any further ahead after those two conversations. And that's frustrating."

MONDAY, 4:38 P.M.

KEVIN GOULET WAS angry. Angry and frustrated. As one of three teachers at the school who took turns directing the fall play, he'd been preparing to take on *Murder in the Cathedral* for months. He had suspected, as soon as he'd heard the news about Sommer's murder, that he would be discouraged from proceeding, but he'd half hoped that he could persuade Alison that his production might have a cathartic, healing effect on the community. That half-hope had been erased shortly after the staff meeting. She'd seemed to listen, but she'd ultimately told him that, no, he would have to choose something else.

Now, for the eighteenth time, he and his student stage-manager, Meadow Strong, were facing a hopeful auditionee, and he had to deliver a little speech about how things were in a state of flux. "Patti," he said, glancing at the audition form she'd just handed him, "I have to tell you that there's been a big change in our plans today. We're no longer doing the play I'd intended, and I'll be making another selection tonight."

"Do you have any idea what it will be?" asked Patti. She was a trim, smiley grade eleven student, a resident of Eaton House, and she was wearing a T-shirt advertising the Broadway production of *The Lion King*.

"I'm not sure yet. I'm thinking it might be another play by Eliot, *The Cocktail Party*, or maybe I'll go in a completely different direction and do a comedy. Still haven't decided."

"Is *The Cocktail Party* a musical? I love musicals!"

"No," said Kevin shortly. "*The Cocktail Party* is not a musical. But it's a brilliant play, with some wonderful roles." Meadow hid a smile behind her hand. She'd taken two years of drama with Kevin Goulet, and she knew that he was not a big fan of musicals. He often said that he liked theatre that made people think, not simply snap their fingers. She herself wished that he would do a comedy: the mood on campus darkened as the nights came on earlier and earlier, and she thought that a comedy would cheer people up. She secretly felt some relief that *Murder in the Cathedral* was off the table.

"Now," said Kevin, "Meadow has given you an advertising jingle for Smarties that was popular for a few years. I want you to read it in a way that makes it come alive—that gives it colour and warmth. I know this may seem a little weird, but I'll get a real sense of how you handle language and how you project."

"When you eat your Smarties, do you eat the red ones last?" said Patti, tentatively trying out the first line.

"Yes. But take a moment, read the full thing through in your head, and then try it. Don't feel rushed."

Patti did not distinguish herself with her delivery, but, with a bit of coaching, she managed to find a rhythm and bounce that gave her a shot at a role—depending, of course, on the play Kevin ultimately chose. Kevin thanked her for her audition, scrawled a note on her form, and was about to ask her to send the next person on his list into the theatre when Patti said something that captured his full attention. "Last night was really weird," she said. "You could smell marijuana over the whole campus."

"What?" said Kevin. "Pardon?" Meadow looked up in alarm.

"Oh, yeah," said Patti. "I went to the library during study period, and the smell was really strong. It was like coming in waves."

"Have you any idea where from?" asked Kevin. Meadow widened her eyes and tried, with small shakes of her head, to signal to Patti that she should shut up.

"I think it was from Ingram House," said Patti. "That direction....I mean, obviously, not from Ingram House *per se*, if you know what I mean." She had noticed Meadow's expression.

"But from campus? From *on* campus?" asked Kevin.

"I don't know," said Patti, now realizing that she had made a huge mistake. "Maybe I imagined it. Probably I did. It was probably just... a bonfire, or something."

"We're sorry to have kept you waiting, Hasan," said Detective-Sergeant Brezicki. "I'm going to tell you frankly that we have fewer suspicions about you than about the other lads. I don't think Detective-Sergeant Stewart will mind if I say that you've pretty well fallen off our list of suspects."

"Not completely," said Detective Stewart.

"No, not completely. True," said Brezicki. "Because it's too early yet for us to rule anyone out. But our antennae aren't twitching when it comes to you."

Hasan said nothing. He looked from Brezicki to Stewart and back again with a blank expression on his face.

"But we have some suspicions about one of your friends," said Brezicki. "I'm not going to tell you which one, because we like to keep our cards close to our chest... But between the two of them, who do you think is more capable of extreme violence?"

"*Extreme* violence?" Hasan repeated.

"Extreme violence. The kind of violence that might take the shape of stabbing another young man repeatedly."

"I... I don't know. It's difficult for me to think of either of them that way."

"Oh, but they're human, Hasan. I mean, any one of us is capable of striking out if he feels provoked, don't you agree? Any one of us. One of them mentioned that you yourself flew off the handle at a rugby game last year." Brezicki said this casually, but as he finished the sentence he looked Hasan fully in the eyes.

This hung in the air for a moment. The three adults watched it dawn on Hasan that perhaps, just perhaps, one of his friends had suggested that *he* was capable of using a knife on Sommer. "*That* guy called me a sand-nigger," said Hasan heatedly.

"And you slugged him," said Brezicki.

"What would you have done?" asked Hasan. "What the fuck would you have done?" And to his horror, he found there were tears in his eyes.

The detective's voice took on a gentle tone. "I've already told you that we don't really suspect you, Hasan. But we were surprised that one of your friends was so ready to tell us about the rugby game. So I guess—"

"Who was it?" asked Hasan.

"I'm sorry, I can't tell you that. But my question is, which of the two might want to distract our attention away from his own actions last night? Or could it possibly be both of them?"

"They did both manipulate the pointer," said Detective Stewart.

"Yes, they did," said Brezicki. "They certainly did. And sometimes people admit to something minor to make their denial of something major more credible."

A long silence. Hasan rooted around in his pocket to find a tissue and, eventually, hauled one out and wiped his eyes. "I know Marcus didn't do it," he said. "We were together from the time we left Stephen's room. I don't think Stephen did it, but I can't guarantee you he didn't. I know he was pissed when he found out Sommer would be in his house."

"He was drunk?" Detective Stewart asked, misunderstanding Hasan's use of the word *pissed*.

"No, *angry*," said Hasan. "Really angry. But I thought he'd got over it."

Dinner began at 5:30 p.m., and math teacher Ben Hendricks—
who'd only realized in the afternoon that he was teacher-on-duty
that day —had showed up on time for the meal. (He was grateful
that lunch had been served in the residences, so his forgetfulness
had not been discovered.) The senior students who were theoretically on duty with him straggled in several minutes late, but
to atone for his own memory lapse he did not reproach them.
Duty days were a particularly resented fact of life for teachers:
every three weeks or so, one was expected to patrol the dining
hall at breakfast, lunch and dinner, making sure that students
cleaned up after themselves, chivvying them along to get to
chapel or class on time, reminding the boys that they couldn't
wear ball caps in the dining hall, and reminding the girls that they
couldn't roll their skirts or expose their midriffs. If some of the
younger female faculty disliked telling the senior boys to remove
their ball caps (and they did), male teachers dreaded telling the
girls to lengthen their skirts or cover their midriffs. They com-
plained regularly to Dick Cargill that the girls must think they
were obsessed with their legs or their bellies. Ben Hendricks
himself rather liked short skirts and bare midriffs, but he had
learned, with some difficulty, to keep his appreciation private.

The TOD sat at the first table inside the entrance to the dining hall, with, if they showed up, the senior students who were
on meal duty. The idea was that they watched students come in,
checking that no one was wearing cleats or sports gear (or ball
caps or crop tops), and, similarly, keeping a watchful eye as students made their way out of the dining hall at the end of the
meal, noting whether they were carrying a tray, and reminding
them to scrape any uneaten food into the compost bins and place
their plates, bowls and utensils in the proper receptacles. It was a

tedious task, made all the worse by the fact that some students made a game out of defying the system, leaving trays piled high with untouched meat, vegetables, soups, salads, and fruit where they had been sitting. The wealth of the student population, and the fact that you could take whatever you wanted from the food stations, meant that as much food was wasted every meal as was actually consumed. Teachers who had spent some time overseas in developing countries were horrified when they first encountered this state of affairs, but over time they became inured to it. Over time, indeed, many of them slowly began to exhibit the same behaviour, becoming more and more casual over how much food they piled on their plates, and justifying the excess by thinking that they were contributing to a nutritionally rich supply of compost.

Having greeted his students-on-duty, Ben began one of the nine or so perambulations around the dining hall he'd make over the course of ninety minutes. "Hughes. Hughes!" he barked at one large and athletic young man. "Take off that cap! You know the rules."

"All right," said Hughes, rolling his eyes at his fellow athletes clustered around the same table. He put his ball cap on his lap, then, a moment after Ben had moved on, clapped it back on his head. He and his pal Pete Grose began the messy but interesting process of turning full glasses of chocolate milk upside down on their trays in such a way that when the kitchen staff picked them up, the milk would flood the tray.

Having completed one circuit, Ben returned to his spot to find that one of his seniors was no longer there. "Where's Morrison?" he asked the other boy.

"Maybe he went for a dessert?" the boy replied vaguely. "I don't know. He didn't tell me."

Ben grunted. The school went to extraordinary lengths to encourage older students to take on responsibilities, to exercise leadership. Every student in grade twelve had a portfolio: there were, naturally, the two head students—male and female; and there were also student heads of every residential house and the notional house made up of local kids who lived at home. But there was also a student-in-charge of library services, a student-in-charge of boys' sports, a student-in-charge of chapel, of assemblies, of student tutors, of charities, of the tuck shop, of the art room, of debating—on and on and on, sixty positions in all. It meant that every graduate of St. Cuthbert's College could list at least one sphere of community responsibility on his or her university applications, and so gain a leg-up over their public-school counterparts. But the fact that a portfolio was given was no guarantee it would be discharged responsibly, and the same was true for more pedestrian things like meal duty.

The dining hall landscape would present an interesting sociological study, if one wished to launch one. The school was more racially diverse than public high schools in the Kingston area, and had been for some years, and the school's house system did a great deal to encourage friendships across racial divides. That meant that many of the school's international students from places like Mexico, Saudi Arabia, Colombia, Spain, Germany, Jamaica, Bermuda and the Bahamas were seated side by side with their mostly Caucasian Canadian counterparts. But most of the growing number of Chinese students kept themselves apart, forming long tables dominated by lively conversations in Cantonese or Mandarin. There was no discernible animosity between the Caucasians and the Chinese—no racially-motivated taunts or fights—but there was also very little interaction during mealtimes. Jim and Dick and Heather and Luke and other school leaders had talked about this situation for years but were no closer to changing it.

Sexual integration was a different matter. To a significant degree, boys and girls sat together with every sign of comfort and ease. That was more true, perhaps, at the senior level, but there were many mixed social groups in grades nine and ten, too.

A grade eleven girl came into the dining hall wearing a very short skirt. The remaining duty-student looked at Ben, expecting a challenge—but Ben simply watched her enter, pass by, and take her place in the line wending its way into the kitchen. The student recognized the hunger in his eyes and tucked the knowledge away: an interesting tidbit to share with his roommate later that evening.

Not surprisingly, Sommer's death was the focus of conversation everywhere in the dining hall. "My mom wants me to come home." "My dad says he's going to call Harvey." "This is nothing. There are murders every day back home." "He's that guy who made Angus eat dog shit last year." "It's gonna be on the news tonight, big time." "What was he doing in the chapel, anyway?" "He's in Roper. A lot of goons in there." "I saw him with that 'vampire' guy at the bowling alley on Saturday."

And here, at a table in the corner, was something a little more substantial than speculation and gossip. "Keep calm. No one knows. No one needs to know."

With most of the girls—those not in study hall—back in the residence after dinner, Wilcox House's residential don Jiao, and student head of house Lauren, met in Lauren's room to discuss whether they should follow up on the day's events. "I feel like we should check in with everyone," said Lauren. "I mean, I don't think anyone's traumatized, or anything, but it's a pretty big thing to have happened."

"I agree," said Jiao. "How about we go room to room during study period and ask, you know, 'how are you doing?'"

"Yeah, I think so," said Lauren. "Better that than another meeting. Talk to the girls on their own turf. Do you think we should see if Karin wants to come with us?"

The two women looked at each other, neither wanting to say out loud that she didn't trust the judgment of the head of house. "I don't think so," said Jiao. "She's probably busy marking and prepping classes. We can always tell her if we run into anyone who's really upset."

"That makes sense," said Lauren gratefully.

Their first port of call was a room shared by two particularly studious international students, Yin and Jasmine. Jiao knocked on the door, waited, then knocked again. "They're probably at the library," she said, opening the door to make sure. Neither Yin nor Jasmine was there. Before closing the door, Jiao observed, with quiet approval, the made beds, the stacked books, the absence of clothes strewn around the room. It was the room of two young women who would earn scholarships to university and scholarly distinctions while there. It was the room of two people on the road to success.

The next room belonged to Bonita and Krista. At the House meeting, Jiao had noted that Bonita seemed shocked by the news of Sommer's death, and that Krista, not the most demonstrative of girls, took her hand. Remembering this, Jiao reproached herself for not checking up on Bonita before.

Like Yin and Jasmine, Bonita was an international student, but from Spain. She was a petite young woman, just a fraction over five feet, dark-haired, very pretty, fond of music. Krista, on the other hand, was tall, rangy—as in slender and long-limbed—and strong: a first-class, Canadian-grown athlete. Not a bad student, but hardworking rather than naturally skilled. She was, Jiao reflected, a likely candidate for female head student next year, and if she failed there, she would probably be appointed a student head of house, perhaps in Wilcox itself. They were not a natural pairing, Bonita and Krista, but they seemed to be good friends. For just an instant, and remembering the affection Krista had showed Bonita, Jiao wondered if they might be something more than friends. But no. Probably not.

Lauren took the lead. "Hi, guys! We're just checking in to see how everyone's doing, you know, after the crazy morning we had. Are you both okay?"

"Sure," said Krista, chirpily—which was a little odd, because chirpy wasn't an attitude one would normally associate with her. "We're just fine, aren't we, Bonita?"

"Yes," said Bonita, the affirmation catching in her throat, however. She coughed. "Yes," she said, more clearly. "I'm just feeling a bit crazy with all the work."

"Yeah, the teachers are really piling it on," said Krista.

"That's what they do," said Lauren, perching on the end of Bonita's bed. "What sports are you guys in this term?"

"I'm in first field hockey," said Krista.

"You made the first team?" asked Jiao.

"Oh, yeah," said Krista, perhaps a little surprised by the question. "I made the first team last year, too."

"That's so unusual for a grade ten student," said Lauren.

"I'm in grade eleven," said Krista—and then, "Oh, you mean, last year."

"Yes," said Lauren, smiling. "It was a real achievement. You're a star!" Lauren knew how to make her girls feel valued. "How about you, Bonita?"

"I'm doing dance."

"Is that with Libby?"

"Yeah."

"I really like Libby," said Lauren. "I bet she's fun to work with."

"Yes," said Bonita.

Lauren paused, hoping, perhaps, that Bonita might volunteer more, but she didn't. Lauren got up. "Well, anyway," she said, "Jiao and I just want to check in with everyone, and you guys seem okay so we'll move on." She smiled. "See you later, alligators."

"See you later," said Krista. "Thanks for coming by."

Jiao paused at the door before going out. "You guys would tell us if you were upset, wouldn't you?"

There was a fraction of a second during which Jiao thought she saw real distress in Bonita's eyes, but Krista spoke up almost instantly. "We're fine. Really. Hearing about Sommer was a shock more than anything—you know, to think a murder happened here. But we didn't really know him, did we, Bonita?"

"No," said Bonita. "We just saw him around."

"Okay," said Jiao. "Okay, then." She nodded and followed Lauren out.

Presiding over study hall was insult on top of injury. If Ben were not the teacher-on-duty, he'd have been knocking back his third whiskey of the evening by 7:30 p.m.—not glaring balefully at a room full of academic underachievers, all assigned to study hall for failing to reach an average of 70% at the end of their first fortnight at the school. Never mind that no evaluation could really be judged meaningful so early in the year; the point, at least in Ben's eyes, was to get troublemakers out of the residences so they wouldn't bother their heads of house. And getting them out of the residences meant making *him* responsible for them, and making him responsible meant no whiskey until 10:08 that evening because he wouldn't finish his appointed rounds before 10:00.

When two grade nines came in a couple of minutes late, Ben saw his opportunity to displace some of his frustration. "Come here," he said, beckoning to them. "What are your names?"

"Gary, sir," said one of them.

"Gary," said the other.

"Surnames," Ben growled, consulting his list of study hall designees.

"Trotter," said the first, and "Edwards," said the second. The second Gary seemed particularly unwholesome, Ben reflected. Mind you, he didn't like the look of either one of them. Additionally, and Ben's eyes lit up at the recognition, they smelled of smoke. And not tobacco smoke. Grass. Marijuana.

"Take your seats," he said, "and don't let me hear a word from either of you." The boys scuttled away, but immediately saw they had no choice but to sit at the front of the classroom: the desks farther back were all occupied by students who had arrived on time. Ben watched them settle, then opened his laptop, went straight to his school software suite, and fired off an email to the senior master: *Dick, I've got a couple of boys in study hall, Gary Trotter and Gary Edwards, who stink of marijuana. Do you want to haul them out, or shall I send them to you?* Five minutes later, an answer pinged into his inbox: *I'm on my way.*

While Ben waited for Dick Cargill to arrive, he surveyed the room with a growing sense of grievance. The kids were all so young, so healthy-looking. Ben himself didn't feel young or healthy. Fifty years old, divorced, overweight, elevated blood pressure, high cholesterol, a need to knock back seven whiskeys a night—he was scarcely a walking advertisement for the values the school claimed to celebrate. But he was, for all that, a fine math teacher: patient with the slow learners, open to trying different strategies with different students, willing to overlook small behavioural transgressions if they didn't disrupt his classroom. No, during the academic day, Ben was everything the school could ask for; it was the after-hours activities—the dining hall duty, the study hall, the patrols of the buildings and grounds—that soured his mood. Every single duty day he asked himself the same questions: Why the hell was he teaching in a residential private school when he could have made a perfectly good living in the public-school system, getting to school at 8:00 and leaving at 4:00? What was the point? What was the freaking point?

The senior master erupted into the room from the door at the back of the classroom. Every student turned and looked at him with some surprise—not just because he would not normally show his face during study hall, but also because he was radiating annoyance. Dick nodded at Ben, then began a slow march up and down the aisles, breathing heavily. Ben saw what he was up to and felt a flush of gratitude and respect: Dick did not intend to reveal that it was Ben who had sent for him. He was going to pretend that he had another secret source of information, and he was going to ferret out the smokers by smelling the grass on them.

And that's exactly what happened. When Dick's patrol brought him level with the two Garys, he stopped and sniffed loudly. He then looked from one to the other. "Edwards,

Trotter," he said—and this would have been impressive if he hadn't mixed the boys up—"gather your things and come with me."

The boys looked scared: they knew, as all the students knew, that smoking marijuana was grounds for expulsion. They gathered their books and their laptops while Dick (and everyone else) watched, and then followed him out of the classroom. But as they went through the door at the front of the class, Gary Edwards suddenly let out a strangulated sob… and Ben found that his resentment disappeared in that instant, to be replaced by a deep sense of shame and sadness. He closed his eyes and lowered his head.

DENNIS MURDOCH OPENED his wife's study door into the girls' residence and called over his shoulder, "I'll just check up on everyone!" It was an evening ritual. Usually, he would do the first patrol, Julie Murdoch another about forty minutes later, then Dennis, then, at the end of study period, Julie again. And Julie and the residential don, Barbara Meeks, would do the final visits—when the girls would be exiting the showers or climbing into bed. It seemed to work. It made sense.

To the common room first, to make sure the television was off: it wasn't, but no one was watching it, so Dennis switched it off without having to shoo girls back to their rooms. Then down the hall, knocking quietly at door after door, opening it at the invitation, and peering inside to make sure the girls were at their desks. Most were, and Dennis wasn't concerned if some were perched on their beds reading or working on their laptops. The crucial thing was to ensure that the residence was reasonably quiet, so that those who wanted to work, could.

Then, at the end of the hall, Barbara's room. Dennis bent his head close to the door, raised his hand, rapped four times in a recognizable pattern. "Come in!" from inside. He entered, and closed the door. Barbara had just emerged from her tiny three-piece bathroom, a plush towel rapped around her petite form, her blonde hair dripping wet. "Hey, soldier," she said, smiling at him seductively.

"I'm standing at attention," said Dennis, his mouth suddenly dry.

Barbara considered a moment, then slowly opened the towel, revealing her pert breasts, her flat belly, her shaved pubic region. She dropped the towel: Aphrodite emerging from the waves. A fully naked Marilyn Munroe. A living Penthouse Pet. Dennis, mesmerized, took a step forward—

Suddenly the door was flung open, and grade eleven student Leslie Ng burst in, full of important news that she *had* to share with her beloved don. "Barbara, you'll never—" she stopped, her left hand clapped to her mouth in an almost cartoonish gesture of shock and embarrassment. "Oh my God, oh my God, oh my God! I'm so so sorry!" And she turned and fled from the room.

"Oh, fuck!" said Barbara, bending to collect her towel. Dennis just stood there, mouth open, aware, suddenly, that he had just placed his marriage, his children's happiness, his career, his whole life's course, in real jeopardy.

THIS TIME IT was the head of house who came to Angus's door. He knocked, and the door was opened immediately by Pablo, Angus's roommate.

"Hi, Pablo," said David. "Is Angus here?"

"No, sir. I think he's in the library—." But at that moment Angus came down the hall, carrying a small tree branch.

David was curious about the branch, but he was on a mission. "Angus, I'm afraid I have to ask you to come back to my apartment."

"Why?" Angus didn't look worried, David noticed. If anything, he looked defiant.

"The detective would like to ask you a few questions."

"I don't really have anything more to say."

"You have to come, Angus," David said firmly.

Angus held out the tree branch to his roommate. "Could you put this in the corner for me, Pablo?"

"Sure," said Pablo. "What's it for?"

"An art project," Angus said, and he followed his head of house down the hallway, through his study, and back into his living room.

"Detective-Sergeant Stewart, this is Angus Graves," said David. He waved the boy toward a chair and took a seat himself. Paul Makepeace, Angus's faculty adviser, was there, too.

"Hi, Angus," said Detective Stewart. "I appreciate you coming to talk to me."

"I didn't realize I had a choice."

She changed her tack immediately. "You don't. This is a murder investigation. It's very serious."

Paul Makepeace spoke up. "Angus, Mr. Waters and I are here to stand in for your parents. The detective has assured us that you aren't a suspect, at this point, but she does have some questions for you."

"I think I probably am a suspect," said Angus.

"Do you wish to have legal counsel?" Detective Stewart asked. "If you're at all concerned, you have the right to request an attorney."

"I don't need a lawyer because I didn't do it."

"I'm going to repeat myself because it's an important point," she said. "The truth is that if you say something I later determine not to be true, that could be held against you in a criminal proceeding. So if you want a lawyer, please speak up now."

"I didn't do it and I'm not going to lie."

"Are you okay with Mr. Makepeace and Mr. Waters being here in your parents' stead?"

Angus shrugged. "Yeah. Mr. Makepeace was there for me when Sommer made my life miserable."

"Would you sooner Mr. Waters left?"

"No, I didn't mean I don't trust him. It's just that I was in a different house last year."

"Okay," said Detective Stewart. "Then I think we know where we all stand. And, yes, some of this is going to be tedious for you because I have to go over ground you've already covered with Mr. Waters." She took out a pen and notebook.

"All right," said Angus.

"So. I understand Dave Sommer attacked you last spring."

"Yes. He beat me up. He's nearly two years older than I am."

"Do you have any idea why he did this?"

"He said I must be a *fag* because I like birdwatching."

"And you think that was the reason?"

"He said it was."

"He said that explicitly to you?" The detective looked up from her notebook.

"Yeah."

"He did," Paul chimed in. "I mean, he didn't say that to us, but other students told us that's what he'd said to them."

"Okay," said Detective Stewart. "That's disgusting. He beat you up badly?"

"He kicked me in the head and stuffed dog shit in my mouth."

She took a moment to write herself an extended note. "So you had every reason to hate him." It wasn't a question.

"Yes. But I didn't kill him."

"All right. What was your frame of mind when you returned to school three weeks ago?"

"I felt okay about it."

"In spite of knowing that Sommer would be here?"

"No, I had no idea he'd be here. I didn't think he'd be coming back."

"It was a shock to see him again?"

"Yes."

"How had you spent the summer?"

"I worked out quite a bit. And I started taking ninjitsu."

"The martial art?"

"Yes."

She allowed herself a small smile. "I have a black belt in karate, myself."

"Karate is good, too. But I wanted something better for street fighting."

"Were you taking it explicitly with the intention of hurting Dave Sommer?"

"No, because I didn't think he was going to be here. I took it with the intention of fighting anyone *like* Dave Sommer. I didn't want to be a victim again."

"I understand that."

Angus nodded. "I never want *anyone* to be able to shove dog shit in my mouth again."

"I get it." The detective paused. "Angus, where were you between 9:00 and 10:00 P.M. yesterday?"

"I was here."

"And by here do you mean in the residence?"

"Yes." Angus looked steadily at the detective.

"And where were you in the residence?"

It was Angus's turn to pause for a moment. Then: "I spent some time watching *Law & Order*."

"Where were you watching it?"

"In the common room."

"Was anyone else present while you were watching it?"

"Shane and Alastair."

David cleared his throat. "Those are the two boys who said they were watching that show last night."

"But they don't remember Angus being there?"

"They said he *may* have been there for a little while."

A flicker of irritation crossed the detective's face. It was frustrating to be in a situation where witnesses with whom she had not herself spoken apparently changed their stories. It was frustrating to be in a context where people other than herself were investigating and reporting different accounts over a period of just a few hours. There was a lot to be said for isolating witnesses and being able to confront them with past statements if they suddenly gave a different report.

"For a little while," Detective Stewart repeated. "So, did you slip out to the bathroom at some point?"

"No."

"—You told us this afternoon that you might have," said David.

"I was wrong," said Angus. "I've thought about it. I don't want to lie to this lady. I didn't go to the bathroom."

"Okay," said the detective. "I appreciate your desire to tell the truth. Can you tell me where you were when you weren't in the common room?"

"Can I speak to you alone?" asked Angus.

She closed her notebook. "Why?"

"Because I have something I can only say to you alone."

David leaned forward. "Angus, I don't think we can allow that."

"Why not?" said Angus.

"Because you're a juvenile, and Mr. Makepeace and I are worried that you might say something you later regret. We don't think your parents would allow you to be questioned without either themselves or legal counsel present. Do you agree, Paul?"

"I do."

"Then I can't say anything," said Angus.

"I just want to be clear," said Detective Stewart. "There is something you want to tell me, but you can't say what it is in the presence of St. Cuthbert's staff?"

"That's correct."

"And you are continuing to assert that you had nothing to do with the death of Dave Sommer?"

"I had *nothing* to do with it. Absolutely nothing."

"You're putting me in a very difficult position, Angus."

Angus stood up. "Look, I'm fed up with this bullshit. I hated that fucker. I'm glad he's dead. But I didn't kill him."

"Angus—" said David, getting up.

"I'm going to call my parents," said Angus. "I'm out of here." He stormed out of the room.

There was a silence in the wake of his departure. Diane slowly put her notebook and pen back into her pocket. "Well..."

"What are you going to do?" asked Paul.

"I'm going to consult with my partner, Drezicki."

"Do you have any thoughts about what he said?" Paul again.

"Yeah. I think he's probably telling the truth. I don't think he's involved. But I have to know where he was so I can clear him. And it's possible that he knows something that I don't know about, and that could be very important." She rose. "Gentlemen, thank you for making yourselves available."

"We're on duty twenty-four, seven," said David, wryly.

"Just like the police," said Diane. "I'll see myself out."

BARBARA PICKED HER towel off the floor and began hurriedly dry-ing herself—while Dennis stood mute and open-mouthed before her. "What are we going to do?" he asked.

"I don't know what *you're* going to do," Barbara replied. "But I'm going to throw some clothes on and go do damage control."

"Should I come with you?"

"No. I can't think of anything crazier." She grabbed a thong from her drawer, slipped into it, then looked around for a pair of sweatpants and a T-shirt. "Go," she said. "Keep doing your rounds or go back home. We both have to stay calm."

"I can't believe she just walked in like that."

"Yeah, well, she did. And now we have to deal with it. Go, Dennis."

Dennis went. Barbara gathered her still-wet hair into a bun, secured it with a couple of pins, slid into a pair of flip-flops and hurried out the door.

BEN HENDRICKS HAD taken out a sheaf of grade eleven quizzes to mark but couldn't find the focus he needed to look at them. He normally prided himself on his ability to churn through a set of class tests, perhaps twenty to twenty-five papers, in half an hour, and privately thought it hilarious that his English and history colleagues could take that long to mark a single essay. But this evening... No. He couldn't bring himself to wield his green pen. Besides, he was left-handed, and his left arm hurt: he massaged his shoulder absent-mindedly.

"Can I go to the bathroom, sir?" asked a boy he didn't recognize near the back of the room. Another reason for irritation: students were supposed to visit the toilets, if they needed to, before study hall began. There would be a break at 8:30, which, surely, was soon enough. He toyed with saying as much.

"Go," he said. "Don't be long. Next time go before you come here."

"Thank you, sir," said the boy, heading towards the back door. Large and sturdy, broad shouldered. Ben reflected that if the school still had its football program, phased out when St. Cuthbert's went co-ed, this new fellow would probably have been on the line of the junior team. Perhaps he'd have some potential as a rugby player: that's where some of the football players had gone. Mind you, rugby required greater conditioning—the ability to run and keep running. Good game, rugby.

His son, Robert, was a football player—a tight end. He'd gone to a public high school, though, not to St. Cuthbert's. Ben's wife, Marcia, had moved to Ottawa when she left Ben, taking their five-year-old son with her. Ben had been shocked when she left—hadn't seen it coming. Sure, the romance had gone, but didn't the romance leave all marriages after a few years? He'd been a good guy: faithful, remembered birthdays and anniversaries, a solid provider. The first night he'd spent alone in the old house he'd found himself howling—and, sure, it wasn't Marcia he missed so much as little Bobby: the physicalness of him, the warmth of his small frame, the fact that he came to hug his dad before he went to bed, the times they made snowmen or tossed a ball in the backyard. And no, come to think of it, it wasn't just the physicalness: it was the whole package—the vulnerability, the self-doubt, the occasional need for reassurance, the times he'd asked, "Do you love me, Dad?"—and Ben had answered, honestly and from a full heart (though he wasn't the world's most affectionate guy):—"Of course I love you, Bobby. Always will."

And because Ben worked crazy hours at St. Cuthbert's—including Saturdays, for Christ's sake—he hadn't seen his son as much as he'd wanted and needed. He'd sent the damn support cheques, and he'd sent the birthday and Christmas presents, and he'd had five days with him at Christmas, and a week over March break (when Marcia and the second husband jetted off to the Caribbean), and a month over the summer... but he'd missed out on the T-ball games, and the Cub meetings, and the homework help, and, yes, the football games, and then, yes, maybe the whiskey had got in the way of the odd weekend visit, and fuck it, fuck it, fuck it, he'd fucked up royally from Monday to Sunday and now his boy was at university and they rarely spoke and Gary Edwards had sobbed in the same way Ben remembered his own son sobbing when he'd left his dad, at the end of the summer holiday, one year into his parents' separation. And God he hated Marcia, and God he wished he'd paid her more attention instead of channelling all his energy into this fucking job, and God he needed a whiskey.

Ben checked his watch. Six minutes. The potential rugby player should be back from the bathroom by now. He could almost feel his blood pressure rise.

Barbara Meeks arrived at the room Leslie Ng shared with her roommate, Trish, and gently knocked on the door. There was silence for a moment, then Trish's voice called out, "Hello?" Barbara entered. Leslie was sitting on the side of her bed with her head in her hands, her face completely covered. Trish was sitting at her desk but pivoted to face Leslie: her eyes were wide open. *What did Leslie tell her?* Barbara wondered. *Is the cat already out of the bag?* "Trish," she said, "would you mind giving me ten minutes alone with Leslie? There's something we need to talk about."

"Sure," said Trish, getting up from her desk and grabbing her history textbook. "I'll go read in the common room for a little while."

"Thank you." After Trish left, Barbara rolled her desk chair across the floor and sat down in front of Leslie. "Leslie," she said, "I don't know what you think you saw, but it wasn't what you thought it was."

"I'm so sorry!" said Leslie—and Barbara saw there were real tears on the girl's face. "I didn't mean to interrupt—I really didn't!"

"You didn't interrupt anything," said Barbara, trying hard to make the lie credible. "I had just come out of the shower, and Dennis had come in to talk about one of the girls, and I—I accidentally dropped the towel. It came untucked. It was a dumb, stupid mistake. And it's just tough luck all around that that's when you came in."

"I'm so, so sorry," said Leslie, rocking back and forth. "I should have knocked. I should have knocked."

"It's okay, Leslie. I'm not angry with you. I'm angry with myself for dropping the towel. *I'm* embarrassed—you don't need to be!"

Leslie uncovered her face, and Barbara saw that it was bright red—and she realized, in that instant, that the girl was deeply embarrassed for *herself*; that her culture, or her home environment, or, or—who knew what else—made her feel shame for, yes, herself, rather than for Barbara. And there was hope in that.

"Let's erase what you saw," said Barbara, making a sweeping motion with her hand. "There, it's gone! Now, tell me what you wanted to tell me."

With some prompting, Leslie composed herself enough to tell the story she'd originally intended to share. She was, she said, a good friend of Angus Graves's roommate, Pablo, and Pablo had told her a few days back—casually, just in passing—that Angus had said to him that he hoped Sommer *would* attack him again, that he'd have a surprise for him if he did.

"And I really like Angus," said Leslie, the blush gradually fading from her face. "I don't think he'd ever set out to kill anyone, but Pablo told me that Angus was ready to fight if Dave started something."

"Okay," said Barbara. "I'm glad you told me this. I will pass it on to... to Dennis or, or to Julie, to see if they think it should be passed on to the police. And you've done nothing wrong, Leslie, so you don't need to be upset, yeah? Let's just forget about what happened in my room, and focus on what's important. Solving this, this murder, if that's what it is."

"Okay," said Leslie, swallowing against the lump that had formed in her throat. "I'm calm now." She took a deeply theatrical breath of air.

"That's my girl," said Barbara, getting up. "And now I've got to find a way of apologizing to Dennis for embarrassing him by dropping my towel. Sheesh! What a night!" She left the room, praying that she had deactivated a bomb.

IN MID-1817, LOYALIST settler James Lilleystone and his wife, Alice Bronwen Lilleystone (née Darvill), bought a parcel of land on Lake Ontario near Kingston, and over the years carved a farm out of the woods that sloped down to the water. The property stayed in the family until 1872, when a distant cousin, the Reverend Christopher Graham, purchased the farm and turned the farmhouse into a small Anglican private school. Over the decades and generations, and through two world wars, the school grew—adding a chapel, a classroom block, playing fields, other residential houses, a dining hall, a boat house, an infirmary, an outdoor theatre, a firehall, an indoor theatre, and a scattering of modest private residences to house faculty who wanted to live on campus but didn't wish to serve as heads of house. The school was single sex until 1982, but in the fall of that year admitted a handful of girls to grade thirteen, and thereafter expanded down by one grade a year. By 2004, by which point grade thirteen had been eliminated from Ontario schools, a roughly equal number of both sexes attended the school.

What was constant, through all those years, were the woods and the lake. Although the school gradually expanded, pushing a little deeper into the forest with each new building or playing field, many more acres of trees remained than acres under human settlement. It was still possible, in the early twenty-first century, to walk straight into the woods for twenty-five minutes before seeing a cultivated field or building on the other side.

St. Cuthbert's had strict rules against smoking, and expulsion was automatic, at least theoretically, if a student were caught lighting up in a school building... so, of course, students went into the woods to smoke. At any time during the day there might be five or six senior students taking advantage of spares, and that number shot up over lunch. But in the evenings, during and especially after study period, there would be as many as forty or fifty. Most of them found their way to favourite spots without the help of flashlights: Doug Nave, a particularly zealous anti-smoking head of house, was known to patrol the woods regularly, a headlamp fixed to his forehead. For a large man, he was remarkably stealthy, turning the headlamp on only when he was a few feet away from his quarry.

One of the attractions of smoking in the woods was the small thrill of transgression—the sense that one was taking a risk. Another was the opportunity it afforded to get to know students in other grades on a more or less equal footing. A grade twelve student, with all his or her senior authority, couldn't very well "bust" a grade nine student if they were both engaged in doing something they knew they shouldn't—and this was especially true if what they were smoking was marijuana rather than tobacco. But one of the dangers of smoking in the woods was that sometimes you couldn't see who else was in the circle, which meant that every now and then someone made a remark like, "Marty Bateman is such a fag," or "I wanna fuck Jason Dunphy's little sister," only to discover that Marty or Jason were standing just five or six feet away.

Shortly before study period officially ended at 9:30 P.M., a steady trickle of students began heading into the woods from across campus. For some, on the west side, it was a simple matter of walking out their front door and slipping around the side of the house. (A few, indeed, could exit through their windows.) For others, on the east side of campus, it was more of a trek—but the trek could be justified, if a don asked, by saying that you were on your way to the library, or to drop off an assignment in a faculty mailbox, or to visit a friend in another house, or to have cookies and a glass of milk in the dining hall.

And so, on the evening after a murder had taken place on the school campus, fifty or sixty or seventy students—desperate to talk with friends in other houses—tucked their cigarettes into pockets or sleeves, grabbed their lighters and empty soft-drink cans, and made for the woods. Three here, five there, eight behind the big rock, twelve in the ruins of the outdoor theatre.

"Holy fucking Christ, so what was it like in Roper House today?"

"Do you think it was Angus? Has anyone seen Angus?"

"Sommer was hanging around with those townies, wasn't he? The vampire dudes?"

"You shoulda seen Rogstad at dinner. She was like three sheets to the wind. That lady has nine empty bottles of wine in her recycling every week—I'm telling ya!"

"So what happened in study hall? Why did Cargill drag those new boys out of there?"

"That detective? She's hot. I'd slip it to her. You wanna interrogate me, lady? Interrogate this!"

"My mom said she wishes she'd sent me to Lakefield."

"Did you see the hearse? That thing gave me the creeps."

"Hey, Hoover. Hoover! Cup that dig, okay? We don't want Nave seeing us. That guy's got eyes like a cat."

"I saw that Arthurs woman crying this afternoon."

"I never liked the guy. Jake says he has a stash of the weirdest porn he's ever seen. Shit and vomit and stuff. German magazines."

"How the hell was he accepted back? Do you remember Kagan? Kagan got caught with a little baggie of weed and he was gone, gone, gone. Sommer stuffed dog shit in a guy's mouth and kicked his ribs in."

"So I guess the Lukester thinks he's like some big-time detective now."

"Does anyone have any weed?"

"Was he stabbed? Or was he shot?"

"What the hell was Sommer doing in the chapel anyway? It's not like any girl here would do him."

"It's going to be so weird going back in the chapel."

"My brother called from Ridley. They all know. Everyone knows. He said the cocktail circuit in TO is already buzzing."

And then, as students began to think about making their way back to their residences, fresh news: "Hey, guys! Leslie Ng walked in on Babs fucking Dennis Murdoch!"

THE FIRST WHISKEY went down quickly—tossed back. A catch-up drink. Normally Ben would have had four by this time, so there was no need for moderation. The second... well, the second went down quickly, too. It tasted good. And the third. And the fourth. Ben began to relax. The world took on a pleasant haze—maybe even a bit of a glow around the edges. He cut himself a hunk from the Mennonite farmer's sausage in the fridge. And some cheese. Very European. Meat and cheese and whiskey.

Was there anything on TV? He'd missed the news. There was always something on the soft-porn channel, but he couldn't work up any enthusiasm about it. Some of those girls at the school, though... He wished he were younger. Wished he were back in high school, knowing what he knew now. *Take what you can. Grab it. Don't get hooked too soon. None of this falling in love business. Been there, done that, bought the goddamn t-shirt. Look at me now: you fall in love, you do the wedding thing, you put in the long hours and buy the house. You support her while she stays home with the baby. No more evenings out with the boys. No more uninterrupted nights. No more sleep-ins. You start losing your hair and put on a few pounds—she takes off—taking the kid. Who you love. The kid, that is. I miss you, Bobby. God, I missed out. God, it's all fucked up.*

Number five was slugged back. *Why* slugged? *Where does that even come from, anyway? Maybe I should take a shower. Bit ranker than I should be after a whole freaking day at that freaking place. Gotta smell nice tomorrow. You never know when some honey might take an interest. Some of those female dons, man. That Barbara what's-her-name in Scott House. Girl who looks like a gymnast. What a bod. Bet she smells nice. Bet she feels good. I'd make her feel good. I'd go down on that.*

Ben brought the bottle with him to the bathroom, gulped down a shot before he turned the taps on. Struggled out of his clothes. *Left arm feels weird. Jaw's aching a bit.* Took yet another swig before stepping in. (Whiskey can make a man think he'll live forever.) *Shit, water's hotter than I thought. Shit—what? Oh, Christ—*

MONDAY, 11:32 P.M.

TWO-HUNDRED AND fifty miles away, in London, Ontario, Bobby Hendricks, first-string tight end for the Western University Mustangs, woke with a jolt. He had a game Tuesday, and he'd gone to bed early. His girlfriend was working on an essay in the living room. "Hey, babe!" he called out. "Was there a loud noise outside just now?"

"No," she called back. "Why?"

"Something woke me up. I was fast asleep."

"I didn't hear anything. Go back to sleep, Bobby."

Bobby shifted his position in the bed, flipped the pillow over, closed his eyes again. An image of his dad swum into his head—a memory of a moment, years and years before, when they'd gone for a walk together along the Kingston waterfront, and they'd played together around the Time sculpture. He felt a little tug at his heart—a metaphorical tug.

It happens, you know. It happens.

"MOLLY IS RESTLESS tonight," Paul Makepeace observed to his wife, lowering his book. Their five-year-old daughter was tossing and turning in her sleep in the bedroom opposite theirs.

Uncharacteristically, Leah was awake and reading a magazine. "I know. I think she must have picked up on the energy in the dining hall this evening." The family lived in one of the grace-and-favour houses on campus, and sometimes took advantage of the opportunity to eat dinner with the rest of the community. "I'm surprised you're not doing prep."

Paul shrugged. "I'd prepared my lessons for Monday," he said, "and I didn't use them so I'm good to go tomorrow."

Molly cried out in her sleep: "No, no! It isn't the green one!"

"The green one?" said Leah. "What is she dreaming about?"

"I'm going to check on her," said Paul, slipping out of bed. He went through the hall and quietly pushed open the door to his daughter's darkened bedroom, illuminated softly by the fairy toadstool nightlight on the bedside table. Molly, fully asleep, had thrown the sheets and blankets off and was half lying on her soft plush poodle. "Hey, baby," he whispered, "you're okay. You're okay." He gently slid the poodle out from under her and placed it in her arms, then covered her up to her neck with her bed clothes. He stroked her back for a moment, gazing into the sweet face that, more than any other, gave him reason to get up in the morning. "I love you, little one," he said, quietly, then went back to the master bedroom.

"She okay?" asked Leah.

"She's fine. Just a bit restless. She'd thrown off her covers. I covered her up again."

Leah put down her magazine. "You really don't think Angus did it?"

"No. I don't."

"Do you mind if I take Molly away for a few days?"

"Where would you go?"

"We have a standing invitation to visit Nancy."

"I don't mind. If you don't feel safe here."

"It's not—it's not that I don't feel *safe*, exactly. I just don't feel comfortable."

Paul nodded. "Then go."

"You really don't mind?"

"Nope. I don't." Paul placed his book on his own bedside table, stretched, yawned and reached for the lamp.

"I'll give Nancy a call tomorrow morning." Leah stared at her magazine. "I'm not sure I'm going to be able to sleep."

"Do you want to make love?"

"No. Not tonight."

"It might relax you."

"No. It wouldn't."

Jason McArthur, a grade twelve student in Scott House, sat at his desk staring at the assignment sheet in front of him: *Write five-hundred words comparing the two different creation stories in Genesis, and explore the contradictions.* While open-minded about many things, Jason was trying to understand why he was having to do this for an English course. Makepeace had told his English class that a familiarity with biblical stories was essential to understanding a great many literary classics, but was a deep dive into these things really necessary? He glanced over at his roommate, Henry Cundill, snoring quietly in his bed. Henry was always the first to fall asleep: he was the kind of guy who actually worked during study period, then showered and went to bed. Jason couldn't bring himself to be organized in the same way. He liked to wander around during the middle evening, visit friends, listen to music, make popcorn in the common room microwave.

At this hour, however, Jason wished he had applied himself earlier. Reading the creation stories was no great hardship—they were short enough. But writing five hundred words was a serious challenge. *I mean, what is there to say? Surely you could do it in a paragraph or two? Fucking Makepeace. What a dick. This was an English class, not Sunday school.*

Glancing again at his roommate, Jason reached for and opened a small container. He removed a couple of pale yellow tablets, each 20 milligrams of Ritalin, and put them on a clean sheet of paper. He took a wooden ruler from his drawer and pressed down on the tablets, crushing them, then rummaged around in the drawer for a straw.

This would set him up, he thought. This would help him do what he had to do. He made sure he had tissue ready for the inevitable nosebleed.

Luke had prayed well into his mid-teens. It wasn't something he did ostentatiously—in fact back then he never did it in front of anyone else. But he did pray. And he did believe that God heard his prayers, though his sense of who and what God is was ill-defined, nebulous.

In his late teens, and all through his university years, Luke abandoned prayer, largely moving away from the faith he'd been raised in. If someone had asked whether he believed in God, he would have probably said yes, but it would have been a qualified yes, swiftly followed by, *but it depends what you mean by*, or *but not in some ancient father figure in the clouds*, or something of that sort. It was, then, a *lukewarm* sort of belief, a pun that his pious father had once deployed against him.

Then, in the year Luke turned twenty-two, and just after he'd graduated from Queen's with a degree in politics, he'd had an experience that reanimated his faith. It wasn't a story he'd told more than a handful of people—his best friend Max, the Reverend Jennifer Reid (his spiritual adviser at Trinity), eventually his fiancée, Claire, and, yes, his father. He'd been hiking alone in Petroglyphs Provincial Park, about forty-five minutes north of Peterborough, Ontario, when he'd found himself on a cliff overlooking a small, turquoise-blue lake, sparkling below him like a polished jewel. The colour was astonishing—more Caribbean than southern Ontario. The trail he was on diverged, he saw, and the path that led off the main branch seemed to lead down, steeply, to the water.

Luke's descent took longer than he anticipated and was more hazardous: twice he had almost lost his footing, and he had jolted one of his knees. When he arrived at the base of the cliff, however, all thought of discomfort left him. He was on a sandy

beach. The sand curved away to the left of where he was standing, coming to a point about fifty yards farther on. It looked as
though the beach might continue on the farther side, but he
couldn't be sure. The water was just as brilliant and sparkling at
this level as it had seemed from higher up, but beachside he was
struck also by its placidity: it was, at that instant, absolutely still
and calm.

The day had not been noisy, but there had been the sound
of birds and insects of one kind or another. As Luke took several
steps forward onto the beach, however, the world suddenly grew
very quiet. His hair was blown about just a little by a breeze that
wafted in off the lake. And then he heard, after a moment or two,
a sound like wind chimes—and the sound grew and gathered
form and force and became like transcendentally beautiful sym-
phonic music—rich and resonant one moment, thrillingly crys-
talline the next: a lover's knowing laughter; thunder like can-
nons; a mother's soothing hush. It seemed to be coming out of
the rocks, or the lake, or the forest, or the air itself. It was
extraordinary. It made no sense. Luke had never experienced
anything remotely like it. His eyes filled with tears, and he sank
to his knees overwhelmed by what he was experiencing. Awed.
The music did not end decisively: when the melody and har-
monies had resolved, the wind chimes returned, and they continued for a while, simply diminishing in volume as time passed.

And that was that. Another man, or woman, might well have
interpreted this event differently, but Luke saw it as a summons
back to full-bodied Christian faith. A year later he had enrolled
in a theology program, and five years after that he'd been
ordained a minister in the Anglican Church. Four months later
he'd met Claire, and they had begun the process of intertwining
their lives. A year and a half after that, she was dead.

Luke knelt at his bedside and prayed: he prayed for wisdom,
he prayed for guidance, and he prayed that the strange pleasure
he'd felt at trying to ferret out the truth of Sommer's murder
would burn away, and that he would once again be able to focus
on the work that his ministry required him to do.

DIANE STEWART'S PARTNER, Emily Hill, was accustomed to Diane getting in late when she was working a case. She had learned patience over the years. When Diane slipped into bed just before midnight, fresh from a shower, Emily rolled over and embraced her. "Long day for you, Di."

"It's going to be like this for several days, Em. We need to cover a lot of ground."

"Have you got your eye on anyone in particular?" Emily nuzzled into Diane's neck.

"No. Not at the moment. A lot of moving parts. But I think we may have ruled out one suspect today."

"It's all over the news, you know."

"I'm not surprised. It's the sort of story the media laps up."

"Who are you working it with?"

"No one you know. A Callum Brezicki from Toronto. He's with the OPP."

"Because Kingston is so stretched at the moment?"

"Yeah. And I think, maybe, because the victim's parents are big shots in Toronto." Diane gently stroked Emily's hair away from her face, tucking a couple of loose strands behind her ear.

"Do you like him?"

"He's okay. I've known worse. We've not had a murder down here since 2002, so it's good to have someone who's worked a number of others... How was your day?"

"It was quiet. Robin's asleep. He told me to give you a hug." Emily hugged Diane by way of honouring their son's request.

Diane returned the hug. Three minutes later, Emily had fallen back to sleep. Diane lay awake for some time, Emily's head on her breast.

CRYSTAL KING, A grade twelve day-student, robust of figure, red-haired, was delivered to the school by her parents Tuesday morning to do something she'd thought about for the three years she'd been at St. Cuthbert's. The school had a decades-old tradition of allowing students in their graduating year to give a talk in the chapel about who they were, what their experience at St. Cuthbert's had been, what advice they might have for younger students. Often the opportunity was used to salute friends and thank members of staff or parents. Usually, the talk was preceded by a piece of music, selected by the speaker, which played while she or he proceeded from the back of the chapel to the lectern at the front. Usually, too, another piece of music, also selected by the student, played while he or she left the lectern and walked down the aisle to the back and then into one of the side aisles. While most of the students (and those staff in attendance) left the chapel, a "hug line," consisting of the speaker's friends and well-wishers, would form in that aisle.

Luke was not fond of the tradition—nor, for that matter, were most of his colleagues (though many of them attended, from time to time, in the hope that they might be thanked or otherwise singled out for praise by the speaker). The problem was that so many of the speeches delivered the same set of messages: "you get out of the school what you put into it," "I had the best friends," "I wish I hadn't quarrelled with so-and-so in grade ten, and I'm so glad we're good buddies now." Dick Cargill had agitated strongly for ending the practice, but each graduating class had fought hard to defend what they saw as a rite of passage, and the headmaster was reluctant to defy students who could make or break the school community's spirit. Besides, every now and then a young person said something unexpected, revelatory, helpful.

As a day-student—someone who attended classes and meals and practices and games and performances but lived in Kingston—Crystal had not been as much affected by the murder as some of her residential peers: in fact, she hadn't come to campus at all the previous day, skipping field hockey practice to refine her speech and agonize over her music pieces. She was initially dismayed to learn that she would have to deliver her speech in the theatre rather than the chapel (which wouldn't be professionally cleaned until later that afternoon), but she had swiftly adjusted to the idea and took some consolation in the fact that the theatre had a better sound system for her musical selections, and a bigger screen for the slides she wanted to show of her friends and family.

With the school assembled in the raked seating of the Mark Danby Theatre, Crystal signalled to the young man in the tech booth that he should dim the lights and start her music. A moment later, Beyonce's "Crazy in Love" blasted out through the speakers. One minute in, Crystal began descending the steps to the podium on the theatre's stage, and, according to tradition, the whole school stood.

It wasn't a bad speech. There were a few funny anecdotes, some affectionate callouts to Crystal's best buddies, some fine photos of beautiful young people, and a teary thank-you to her parents for sacrificing in the way they had to make her attendance at the school possible. Standard stuff, yes, but warm and pleasant: besides, Luke reflected, who among us has anything profound to say at the age of seventeen? But shortly before Crystal finished her speech, just as she was bringing things to a close, she said something that made Luke and several other faculty members snap to attention.

"I'm not a very religious person," she said, "and I don't know much about any religion. But I do believe in karma—I guess that's from Hinduism? I do believe that if you put a lot of bad energy out into the world, you get bad energy back. What goes around, comes around." This was close enough to the boiler-plate chapel-speech message, "you get out of the school what you put into it," that it didn't seem to fizz on most students, though there were a few, here and there, wide-awake and bright-eyed, who also likely picked up on the subtextual message that Luke, Jim, Dennis, Paul, and Jiao heard clearly: *What goes around, comes around.* Dave Sommer got what he deserved.

Crystal finished her talk with a little flourish and came back up the stairs to the strains of James Blunt's "You're Beautiful." An intelligent lass, she saw that there wasn't as natural a place for a hug line to form as in the chapel, so she squeezed herself against the wall near the tech booth, gambling that her friends and parents would similarly keep to the wall as they lined up to hug her. Luke stood off to one side, resolving to be the final person to speak with her, if he possibly could.

"CANDACE," SAID CORONER Baz Van Herten, "I'm going to ask you to take the photos." The two of them—the brusque, middle-aged coroner and the quiet and youthful anatomical pathology technologist—were clothed in blue scrubs, white Wellington boots, face-visors, gloves and gauntlets. Dave Sommer was laid out on the table in front of them, wearing what he was wearing when killed, but destined, after the first set of photos, to be stripped, photographed again, finger-printed and X-rayed; to have blood drawn from a vein, urine from his bladder, and deposits scraped from under his fingernails; to have his body cavity opened, his organs examined, his eyes checked, the top of his head removed and then the brain—and everything noted, via Baz Van Herten's gruff dictation, so that the boy who once lived and breathed, became, in the legal record, a list of characteristics, descriptions, measurements, statistics, scans and photos.

But the coroner and the technologist were not the only ones in the room with the deceased. Detective-Sergeant Diane Stewart was also there, though she was several paces away and wore a surgical mask rather than a face-visor. A forensics officer was there too, and he took Sommer's clothes, when once they were removed, placed them in a thick plastic bag, then spirited them to a locker in a secure storage room at police headquarters. Diane had not attended many post-mortems, but she had a strong stomach and watched the whole procedure with a composure that Dr. Van Herten found mildly irritating. He liked his police colleagues to blanch a little when he pulled out the organs.

"So," Baz concluded three hours later, "two stab wounds to the belly and neck from a double-edged military grade knife. Cause of death: severing of the descending aorta and exsanguination. The person who wielded the knife was strong, and the wounds were not self-inflicted. Likely time of death, between 9:00 and 11:00 P.M. Sunday."

Candace nodded, wondering whether she should proceed with the clean-up, or take a quick pee-break. Her focus in the last half-hour had been a little compromised by her drinking a large green tea before the procedure.

"God Almighty," said the coroner. "Nothing like a post-mortem to whet the appetite. Would you like to join me in a nice curry, Diane?"

CRYSTAL'S HUG-LINE WAS a little shorter than those that usually formed after a chapel talk: eight members of the girls' field hockey team, six other day students, an old friend from the local high school she might have attended if her parents hadn't sent her to St. Cuthbert's (a happy surprise, this), and her parents. Sometimes a grandparent or two might attend—particularly if they were helping pay the fees; sometimes there would be a boyfriend or girlfriend from another school; sometimes, especially if the speaker were from one of the residential houses, nearly every girl or boy in the House would line up for a hug or, in the case of boys with boys, a handshake. But Crystal seemed pleased with the response to her talk: she whooped when she saw her public-school friend, she hugged everyone enthusiastically, and she got a little teary-eyed with her parents.

By the time the hug-line was finished, the theatre was pretty well empty except for Crystal, her parents, her public-school friend, and a couple of girls from the field hockey team. Luke moved in quickly. "Crystal, can I speak to you for just a couple of minutes?"

"Can it wait until break, Mr. Nash?" she replied. "My parents want to take me and my friends out for breakfast." This too was a tradition, and not one the school's academic leadership approved of at all. It meant that any student who went out on these breakfast trips missed at least two classes, and sometimes those classes featured tests, presentations, lab-work, or performances that, when skipped, caused profound inconvenience for teachers and other students. But, again, Jim Harvey was reluctant to step in and close them down: denying parents the opportunity to have breakfast with their children would not be good for relations within the school community, and pleasing parents trumped the integrity of the academic program every time.

But Luke had a murder to help solve. "Just two minutes," he said—and, smiling at her parents, added, "I really won't detain her long, but this relates to what happened yesterday." He drew her away from the others. She followed, though her own smile had faded a little.

"Crystal, I have to ask you: when you spoke about putting bad energy out into the world, and then getting it back, was that a general comment? Or were you, in a clever way, speaking about Dave Sommer?"

Her face took on a certain wariness. "I think it's just generally true," she said, "so it would apply to Dave Sommer, too."

"Okay," said Luke. "I agree with the principle, but is there something about Dave Sommer that Mr. Harvey and I and the police should know? Did he do something horrible to someone that we should follow up on? Because this is a death, Crystal, and it's really important for all of us at the school that we get to the bottom of this."

Crystal hesitated, an internal struggle suggested by fleeting expressions on her face. "He wasn't good with girls," she said after a moment. "There are a couple of girls who he maybe tried to pressure in some ways, like, after dances. He pushed. He didn't like to be told *no*. That's what I've heard. It never happened to me, but I'm not the sort of girl he'd go for."

"Can you point me in the direction of a particular girl or girls?" Luke asked, sensing that something tangible or palpable might be in his grasp. An outraged boyfriend? A vengeful father? An older cousin?

"No," said Crystal firmly. "It's just something I've heard. Girls talk. Word gets around....I've gotta go, Mr. Nash. My parents are waiting." And she went, raising her arms in triumph as she returned to the small group waiting for her: "Waffles!" she cried. "I can smell the maple syrup and bacon!"

TUESDAY, 8:30 A.M.

JIM HARVEY KNEW it was going to be a difficult day: that was a given. The headmaster suspected, in fact, that he was in for a lengthy stretch of very difficult days. He'd already received several sympathetic emails from other heads of school in the Canadian Association of Independent Schools, and while at one level, he was grateful for them, at another level he wondered if there wasn't just a little *schadenfreude* at work: if St. Cuthbert's applications declined precipitously, the slack would almost certainly be picked up by Trinity College in Port Hope, by Lakefield College in Lakefield, by Ridley College in St. Catharine's. A good part of his job was simply selling the school to parents prepared to pay, for a single year's tuition and residence fees, the equivalent of a new luxury car; and doing that would be much more challenging in the wake of the murder of a student on the premises.

He returned from Crystal's chapel talk in the theatre to face the reality of making, and receiving, phone calls—and no sooner had he sat down at his desk than Debbie appeared at his door. "Jim, can you take a call from Angus Graves's father? He's on line one."

Jim nodded, picked up. "Jim Harvey."

"Mr. Harvey," said the stern voice at the other end. "I'm going to have a hard time staying calm during this conversation."

Mr. Graves did, mostly, stay calm, and his phone call was the more effective for his composure. He made it clear to Jim that he and his wife were furious with David Waters and the chaplain and Paul Makepeace for *harassing*—his word—their son. He said that they still could not understand why Dave Sommer had been permitted to return to the school. "We've already discussed this, Mr. Harvey," he said. "It was a serious error of judgment on your part. And that error of judgment has led to my son suffering the indignity of a police *interrogation*." He said that he—and his wife—were a hair's breadth away from pulling Angus from the school and enrolling him at Ashbury in Ottawa. He made the point that he didn't think he'd be able to find the motivation to pay the residence fees that the accounts office was requesting, and that if his son *were* to remain, the school should very seriously consider a suspension of all financial demands, and that step alone might forestall punitive legal action. In brief, he conveyed a great deal in a relatively short time, and hung up, dramatically, when Jim began to reply. Jim sat and, metaphorically, bled for a couple of minutes after he had also replaced the receiver.

But only for a couple of minutes, because he then had the joyful task of calling the parents of the two Garys—Edwards and Trotter—to let them know that their sons were being sent home for smoking marijuana, that the chaplain would be putting them on the bus later that morning, and that there was a real possibility they wouldn't be allowed to return to the school. In each instance, his call was taken by the mother, and in each instance the mother wept—Mrs. Trotter uncontrollably. Mrs. Edwards wanted to know how the school had allowed her son to access marijuana, because he certainly hadn't been smoking it while he was under her roof. Jim had always seen himself as a man's man, and would sooner take a punch to the gut than deal with a weeping mother. He wished that he could lose his business suit and go for a long run—either that, or chug several beers.

Neither running nor beer-chugging was even a remote possibility, however, because as soon as he'd finished his call with Mrs. Edwards, Debbie again appeared at his office door. "Jim, Dave Sommer's parents are here. I've put them into the board room and ordered coffee from the dining hall."

"Thank you, Debbie," said Jim, "but I don't think I'll meet them there. Glenda has made some banana bread and she has the coffee on, so I'll talk with them in my living room. Could you locate Luke and ask him to join us?"

"Why don't I take them in?" said Debbie. "Give you a moment to recover." She was an excellent secretary.

"Thank you," said Jim gratefully. "Yes, take them in, and tell them I'll be with them in three minutes. Could you close the door?"

Debbie smiled as she closed the door. Jim took his blood pressure medication out of the middle drawer of his desk and swallowed a pill.

Paul Makepeace was primarily an English teacher, but his five-course load included one class of grade twelve drama. It wasn't a course he had asked to teach, and his colleague Kevin Goulet had expressed horror upon learning that someone who lacked a drama degree was assigned a senior course—but Paul had worked as an actor for a couple of years before going to teacher's college, and the director of academics felt that was qualification enough. Over the course of a few years, moreover, Paul had come to enjoy teaching the subject.

First period Tuesday morning the class was beginning a series of long-form improvs. They had spent the previous two weeks reviewing the conventions of improvisation and performing short scenes, but Paul felt they were now ready for something more ambitious. He divided the class into three groups and gave each group a setting (a public park, a hotel foyer, a residence common room); a prop (a small beanbag, a roll of masking tape, a pen); and a line of dialogue that had to be spoken at some point in the improv. Each group then had five minutes to create a kind of plot and was asked to perform their improvisation for the class. Paul was alive to the fact that there was a tendency to go for big events—terrorist bombs going off, earthquakes, gang murders—and he encouraged them to think of more modest, smaller-scale events that might allow them to focus on characters with some depth, some dimensionality.

The first group did perfectly competent work. A child went missing in a public park when he kept throwing his beanbag farther and farther away from his mother. A young woman played the boy-child, which struck Paul as an interesting choice. The actress playing the mother did so in a straightforward, credible way. A male student played a vagrant who at first appeared sinister but turned out to be harmless. The other actors had lesser roles, but that was okay: Paul had stressed that in theatre, as in the real world, no one had to be front-and-centre all the time.

The second group pushed their improv back into the comic realm where they had spent the first week of their explorations: an elderly gentleman fell and broke his leg in the hotel foyer, and the concierge helped him up and, with assistance from the front desk clerk, wrapped masking tape round and round the leg to brace it. The piece started well, but soon ran out of steam. The actors did their best to mask its failure by pumping up the energy, but it just didn't work. Paul made a note to tell them that the fact it didn't work was not in itself a problem: we learn from our failures.

As the final group moved into place, Paul was aware of a subtle change in the energy of the room. Tracey-Lee Goodman, a talented actress, quickly revealed herself to be playing a victim of sexual assault. The scene opened with her sitting in a common room with another female friend, to whom she disclosed that she had been raped by a male student the previous evening. The scene's resolution, however, was unexpectedly and credibly violent: the assailant showed up in the common room for a second helping, and the friend of the victim leapt forward and stabbed him, repeatedly, with a pen, ultimately killing him. The performances were so compelling that several students in the other groups gasped.

What am I to do with that? Paul wondered. Portraying the killing of a male student so soon after a real murder a stone's-throw away was in questionable taste, but maybe this was the way that adolescents needed to work through the issue. Maybe he should simply accept that they had done what he'd asked them not to do and move on. Or should he, perhaps, initiate a conversation? Were the kids effectively asking for an opportunity to talk? He was still wrestling with the question when he rose and moved to centre-stage to deliver his critique of the three scenes.

When Jim Harvey arrived in his living room, his secretary was serving the Sommer parents coffee, while his wife cut slices of home-made banana bread on the coffee-table. This business of "living-over-the-shop," as he sometimes called it, might have strained many another marriage, but Glenda had embraced her role, playing hostess at all sorts of official functions, cheering from the sidelines at important games, appearing engrossed at concerts, plays and dance showcases, and soothing some of the feathers her husband inevitably ruffled in the course of his daily governance of the school. Many another wife might have taken a dim view of her husband's secretary having free access to her home, but, again, it just didn't seem to be an issue: Glenda and Debbie got along famously. In an era of vigorous feminism, his wife showed every sign of embracing her supportive role. While Jim ruled, Glenda charmed. If there was space between them, the public never saw it.

Leopold and Greta Sommer were difficult to read. Jim knew that grief did different things to different people, but he was still surprised that neither parent was teary. Leopold seemed simply cold, while Greta appeared almost detached. Comparing notes later, Jim and Glenda both wondered whether Greta had been heavily medicated, but there was nothing sluggish about her speech or movements.

"We are thinking that we would like to have the funeral here," said Leopold, after the handshakes and obligatory expressions of sadness and support were exchanged. "We are not church goers, so we don't have a church in Toronto, and we would like David's friends to have a chance to say their good-byes."

"Of course," said Jim. "Our chaplain, Luke, will be here any minute to discuss how you would like things done."

"Our son was very fond of this school," said Leopold. "It was important for him to return. He had resolved to make a good impression after the unfortunate events of last spring."

"He had clearly undergone some positive changes," said Jim. "Several faculty members have said as much." This was, of course, a lie, but it seemed a forgivable lie, under the circumstances.

"Yes, he had some troubled times, but Greta and I felt he had turned a corner. We believe he would have made a fine head student if the opportunity had been given him. He was very interested in helping younger students."

"A natural mentor," said Greta.

Jim was struck, as he had been many times before, by the degree of self-deception or outright delusion some parents had around their progeny's strengths and weaknesses. "I think those qualities would have become even more evident at university," he managed to say. And at that moment, fortunately, Luke entered.

Jim began to make introductions, but Leopold signalled they had already met. "We would like you to conduct the funeral service," Leopold said to Luke. "I am sure you will find some wonderful things to say about our boy."

"I will gladly conduct the service," said Luke, thinking privately that the second part of the mandate would be a bit of a challenge.

"Perhaps we could go to the chapel and see where things will go," said Greta. "I would like to order flowers for the altar and the window ledges."

"I'm afraid we won't be allowed into the chapel itself," said Luke. "But we can certainly go to my office and go over the order of service and any musical requests you may have."

"Why can we not go to the chapel?" asked Leopold with a trace of belligerence.

Luke hesitated. "It's being cleaned—professionally cleaned."

"Well, surely that isn't a problem," said Greta. "We can walk around the cleaners. I want to make some important decisions about the service, and I need to see where the service will take place."

It was in that instant that Luke and Jim realized that the Toronto police hadn't told the Sommers that their son had been killed in the chapel.

First period began at 9:10 a.m., at which point all students were theoretically to be in their seats and ready to learn. A couple of minutes later, Ben Hendricks still hadn't arrived to unlock his classroom door. His grade eleven math students were beginning their usual chatter about the mythical "five-minute rule," a rule that, some believed, gave them permission to leave if a teacher had not appeared five minutes after a class was scheduled to begin. In a school where faculty members often received telephone calls from parents at all hours—calls they were obliged to take—the odd late arrival was almost guaranteed. The chatter came to an end, however, when Karin Rogstad, on her way to the staff room, produced her own keys and unlocked the door. The students filed in, grumbling a bit.

Angus Graves headed for the back of the classroom. He was a reasonably strong math student, but he preferred not to be under any teacher's easy scrutiny. Pablo, his roommate, shared this class with him, and he followed Angus toward the back, taking a seat across from him: the two young men had little in common, but they got along well together. Bonita from Wilcox, Patti (who had auditioned for the school play), and Leslie (who had burst in on her don), were also in the class. There were others too, of course: twenty-three in all, boys and girls, strong students and weak, residential and day.

One of the day students, Struan Lynch, wore a sour expression. His parents were in the midst of a break-up, his girlfriend had recently dumped him, and he had been dropped from the first soccer team. It was a poisonous mix. He sat down, dumped his bookbag on the floor, pulled out his math text, notebook and calculator, then looked around moodily. His eyes came to rest on Bonita, sitting one seat ahead of him in the row to his left. "Hey,

Bonita," he said, emboldened by the teacher's absence and who-knows-what else: "How does it feel to know that the guy who screwed you is dead?"

Bonita turned and looked at him in bewildered horror. Other students immediately raised their voices in protest. No one laughed. There was an instant recognition that Lynch's question went far outside the bounds of acceptable banter. "What do you mean?" said Bonita. "Who screwed me? What are you talking about?"

Struan was all-in now; there was no turning back. "Everyone knows that Dave Sommer screwed you," he said. "No use deny-ing it. So at least he lost his cherry before he died, eh?"

Bonita burst into tears.

That was all Angus needed. He had been a decent young man before Dave Sommer had beaten him up the previous spring. His summer of reflection, and of martial arts and weight training, had nurtured in him a willingness to step forward to confront bullies wherever they showed up. He rose, walked up his aisle and down Struan's.

Seeing him coming, Struan stood up, too. "You wanna play the hero, Angus?" he said.

"You wanna be next?" asked Angus.

"Next for what?" But Angus's implication had been clear. Struan moved his hands toward Angus's chest, intending to give him a shove—but Angus was more than ready: he moved for-ward into the shove, and followed through by kneeing Struan in the groin. Struan sank to his knees.

Perhaps thirty seconds later, Pablo and two other boys felt compelled to pull Angus off Struan... but before that happened, Struan's face was a bloody mess: his nose broken, his eyes black-ened, his jaw dislocated, his brain concussed from repeated colli-sions with the classroom floor. Simply put, Angus had lost it.

Dick Cargill joined Jim Harvey in his office, sinking into one of the two armchairs facing the desk. "So. The Garys," he said. "Gary Edwards and Gary Trotter. Chris Wong will be bringing them here in two minutes."

"It's the usual drill," said Jim. "I'll ask them why I shouldn't expel them, and I'll ask where they got the pot. I take it there's no question at all that they smoked it?"

"None," said Dick heavily. "They stunk of it. Kids never seem to realize we can smell it on them a mile away."

"Good for Ben for calling you in," said Jim.

"I don't think he could have ignored it. Every kid in study hall would have known."

Jim thought about that for a moment. "Maybe. Still, some others might have let it slide."

"Yeah, you're probably right."

Jim fiddled with a paper clip, doing his best to straighten it out. "Do we want Chris to stay with us?"

"He has a class second period, so I don't think so. Is Luke coming? Should we have him drive the boys to the bus depot?"

"He's with the Sommers, and he may be some time. Let's get a don to do it. Remind me: who is the don for Roper House?"

"Harper. Lou Harper."

"We'll ask Chris to send Lou to us. Lou can wait in reception until we're finished with the boys."

At that instant, Chris Wong entered the area outside Jim's office with the two Garys in tow. Jim beckoned him to the open door. "Chris, there's no need for you to stay for this. Can you tell Lou to come here directly with his car keys? We want him to drive the boys to the bus depot."

"Sure," said Chris, but he hesitated a moment and dropped his voice so the boys, who had stayed some distance away, couldn't hear: "Jim, they're basically good lads. I know you've got to punish them, but if there's any room for clemency…"

"Let's see what they have to say for themselves," said Jim. "If they come clean, maybe."

"That's what I've told them." Chris turned and spoke to the boys. "The headmaster is ready for you. Go in. Tell the truth." The two Garys, white-faced, entered the office and stood in front of Jim's desk. Dick eyed them sourly from the side.

"So," said Jim. "Are you aware that you've breached one of the cardinal rules of the school—one that we stressed in the acceptance letters we sent you in April, and repeated at the first assembly three weeks ago?"

"Yes, sir," said Gary Trotter.

"We're sorry, sir," said Gary Edwards.

Jim looked sternly at them. "My instinct is to do exactly what we say we'll do if the rule is broken, and that's to expel you. And do you know what that means? That means your parents lose the first installment of your tuition and residence fees, about $25,000, and it also means you have a black mark beside your name if you apply to any other independent school. Do you understand that?"

"Yes, sir," said Gary Trotter.

"Please give us one more chance," said Gary Edwards.

"There is a tiny possibility that you could get one more chance," said Jim. "A tiny possibility." He held up his right hand, his index finger and thumb separated by less than a quarter of an inch, to illustrate his point. "But you need to give me a good reason *not* to expel you, and you need to tell me where you got the marijuana. That's the only way I might see my way clear to giving you another shot."

There was a brief silence as both boys stole a glance at each other.

"We were upset, sir," said Gary Trotter. "We were upset over, over the murder. Because we knew Dave."

"He was nice to us, sir," said Gary Edwards.

"All right," said Jim, a hint of softness showing itself. "I'm going to think about that. It doesn't excuse what you did—not at all—but I'm going to weigh its importance."

"Thank you, sir," said Gary Trotter.

"Thank you," Gary Edwards echoed.

"Where did you get the pot?" Jim asked, leaning forward.

Gary Edwards didn't hesitate, didn't look at Trotter. "From Dave, sir."

"From Dave?" Jim repeated.

"From Dave Sommer. He gave us a joint. As a present, like."

"And did Dave Sommer tell you where *he* got it?"

"He made a sort of joke about it, sir," said Gary Trotter.

"How so? What was the joke?"

"He said he gets all his pot from a vampire," said Gary Edwards.

★

Five minutes later, the boys dispatched to the bus depot with Lou Harper, Jim and Dick were once again alone.

"What do you think, Dick?"

"I'm thinking that Dave Sommer was poisonous from the moment he walked through the door," said Dick.

"I can't argue with that," said Jim wearily. "If there were one decision I could take back…"

"You didn't have a crystal ball," said Dick. "You couldn't have known."

Debbie came to the open door and leaned in. "Ben Hendricks didn't show up to his first period class, and he's not answering his phone. I've just asked Barbara Meeks to go to his house and check on him."

"Okay, thanks, Debbie," said Jim. Debbie nodded, and headed back to her desk.

"He was on duty last night," Dick offered. "He probably slept in and he's enroute now. Barbara will likely pass him on his way here."

"Right," said Jim. "Would you speak to him? Just tell him to set an alarm clock in future. No need to make a big deal of it."

"Sure," said Dick, and he got up. Ben Hendricks missing a first period class was a trivial issue next to a murder.

As a semi-rural independent school, St. Cuthbert's used a lot of buses and coaches to transport students to and from other independent schools in the southern part of Ontario—and, for that matter, to public and Catholic high schools in the Kingston area. On at least two days of the week, teams would be sent to play fixtures in Kingston, Gananoque, Brockville, Ottawa, Belleville, Port Hope, Lakefield, Rosseau, Pickering and Toronto, and occasionally they would venture as far as Ridley College in St. Catharine's. Because the buses usually arrived early, and because team members tended to straggle on board, often several large vehicles would be on the driveway, belching diesel or gas fumes for long stretches of the morning or afternoon.

The bus hired to transport the boys' first soccer team to Lakefield arrived at 9:25 a.m., and sat, its engine on, as the boys came in from their various classes or residences (if they had first period spares). Stephen and Hasan from Roper House were among the players, and the two boys chose seats, Hasan one seat ahead of Stephen, near the back. On a mini-coach of this kind, smaller and more upscale than an ordinary school bus, each student would have a two-person seat to himself, and enough elbow room to work if he were moved to do so.

"Hey, Hasan," called Jason Smith from Colgrave House, as he came down the aisle, "I hear you had some sort of weird séance in Roper Sunday night, eh? With Sommer?"

"It wasn't a séance, dickhead," said Stephen, answering for Hasan. "We were just messing around with a Ouija board, trying to entertain the juniors."

Jason laughed. "That worked well," he said, "seeing as they've just been expelled. I saw them with their bags, getting into a car with Lou Harper. Edwards was bawling away."

"We don't feel good about it," Stephen said, as quietly as the noise of the coach engine allowed. "We don't feel good at all."

"Where'd you get a fucking Ouija board?" asked another boy. "That's some crazy shit."

"It belongs to Marcus," said Stephen. "It's just a game. No big deal. No one believed it was magic."

"Yeah, but the board said he was going to get murdered, right?" said Jason. "That *is* pretty crazy."

"It didn't say—" Stephen began, but at that moment Hasan stood up and shouted, "Shut up! Shut the fuck up! We don't want to talk about it, okay! Just shut up!" He grabbed his laptop and his athletic bag and stormed back down the aisle, pushing past team coach Maurice Kahn as he boarded consulting his clipboard.

"Hasan, where are you—," Maurice said, going after him, but Hasan didn't stop.

"What's that about?" Jason asked, turning back to Stephen.

"His parents called last night," said Stephen. "They're not happy. They may pull him out of school."

"Why?" asked another team member.

"I guess because he's Muslim," said Stephen. "They don't like that kind of thing."

"I didn't mean to get him all riled up," said Jason.

"Well, you did. Sometimes you just need to let things go."

"How was I to know he was going to be such a pussy about it?"

"He's not a pussy," said Stephen. "He's a good guy. He's upset."

The coach reappeared, looking flustered. "Anyone wanna tell me what's up with Hasan? Did one of you say something stupid to him?"

Barbara Meeks was relieved to get off-campus—anything to get away from the anxiety she felt that at any moment she'd be summoned to Jim Harvey's office to explain why a student had found her naked with the husband of her head of house. And even worse than that—much worse at some level—was the chance of a loud knock at her door, and there would be Julie Murdoch herself, the wronged wife, wanting to know what kind of little slut she was to be showing her tits and ass to Dennis. *Dennis… Shit. A nice guy, sure, but just a distraction, really. A challenge. A little excitement. Pathetically grateful for some action on the side. Not worth losing my job over.* She wasn't absolutely certain that Leslie had spilled the beans about what she'd seen, but she suspected she had. No one had *said* anything, but a number of students had given her a queer look that morning when she circulated through the dining hall, urging them to get to the theatre for Crystal's chapel talk. *And holy cow, what was it Crystal had meant by saying "what goes around, comes around"? Who was* that *pointed at?*

The headmaster's secretary had given her Ben Hendrick's address, just a six-minute drive from the school, and she hadn't even needed to plug it into her GPS. She'd met Ben only once, at the opening staff meeting, when he'd introduced himself during the coffee break. She'd had the impression he was giving her the eye, but then most men did. Seeing his car in the driveway she figured she'd knock on the door, give him a chirpy greeting when he opened it, wide-eyed, dressing gown wrapped around him, then head back to campus, perhaps stopping at Tim Horton's on the way back, 'cause a girl needs her double double.

She climbed out of her car and took the little paving stone walkway from the driveway to the front door. There was nothing particularly striking about the house: Ben clearly wasn't a gardener, and the two beds on either side of the front door were overgrown with weeds. She suspected, too, that the lawn hadn't been cut since term began. The curtains in the living room window were drawn, though not carefully. If there were a need, she'd be able to go up to the window, shade her eyes, and see inside. But there wouldn't be a need. She rapped on the door, then rang the doorbell for good measure.

There was no answer. She knocked and rang again. Glanced sideways at the car to confirm that it was his—and, of course, she couldn't be sure, because she'd never seen him getting into or out of it, but it was certainly a car she'd seen on campus. She hesitated, then tried the door handle. The front door opened. "Hello," she called into the interior, which was lit-up; many lights were on, unnecessarily, given the daylight. "Ben? Ben!"

Again, no answer, but she could hear what was probably a shower in the distance. She stood still for a moment, irresolute, but then something compelled her to act. She entered the house and closed the front door behind her. "Ben! Ben? Mr. Hendricks?" Just the sound of the shower. But the very absence of other sounds was a little odd, because, usually, when a man took a shower, you could hear him moving around, or coughing, or dropping something, or even singing. So Barbara sighed and moved through the mud room and around the corner to the short hallway, at the end of which, clearly, was the bathroom. That it was the bathroom was evident from the slow stream of water coming out from under the door and flowing into the hallway.

Whatever Barbara's other failings might be, she wasn't afraid to act in an emergency. She ran down the hall, opened the bathroom door, stepped inside, and discovered Ben Hendricks, flat on his face, in an inch of water on the floor. She knew immediately from his colour that he was dead: there was no need to take his pulse, no sense in trying to resuscitate him. She rolled him over on his back, turned off the shower, then went down the hall to the kitchen, from where she made two telephone calls: one to Glenda at the school, and the other to Emergency Medical Services in Kingston.

So it was that, in death, poor Ben Hendricks fulfilled his late-middle-aged dream of getting naked with a beautiful young woman. And yes, it's a lousy joke, but we need a joke, sometimes, to release the tension.

To her intense surprise, Barbara burst into tears when she ended her call to EMS. She sat in the kitchenette on one of Ben's second-hand dining room chairs, rocking back and forth, back and forth, her body recreating the movements her young mother had once used to soothe her.

Detective-Sergeant Callum Brezicki had opted not to attend Dave Sommer's post-mortem: he was content to have Diane Stewart look after that particular chore. He'd spent the first part of the morning going further back through case files in the Kingston Police archives and consulting the Major Case Management database, which was still fairly new. He could find nothing that resonated strongly with this case—nothing where a possible link popped out at him. He needed a break. He needed to take some sort of action.

Callum assumed that a knife was probably the weapon used to kill the boy, and it occurred to him suddenly that a search for that knife might be a useful thing. But where to search? It hadn't been left at the scene, obviously, so the killer had probably carried it away with him. But what if he hadn't? What if the knife had been discarded somewhere not too far away, but off the beaten track? It wasn't likely, but it was possible. What about along the highway that went past the school? What about in the woods surrounding the school? It was a hell of a large area to cover, but in the absence of a significant lead they had to start somewhere.

Looking out the window of Diane's office at 11 Queen Street, he chewed his lip for a moment, then picked up the phone on her desk and stabbed in a three-digit number. "OPP Detective-Sergeant Brezicki here. I'm working in Diane Stewart's office. Could I ask you to arrange for a squad of community volunteers to conduct a search?... I think you'll find Chief Closs will approve... As many as you can round up... Let's say twelve noon at St. Cuthbert's College near Bath... Thank you." He replaced the receiver and looked out the window again. The skies were clear, so rain was unlikely.

His cell phone buzzed, and he glanced down. A text from one of his daughters.

Jim was poring over a report from the St. Cuthbert's recruitment and admissions office when he heard a gasp from Debbie at her desk in his outer office. He rose and walked over to the open door just as she was replacing the receiver. "What's happened?"

"Ben Hendricks is dead," said Debbie. "That was Barbara Meeks. She's at his house now." Her normally professional demeanor had slipped a little. She looked shaken.

"*Murdered*?"

"No. Barbara suspects a heart attack, but of course she doesn't know for sure. But there's no sign he's been shot or stabbed."

"I assume she's called the police? Can you let Luke and Dick know immediately? One of them should go there and take over from Barbara."

"Barbara called EMS, so I'll call the police. I'm pretty sure Dick is teaching this period, so I'll get Luke."

"Luke may still be with the Sommers. We may have to contact—"

"No, he saw them off about two minutes ago. I'll call him right now." Debbie picked up her receiver again and punched in a number, her professionalism reasserting itself. Jim stood there a moment longer, reflecting, just briefly, that a lousy week had just become catastrophic... then he turned and went back into his own office: he needed to prepare for his afternoon meeting with the chair and vice-chair of the school's executive board. As he sat down, he saw that a cascade of new emails had dropped into his inbox, and he recognized the surnames of several parents with children at the school.

A squad car with two Kingston Police constables pulled into Ben Hendrick's driveway about ten seconds after Luke arrived. He waited beside his car for them to get out.

"Are you related to the gentleman inside?" asked one of the constables, Chad Lowell.

"No, I work at the same school," said Luke, "St. Cuthbert's. So does the young woman who's already inside."

"Okay," said the constable. "I recognize you. I was at the school yesterday. You're the priest, aren't you?"

"The chaplain, yes. Luke Nash."

"I'm going to ask you to wait outside, Mr. Nash, while Raj and I have a look around. Then if we're satisfied there's been no foul play, you can go in."

Luke nodded. "Would you mind asking Barbara to step outside? She may know something I should relay back to the school."

"We will need to speak to her first," said Chad. "But after that, sure." He and the other constable went into the house. Luke leaned against the car, took out his cell phone, and texted a message to Debbie, explaining the situation so far.

As Luke was waiting outside on the driveway, an elderly woman walking a small poodle approached. "Excuse me. Is Ben okay?"

Luke hesitated a moment before replying. "Are you a close friend?" he asked.

"Not a *close* friend," she said, "but we've known each other for at least fifteen years. We're neighbours." She gestured to a house two doors away. "Ben used to clear snow off my front steps sometimes, when my husband was too sick to do it."

"I'm afraid it doesn't look good. A young lady from the school came to check up on him this morning when he didn't show up to work, and he may have had a heart attack."

"I've had two heart attacks."

"This one may have been fatal," Luke said gently.

"Oh, dear. That is sad. We're such frail creatures, aren't we? Come along, Tricky." She and the little dog continued on their way.

Five minutes later Barbara came out of the house, and Luke was surprised to see that her eyes were red rimmed. "Are you all right?"

"Yes, I'm fine. It's just not what I expected when I drove out here. It's so… final."

"I understand," said Luke, thinking, inevitably, of Dave Sommer, and of Claire, his fiancée. And then, instinctively, "Do you need a hug?"

Barbara didn't answer, but simply came towards him and sagged into his arms. Luke put his arms around her, and she burst into tears. Luke was a young man, and of course sensible of her attractiveness, but in that moment his most pressing thought was that Barbara's distress seemed out of proportion to the event, simply because she didn't really know Ben. *Something else is going on here*, he thought.

ON MORNINGS WHEN Jiao wasn't covering a class for a sick teacher, or travelling with a team, she would spend a few minutes every hour wandering around Wilcox House, checking to make sure that no one was skipping class, and chatting with students who had spares. These one-on-one conversations had helped her create good relationships with the girls in the house in the previous year, her first at the school, and she suspected they had also helped ward off some of the difficulties that inevitably arose when twenty-four adolescent females were living in close quarters.

Doris Brooks, the cheerful, middle-aged Wilcox cleaning lady, saw her in the halls and beckoned to her, leaning in conspiratorially when Jiao came up. "Bonita is in her room," she said, jerking her thumb over her shoulder toward the closed door of the room Bonita shared with Krista. "I think she's really upset about something."

Jiao nodded, and, entering into the spirit of hushed confidences, whispered, "Thank you, Doris." She squeezed the older woman's arm and took the few steps that brought her to Bonita's door. She knocked.

A snuffle from inside, then, "Come in." Jiao entered. Bonita was sitting on her bed, shoes off, her knees drawn up to her face. She had been crying.

"What's wrong, sweetheart?" Jiao asked, going to Bonita's bed and seating herself a couple of feet away. She put a hand on Bonita's ankle, just to make contact.

"Everything's fuck up," said Bonita. While fluent in English, Bonita still had a Spanish accent, and sometimes dropped her final consonants. When she spoke at greater length, the words tended to tumble out, and the unusual rhythms of her speech meant that it took a moment for one's ears to adjust.

"Tell me," said Jiao.

"Estruan is such an asshole. An *assohole*," she said, vehemently. "He said to me, he said, *How does it feel to know that someone who screw you is dead.* And I didn't screw him. I didn't screw anyone!"

"Hold up," said Jiao. "You're leaving me behind. This is Struan…?"

"I don't know his last name," said Bonita. "He's in my math class."

"When did he say this?"

"*In* math class," said Bonita, frustrated that Jiao hadn't caught on immediately.

"He just blurted it out?"

"Yes, in front of everyone."

"And who was he talking about? Who was he—oh, did he mean Dave Sommer?"

"Yes! And I didn't screw him. I never screwed anyone. I am a *wirgin!*"

Sympathetic though Jiao was to Bonita's distress, she had to bite her lip to prevent her from giggling a little at her pronunciation. "What did the teacher do?"

"Nothing. He was not there," said Bonita. "He was late. Karin let us into the classroom."

"Well, we're not going to let Struan get away with that sort of behaviour, are we? Have you any idea where he is now?"

"I hope he's dead. He is an *assohole*."

"Yes, but do you have any idea where someone could find him?"

Bonita looked at her with astonishment, clearly surprised that everyone didn't know. "They took him away. Angus beat him up. He beat him so bad."

PAUL MAKEPEACE SAT at his desk, filing his attendance reports online, and responding, as best he could, to the barrage of emails that came in every morning—some from students, some from parents, some from colleagues, some from administration, some from former students, others, inevitably, from Nigerian princes wanting to transfer millions of dollars to his bank if only he would provide his account number and password. He was just firing off his fourth reply when Laura Black came into the office.

"Jesus," she said, dumping her books on her desk, "the kids are in a weird space this morning."

"I can't say I'm surprised," said Paul, turning around to face her. "My first class was pretty strange, too."

"You know, I gave them a small assignment on Thursday. Last Thursday. Should have taken all of twenty minutes. They had Friday. They had the weekend. No classes on Monday because of, well, because of shit happening—and they can't *believe* I want it today. *But Mrs. Black, Mrs. Black—we couldn't get it done because of Dave Sommer!*"

"Yep, well, there's always an excuse. Would you like a tea? I can put the kettle on."

"Yes, please," said Laura. "Tell you what: you get the water for the kettle and plug it in, and I'll take it from there. I've got a new tin of Ahmad Tea I want us to try."

"Deal," said Paul, rising and grabbing the kettle. He filled it from the water dispenser in the corner and plugged it in at the little tea table the four colleagues had set up in one corner.

"I can't face opening my email," said Laura. "So what happened in your first period class?"

"Well," said Paul, "that was... I'm not sure what word to use: weird, strange, unsettling. I don't know. I had the kids doing extended improvs—you know, where I give them a setting, a prop—"

"I know," said Laura. "Sorry, I don't mean to be rude. I just mean I know what they're about."

"Yeah, okay," said Paul, briefly derailed. "Then I'll cut to the chase. I gave one group a common room in residence and a pen—the line isn't so important—and they created a scene where one female student is telling another female student that she was raped the night before, and then the male student who raped her comes back, um, wanting more—and the friend stabs—*stabs!*— the rapist with the pen."

"Jesus."

"Yeah. *Jesus* is right. And there were two things that struck me: how realistic and powerful the stabbing was—that kind of thing is hard to pull off. And the plot line. I mean, what do you do with that?"

"Do you think it means anything? Do you think someone knows something?"

"I don't know. I've been answering my emails for the past ten, fifteen minutes, but I can't get it out of my head."

"Who was in that group?"

"Okay, let me think. Tracey-Lee Goodman, Marcus Bolduc, Julie... Julie Cranston, Megan Exton, Charlotte Evans, Barney Naughton, Anne Parker."

"But you only mentioned three roles?"

"Tracey-Lee played the girl who'd been raped. Anne played the friend who stabs the rapist. Barney played the, the rapist. Julie, Megan, and Anne played other girls in the residence who came running in when they heard Barney's screams. And Marcus... Marcus set up the stage. He didn't take an active role otherwise. Which, come to think of it, is unusual for Marcus."

Laura thought for a moment. "What residence was Sommer in?"

"I'm pretty sure it was Roper. I think he was assigned the room in the old attic, the single."

Laura turned in her own seat and opened her laptop: "I'm just going to see what houses the others are in." There was a pause while she pulled up the relevant file. "So…Anne Parker is from Wilcox… Tracey-Lee is from Scott House… Julie and Megan are from Buckley. And Marcus and Barney are from Roper." She turned back to look at Paul.

Paul cocked his head. "Do you see some pattern that I'm missing? Apart from the fact that Marcus and Barney are both from Roper?"

"Well, that one's worth thinking about."

"Maybe. But, on the one hand, Barney was in there like a dirty shirt, and, on the other, Marcus wasn't. So…I don't know. I'm not saying it's irrelevant, but I don't know where to take it."

At that moment, the kettle began to boil.

"I DIDN'T KNOW," said Jiao. "I hadn't heard. I've been here in the house since breakfast."

"There was blood—*blood*!" said Bonita. "Angus broke Estruan's nose and smash his teeth."

"All right," said Jiao. "Well, it sounds like Struan got what was coming to him."

"Yes," said Bonita. She paused a moment—then burst into tears. "I am so *tire* of blood!" she said.

Jiao nodded sympathetically, and pulled the young woman to her, holding her and rubbing her back. They stayed like that until Bonita's sobs subsided, whereupon she withdrew and blew her nose enthusiastically. "I cannot be weak," she said. "He is not worth it."

"No, he isn't," said Jiao. But a question had occurred to her. "Bonita, Karin was at a book club meeting on Sunday night, so I did check-in for her—and I was in the common room for about half an hour helping Stacey with a math assignment. You were here when I came by around 10:40, but Krista wasn't. You told me she was in the bathroom."

"Yes," said Bonita.

"Was she really in the bathroom?"

"Oh, yes. Of course. She had to shower and things. She was in the bathroom for a long time. She likes to shower." The answer came quickly, but Jiao felt there was something evasive about her response. The two last sentences struck her as embellishments, little extras thrown in to underline a reply that shouldn't need underlining.

"You're absolutely sure?"

"Yes!" Very clear, but the degree of indignation seemed out of proportion.

"Okay. Sorry. It's just that we're trying to account for where everyone was when we think Dave Sommer died. That's all. We—faculty, heads of house, dons—have been told to check everybody."

"Maybe one of the teachers kill him! Or maybe one of the dons!" said Bonita. "*Nobody* like him."

"Well, maybe," said Jiao. *And maybe that is true.* She got up, straightened her back, which she had twisted a little to hug Bonita, and headed toward the door. "Are you okay now?"

"Yes."

"Oh. I can give you an excused for the class you must have skipped after math, but you really should attend your afternoon classes. Okay?"

"Okay."

"I'll send an email to the academic office for you," said Jiao. "I'll say you weren't feeling well." She left.

Bonita drew her knees close to her chin and hugged them tight.

THE BLACK DODGE van with *Steven E. Silver & Son* stencilled on the side window pulled into Ben Hendricks's driveway. The police and the ambulance had left—both called away by an accident on the 401—and Luke, who had gently dispatched Barbara Meeks back to campus, was waiting on the front steps. Impeccably dressed in black suits and white gloves, Steven and Ernie climbed out on either side of the van, Steven from the driver's side. Ernie went round to the back of the vehicle, opened the doors, and pulled out the collapsed stretcher on wheels that had transported Dave Sommer to the morgue just the day before. Steven Silver, his generous girth carried with remarkable grace, took off his sunglasses and greeted Luke. "Good morning, Reverend."

"Good morning," said Luke. "I'm the chaplain up at St. Cuthbert's."

"I guessed you were, sir," said the older Mr. Silver. "I guessed you were. What a tragic couple of events your little community has experienced in the past twenty-four hours."

"It's true," said Luke. "We have some grieving to do."

"At times like this," said Mr. Silver, "I take comfort in the words of the psalmist: *He that dwelleth in the secret place of the Most High shall abide under the shadow of the Almighty.*"

"Good words," said Luke, hiding his surprise at having a psalm quoted at him.

"Good words from the good book," said Mr. Silver. "What a different world it would be if we all lived by its teachings."

Not altogether sure what to say, Luke simply nodded.

"I take it the deceased is inside the house?" said Mr. Silver.

"He is," said Luke. "In the bathroom. It seems he was in the shower when the, the heart attack hit."

"God alone knows the hour we'll be called," said Mr. Silver. "Let's hope his soul was clean, too.... Ernie." Ernie raised the stretcher to its proper height and began pushing it toward the house. His father fell into line behind him, and the two men entered, Luke having propped the screen door open.

While the father-and-son team were in Ben's home, Luke walked to the end of the driveway and surveyed the neighbour-hood. The street was built on a slight incline, and there were handsome older houses, with fairly large front yards, lining both sides. With its mature trees and well-kept lawns and flowerbeds, this part of the village felt both quietly prosperous and calm. Ben's place was easily the shabbiest and most neglected, but, as a real estate agent might say, the bones were good. Luke had heard the gossip—knew that things had gone downhill for his colleague after his wife left him, taking their son—and he felt a rush of sadness for the man. *How fragile we are*, he thought. *How fleeting our lives.*

As he was standing there, listening to the birds and drinking in the scenery, a late-model Lexus pulled over to the side of the road, and an attractive, well-groomed woman in her early thirties climbed out. "Is it Ben Hendricks?"

"It is," said Luke.

"Heart attack?"

"It looks like it. Are you a friend?"

"Not really, no. I graduated from St. Cuthbert's thirteen years ago. He was my math teacher."

"I'm the St. Cuthbert's chaplain."

She looked at him closely. "Well, it's good that someone from the school is here. He was a bit of lech, but I liked him. He knew his subject."

"Did he behave, uh, inappropriately?"

"No, no." She laughed. "Well, his eyes. He looked a bit too hard. But he never... you know, made overtures or touched any-one. Not me, anyway. He was okay."

"I have to admit I didn't know him well," said Luke. "He never came to chapel."

"Well, he wouldn't." She laughed again. "Will the funeral be at the school?"

"I'm going to guess it will. Unless his son wants something different."

"Oh, yes, there was a child, wasn't there? I remember now." She stared at the house for a moment. "Anyway. I should go. If the funeral is at the school, I'll probably come. Poor old bugger."

"My name is Luke, by the way."

"Nice to meet you, Luke. I'm Sasha." She extended her hand, and Luke shook it. "See you around, maybe." She took one last look at the house, then returned to her car. Luke watched her drive away.

Five minutes later Steven and Ernie Silver re-emerged from the house with Ben zipped up in a body bag. Luke went to the back of the van and waited as they manoeuvred the stretcher down the stone walkway to the driveway, then carefully slid their burden into the vehicle. Ernie finished putting things away and peeled off his gloves, placing them in the back of the van before closing the door.

The older Mr. Silver addressed himself to Luke again. "A fine gentleman, Mr. Hendricks, I'm sure. We will treat him with dignity and honour."

"I've no doubt of it," said Luke.

"Were there family, do you know?"

"Yes. An ex-wife, and a son. I believe the son would be of university age now."

"A young age to lose a father."

"Indeed."

"We'll leave you to your ruminations, Reverend," said Mr. Silver. He produced a set of keys from his pocket. "These were on the hall table. You might like to lock up before you leave."

"Thank you. I will," said Luke.

The Silvers' black Dodge van drove away, turning right out of the driveway and descending the slight hill. Luke closed his eyes and said a silent prayer for the soul of Ben Hendricks.

Callum Brezicki set himself up on the school driveway a few minutes before noon, and precisely at 12:00 the first of four old squad cars, each with two community volunteers, pulled in and parked in the parking lot. The volunteers were dressed in black pants and white shirts with shoulder flashes. One in every pair had a portable police radio clipped to his belt, and Callum saw that they also had yellow windbreakers, though all but one chose to leave these in the cars. In some other police forces Callum had worked with, these men—and they were all men—would be called auxiliary constables, but not in Kingston.

"Welcome, gentlemen," said Callum after they'd all assembled around him. "I'm Detective-Sergeant Callum Brezicki with the OPP, and I'm one of two detectives assigned to this case, along with your own Detective-Sergeant Diane Stewart. She was at the post-mortem this morning, and she'll be joining us shortly."

"She drew the short straw," said one of the volunteers. A couple of the others laughed.

"Yeah. I'm glad to be here with you," said Callum. "Sergeant Stewart tells me the murder was committed using a double-edged military grade knife. *A double-edged military-grade knife.*" He scanned the faces, making sure the detail sank in. "And that's what we're looking for. I'm going to ask two of you"—he pointed—"to search the little stretch of woodland on the other side of the highway. And the rest of you I'm taking down to the soccer field just to the east of where we are now, and I'm going to send you into the woods. Our thinking is that there's a possibility, however small, that the killer might have thrown the weapon away rather than take it with him. So, yes, a long shot, but we don't have many real clues at the moment, and finding the weapon would be very helpful."

"There's not a hell of a lot of woodland on the other side of the highway," said one of the men who had been deployed there.

"No," Callum agreed. "Searching there shouldn't take longer than a couple of hours, even less. When you finish, come on down to the soccer field. We'll be setting up a little command post there, with coffee and some muffins or something, and we'll probably ask you to join the others. Now, there are bathrooms in the school's main buildings, but we're all guys here, so I'm going to suggest that you piss in the woods if you need to. Okay?"

"Okay," the men agreed. The two directed to the other side of the highway turned and went off immediately, while the others fell in behind Callum and headed for the soccer field. There was little conversation: everyone seemed very focused, very sombre.

MALCOLM THATCHER, CHAIR of the school's executive board, and John Hawkins, vice-chair, arrived at St. Cuthbert's together in Malcolm's Mercedes E55. He was proud of his car, proud of his job in securities, proud of his school: he had graduated in the early 1960s, and he saw his chairing of the board as his "giving back." John's background was similar, except that he was younger by a few years and had made his money in real estate. They were, in many ways, typical of graduates from their eras: wealthy, once-divorced, house in Toronto, cottage in Muskoka, hockey-watching, squash-playing, scotch-drinking, members of the Progressive Conservative Party. But it would be wrong to see them simply as types: John had lost his first child, a daughter, to pediatric cancer, and gave both time and money every year to a charity seeking a cure; and Malcolm served soup and sandwiches at a homeless shelter once a month. Both had taken in some of the lessons preached by Luke Nash's predecessors at the school.

Glenda Harvey had ordered lunch for five from the dining hall, and it was delivered to the house at 12:30 by two food service workers. She had set the table, so it remained only for the workers to serve the food, which they did as soon as Malcolm and John arrived. The two visitors sat down around the headmaster's table with Jim Harvey himself, senior master Dick Cargill, and the director of admissions, Sarah Carson. Glenda, a spectacular hostess on less charged occasions, discretely took herself off to a yoga class.

Once lunch was served, and the food service workers had left, Jim briefed Malcolm and John on what he knew about the death, and what he and the school's leadership were doing to deal with the aftermath. He then turned to Sarah.

Sarah put down her fork and took a sip of water. "I'm afraid there's further bad news. Fourteen sets of parents and prospective students have cancelled their campus visits, and two students to whom we gave priority acceptance are now reconsidering. That number could grow dramatically in the next couple of days. If this trend continues, we'll have real trouble filling the school next year."

Malcolm pulled a face. "That's *grim* news."

"We're bleeding," Sarah said. "And even if the police make an arrest very soon, I think there will be damage for some time to come."

"Yes," said John. "We're going to be known for a long time as the school where a student was murdered."

"That's the reality," said Jim.

"Damage control," said Malcolm. "We can see that you're doing everything you can to restore a sense of normalcy. What can we do to change the perception of the school in the public mind?"

"My honest answer is nothing immediately," said Jim. "Nothing until the police have made an arrest. Anything we do to try to change the narrative will be undone by the arrest, and what we do at that point should be shaped by who is arrested."

"Expand on that, please," said John, raising an eyebrow.

Jim pushed back from the table. "There are several possibilities. If the killer is a random madman who came in off the highway, then we should talk about the security arrangements we'll make going forward. Security guards, night watchmen."

"Christ," said Malcolm. Jim looked at him in surprise. "No, I realize there may be no choice, but it will give the school a completely different feel. Nothing like when we were here, eh, John?"

"A more innocent time," said John. "Maybe."

"If it turns out to be a staff member—which seems almost impossible—then we'll need to highlight our vetting procedures, again going forward," Jim continued. "Psychological testing. Independent review of references. That's a hornet's nest."

"But you don't think it was a staff member," said Malcolm.

"No. No, we don't," said Jim, looking to Dick Cargill.

"No," Dick echoed.

"Can we really be confident of that?" Malcolm asked.

"I just don't see it," said Jim. "I know my people. I know them. So a third possibility is that it was a student…"

"Yes?" said John.

"At this moment," said Dick, "that seems the most likely possibility. Sommer wasn't a popular young man."

"This is the boy who made a younger boy eat dog shit, isn't it?" said Malcolm. "Pardon my language."

"This is that boy," said Jim.

"And you suspect the boy he did that to?"

"I do."

"And do the police suspect him?" said Malcom.

"The police are keeping their cards pretty close to their chest. *I* suspect him. Or, maybe, a friend of his. Or both. But I should stress that that's just me. That's just *my* instinct."

There was a pause. "We place a lot of faith in your instincts," said John.

"I appreciate that," said Jim. "I just need to say again that this doesn't come from the police. They haven't told me anything."

"Okay," said Malcolm. "Well…"

"I have one other piece of bad news," said Jim. "Ben Hendricks died this morning—apparently of a heart attack."

"The math teacher, Ben?" said John. "Oh, my Lord."

"Yes. Ben taught grade eleven and twelve math for years. So I'm going to try to find a replacement for him very quickly."

"You've got colleagues covering for him now?"

"Yes. But that isn't doable for long. His colleagues are already busy. I'll need someone for the balance of the year."

"I'm glad I don't have your job this week, Jim," said Malcolm.

"About that bonus…" said Jim. And they all laughed—the laughter releasing a little of the pressure that had built up over the course of the previous thirty hours or so.

Paul Makepeace brought his tray to one of the two staff tables to eat a relatively late lunch. Most teachers had already left, but Jiao Lee was still there. While they were not close friends, they'd had several pleasant conversations the previous year, and had eaten together once or twice since the fall term began.

"Hello," said Paul, sitting down across the table from her.

"Hi," said Jiao, covering her mouth with one hand and waving at him. "Sorry," she said, a moment later: "I was chewing."

"Not to worry," said Paul. "Is it any good?" He regarded his chicken stew with some scepticism.

"It's surprisingly tasty," said Jiao. "I'm enjoying mine. *Bon appétit.*"

"Thank you." He picked up his cutlery. "So what sort of day have you been having?"

"I think all the dons are on edge. It's been a strange twenty-four hours."

"How is Karin handling things?"

Jiao looked him full in the eyes, wondering exactly how much she should share. After a moment, she said, "Okay."

Paul nodded, but the look he gave her suggested that he, too, had reservations about Karin's house-mastering skills. "I was telling Laura earlier today about my first drama class," he said. "I had a group of students do an extended improv—do you know what that involves?"

"Yes," said Jiao. "I took two drama courses at university. We did those."

"Really? Okay. Well, one of the groups gave me a full-fledged drama about a student confiding to a girlfriend that she'd been raped, and then the student who raped her comes in, and the friend stabs him to death with a pen."

"Wow," said Jiao. "That's fairly intense."

"It woke me up, I can tell you," said Paul. "No coffee needed this morning."

"I scarcely slept last night, and I'm wired," said Jiao. "Who was in the group?"

"Charlotte, Anne, Julie, Megan, Marcus and Barney," said Paul, ticking them off with his fingers. "All grade twelves."

"Which Anne? Parker or Schull?"

"Parker. She played the girl who stabbed the rapist. She did a nice job."

"She's in my residence," said Jiao. "Wilcox. Did she—"

Their conversation was interrupted by a sudden burst of activity at a student table halfway across the dining hall. A senior male student had stood up, apparently knocking some glasses over. He grabbed his chest, tried to say something, then collapsed. There were a couple of screams, but two students from his table, and several from others nearby, swiftly converged on him. St. Cuthbert's students were trained in emergency first aid, and some were ready to try out their skills. The teacher-on-duty, Brent Hurley, in the midst of patrolling the dining hall, also ran over. Paul and Jiao got to their feet.

As it happened, the head nurse, Martha Ellis, was just emerging from the dining hall service area with a cup of coffee and hastened over to the knot of students. She pushed herself through them and knelt down on the floor beside the young man.

"Did you see who it was?" asked Jiao.

"No," said Paul. "He went down too quickly."

"Do you think we should go over?"

"If Martha and Brent weren't there, I would—but I think Martha has things in hand. She likes to take control. I'll just stay in their line of sight so they can call us over if we're needed."

A minute went by, and the knot of students began to clear—probably because the head nurse had waved them away impatiently. Two minutes later, there was a bit of a stir as Martha stood up, and Brent leaned in. Together they helped the young man to his feet. It was Marcus Bolduc.

"Marcus!" said Paul. "Well…"

The head nurse and the TOD each took one of Marcus's arms and headed toward the doors into the dining hall. As the three of them began to move, a generous wave of applause went up from students all over the room.

"One of our little customs," said Paul to Jiao.

As Brent, Martha and Marcus drew near, Martha met Paul's gaze. His eyebrows rose in a question mark. Martha mouthed something as she moved on by.

"What do you think it was?" asked Jiao, who had been focusing on Marcus.

"Martha just mouthed *panic attack* to me," Paul said.

"I completely missed that."

"Well," said Paul: "A little unusual, maybe, in a teenage boy. But…" He left his follow-up thought unspoken.

Detective-Sergeant Callum Brezicki had set up a command post on the edge of the soccer field close to the woods—though that post consisted simply of a portable table. On the table Callum had taped a map of the campus, including the forested area, which he'd divided up into many small grids, demarcated by a black felt pen. Spread out along the remainder of the table was a police radio and an urn of coffee, plastic cups, and trays of sandwiches sent, at Luke Nash's behest, by the school's food services. This astonished the detective; in the past, he'd always had to arrange for food and beverages himself. Another four community volunteers had shown up since the operation began, so he now had twelve workers combing the forest. While he was doing everything he could to focus his attention on the job at hand, his mind kept straying to the text he'd received from his daughter while he was at the police station. It revealed that she was planning to leave her husband, and Callum, who loved his daughter and infant grandson but was also fond of his son-in-law, was still mulling over how he should respond.

"How's it going?" asked Detective-Sergeant Diane Stewart arriving at his side. She'd come from behind, and he hadn't heard her approach.

"We've got twelve searchers out there right now," he said. "Your community volunteers—good lads."

"Any news on other fronts?"

"Well, there's no shortage of ex-cons with violent records in the Kingston area, but none of their M.O.s jumped out at me, and none of them have any known connection to the school or anyone who works here."

"Maybe *known* is the operative word," said Diane. She put her hands on the table to study the map, inadvertently giving Callum a glimpse of her cleavage before he looked away.

"Maybe," he replied. "The station has also logged sixteen calls from people claiming to have information, but your colleague Yendt tells me he thinks they're all nutters."

"That's the problem we're having with our case in Joyceville. We've had hundreds of calls about that one, and most of it's garbage."

"Anything else about the post-mortem that struck you?"

"Just one thing," said Diane. "There weren't any signs that Sommer put up much resistance, so it seems likely that the first thrust brought him to his knees immediately. So either the killer knew what he was doing or he was lucky."

"But there were two entry wounds, you told me?"

"Yes. Two, neck and belly. Both deep."

"Which suggests that he wanted to make damn sure the boy was dead."

"Yes," Diane agreed. "Either he was very angry or very determined." She paused. "Or both."

They stood gazing into the woods. Every now and then they could see an individual searcher through a break in the trees. At this early stage, the volunteers had not yet penetrated very far into the forest.

"And what about your interviews?" Callum asked.

"My instinct is that none of the boys we've questioned so far did it, but I still have some unanswered questions. And it's possible that at least one of them knows more than he's telling or knows something he doesn't realize is relevant."

"It's an oddly self-contained little community," said Callum.

"It is." Diane checked her watch. "I've got to go. I have a meeting with the chaplain and the guy they call the senior master."

"Are you still finding them helpful?"

She considered a moment. "The chaplain, yes. The senior master... I'm trying to get a read on him."

Callum gestured toward the urn. "Sounds like you'll need to take a coffee with you."

Jiao had mostly finished her lunch by the time Paul joined her, and she skipped dessert, as she always did. She walked quickly back down the hill to Wilcox House, knowing where she was heading, a little apprehensive about what she was about to do.

Coming to Bonita and Krista's door, she knocked loudly, not expecting an answer. She knew they should both be in class. She waited a few seconds and turned the handle to enter; the girls weren't allowed to lock their doors. She went in, deliberated a moment, then closed the door behind her.

She didn't know what she was looking for. She had no pre-conceived notion of what she might find. In some part of herself, she didn't think she would find anything. But Bonita's behaviour earlier that day, and Krista and Bonita's behaviour on Monday, had made Jiao think that maybe, just maybe, they knew more than they had admitted. She began her search—the closets, the drawers, under the beds.

Having come up short, Jiao scanned the room, her eyes eventually alighting on the small garbage receptacles placed under each girl's desk. She hesitated briefly, a little queasy at the thought of rummaging through used tissues and who-knows-what-else, but then went over to Krista's desk and thrust her hand into the waste-basket. Tissues, yes. An empty Midol package. Fingernail clippings. Nothing unexpected. Nothing suspicious.

And so to Bonita's. Again, tissues. A wrapper of a brand of European candy that Jiao had never seen before. And, at the bottom, a piece of white paper, folded into quarters. Jiao unfolded the paper. On it was scrawled a message in an awkward hand—a hand not skilled at writing: *Meet me in the chapel tonight at 9:40. Make sure you smell good. Take a shower. LOL* Jiao squatted beside the basket, reading the message over and over again.

There was, of course, no name on the paper. No greeting. No signature. But Jiao knew intuitively that Dave Sommer had written the note, and it had been meant for, and found by, Bonita. Perhaps he had slipped it into her mailbox. Perhaps he had given it to her in chapel, or in some class they had together. It didn't matter. It was from him. It was for her. It meant something significant. Shit.

Jiao put the basket back exactly where she had found it, rose to her feet, and headed to the door. She knew that Karin had no class after lunch on Tuesday, so she would almost certainly be home.

Detective-Sergeant Diane Stewart had only a couple of minutes to wait in the board room before Luke and Dick arrived. The three of them sat around the table, Diane calm, Luke pensive, Dick wheezing a little from the exertion of walking from his home on campus. On the table sat a carafe of ice water and four glasses. "Are we expecting anyone else?" asked Diane.

"I don't think so," said Luke. "Dick?"

"I'm not. I'm standing in for Jim."

"Okay," said Diane. "Can I ask whether anything further has come forward from heads of house, or faculty, or dons—or anyone, for that matter? Any leads, no matter how apparently trivial?"

"I haven't heard anything new I give any credence to," said Dick. "I know that Jim remains… *focused* on Angus, and his instincts are always very reliable."

"I have questions I want Angus to answer," said Diane, "but I don't think he murdered Dave Sommer. I'd like to let the issue sit with him a few hours longer, then question him again."

"No. It can't be done," said Dick. "Jim won't allow it. His parents would hit the roof. They're already furious."

"This is beyond your headmaster's ability to control," said Diane mildly. "This is a murder investigation. If my colleague and I feel that someone is of interest to us, we can and will question him."

"The headmaster is vested with the authority to control a great deal that happens on this campus," said Dick, clearly irritated.

"Then it's a simple matter for me to take the boy in for questioning at the police station," said Diane. "If I think that's appropriate."

"Could we ask you to bring us up to date on what the police are doing?" asked Luke, doing his best to defuse the tension.

"Certainly," said Diane. "At present we have twelve community volunteers searching the woods under Detective-Sergeant's Brezicki's supervision. They are looking for the murder weapon—which this morning's post-mortem identifies as a military-style two-bladed knife. Brezicki has gone through a massive amount of computerized information about similar crimes in Kingston and the larger region, trying to find patterns. I, of course—with your very welcome assistance, Luke—have interviewed four students. Our officers back at 11 Queen have been receiving, and following up on, telephone calls from the general public."

"So things haven't really progressed very far?" said Dick.

Diane consciously breathed deeply once, in and out, before replying: "We haven't arrested anyone, no. My instinct tells me that things could change, and change very quickly, at any time. We could find the murder weapon in the woods. A telephone call could reveal that someone driving by saw a strange figure come off the road onto the campus. One of the students we've already interviewed could suddenly remember something important. Someone else in the community could come forward with a critical piece of information. I will offer you two guarantees, Mr. Cargill. First, *someone* on this campus knows something they haven't yet told us—either because they're scared or they don't realize it's relevant, or they don't want us to know it. Second, we will solve this. The Kingston police and the OPP have an excellent record when it comes to solving murders. But solving them inside thirty-six hours is very, very difficult."

Dick sighed—but there was a measure of acceptance in the sound. "Our problem is that we're a business as well as a school," he said. "With every hour that passes without an arrest we lose students who would otherwise have applied and maybe come here. And that's how we keep the doors open and everyone who works here employed."

"I understand," said Diane. "Believe me, I do. Detective-Sergeant Brezicki and I are working very hard to solve this—and we are doing nothing else. Not a single other case between us. But you wouldn't want us to arrest the wrong person, Mr. Cargill."

Luke's cell phone buzzed. He opened it, checked his messages, looked up again. "Marcus Bolduc is in the health centre," he said. "Panic attack." He turned to Dick. "He was one of those at the Ouija board game with Sommer Sunday night."

Karin opened the door to her apartment off the residence corridor looking wild-eyed—almost witchy. For just a second Jiao wondered whether Karin even knew who she was. But recognition dawned. "Hi, Jiao. Is something wrong?"

"Are you busy?" asked Jiao, playing for time, wanting a moment or two to assess whether Karin was in a place to hear her suspicions.

"No. Yes. I was just going to lie down for a little while. I don't teach for an hour, and I thought I'd have a power nap."

"You go ahead." Jiao made her decision. "I can catch you later. Nothing that can't wait."

"Okay, thank you," said Karin, already beginning to close the door. "We'll talk later." And she was gone.

Jiao turned and stared down the hall. *What to do now? Where to turn? Who can I trust with what I suspect? Lauren? No. Not a student, even if she is head of house. Another of the dons? No.* She had two friends among them, Jacqueline and Tammy, but neither could keep a secret if a secret needed to be kept. The chaplain? This possibility Jiao did consider seriously. She liked Luke. She thought he had his head screwed on. But he seemed to be working very closely with the police, and she didn't want this going to the police. Not yet. Not until she was sure. And not until she knew the whys.

"All right, girl," she said to herself. "*You* investigate this further. *You* see what you can find."

CALLUM WAS JUST finishing a brief text to his daughter, Lorraine. *Sweetheart, I've been brooding over your message for the past three hours, and I don't know what to say. Could we maybe have a private chat this evening? Would you be able to find ten minutes for a talk?* He read it, reread it, then pressed Send. An instant later, a cry came from one of his searchers in the woods: "Detective-Sergeant!" Callum tucked his phone into his breast pocket and set off at a run.

A fit black fellow in his late forties had indeed found something. He had wisely not picked it up, but pointed to it as Callum came towards him. To get there, the fellow had followed a well-worn smokers' path, but stepped off it a distance of about nine yards, the equivalent of a gentle underarm throw if what was thrown was hindered to some degree by underbrush. And if what had been thrown was a wicked-looking knife. It had a brown leather scabbard, and a double-edged blade with *F.S., Wilkinson Sword, London* etched on the bolster. Callum pulled on a vinyl glove and picked the thing up gingerly, making as little contact with it as he possibly could.

"It's a Fairbairn-Sykes," the detective said. "British made. Used by the SAS."

"What's the SAS?" asked the volunteer.

"The Special Air Service. It's the British equivalent of the American Delta Force or our own JTF2."

"I've heard of Delta Force."

"You wouldn't want to mess with any of them," said Callum, sliding the knife carefully into an evidence bag pulled from another pocket. "Well done. What's your name?"

"Aaron Firth."

"Aaron Firth, I think you've probably found our murder weapon."

"It looks as though it's been wiped clean," said Aaron.

"It looks that way. But I have faith that our lab people will be able to pick something up from it."

"Are we done, then?"

"Not quite," said Callum. "Let's look a little further around here, just in case our perpetrator threw something else away. But I think this is the holy grail."

"I think she and the OPP detective are doing their best," Dick Cargill said to Jim Harvey, sitting across from the headmaster in his office, the door closed. "But I can't figure out why there are only two detectives on the case. I understand that there's some sort of big investigation going on in Joyceville, but you'd think that the murder of a teenager would get more resources than this."

"There have been other police officers here," Jim pointed out. "Aren't there some searching the woods right now? I don't know, Dick. You may be right. This is a first for me. I don't want to judge this by the shows I've seen on television."

"Well, I haven't had any more experience," said Dick. "I'm just... *frustrated* that they don't have anyone square in their sights yet."

"Which brings us to Angus. As you know, he's the one I'm looking at. And this most recent episode makes me even more suspicious."

"Luke will have him here any minute," said Dick. "He's been holding him in his office."

"Holding him?" said Jim. "Is he resisting in some way?"

"No, no. Figure of speech. Keeping him there until we were ready to talk to him. Probably trying to talk some sense into him. I hope so."

"And how badly is the Lynch boy hurt?"

"Martha says his nose is broken, his eyes are blackened, his jaw is misaligned, and he probably has a concussion. Two other boys had to pull Angus off him."

"Jesus. But you say there was provocation?"

"Yes. But. The attack was way out of proportion. And the kids said that Angus as good as threatened to do to him what he'd done to Sommer. Not in so many words. But."

There was a knock on the door. "Come in," said Jim. Luke entered, followed by Angus Graves. "Have a seat, Angus. Luke, you too, please. I'd like you to stay." The two sat down, Angus looking sullen. The knuckles of his right hand were bandaged. "Have you anything to say for yourself?"

"About what?"

"Don't use that tone with me!" Jim snapped, suddenly growing larger behind his desk. "You have seriously injured another student. He will be disfigured for some time. It's possible he has a brain injury. So. What have you to say for yourself?"

"He had it coming," said Angus, his defiance undiminished.

"He had it coming," Jim repeated. "He had it coming? You think it's right to cause serious physical damage to someone who has used inappropriate language? You think that a brain injury is a suitable punishment for stupidity?"

"Not for stupidity," said Angus. "For cruelty. He was cruel. He tried to hurt Bonita. He was a bully. I have no respect for bullies."

"Really?" said Jim "Well, some might call *you* a bully. You certainly whaled away at Struan much longer than was necessary to shut him up."

"Bullies need to learn not to bully," said Angus. "Struan had it coming. When people like you don't do their jobs, people like me have to take action."

There was a silence in the room. This went well past ordinary teenage defiance: this was open rebellion. Jim hadn't encountered this in a long time, but he hadn't been appointed headmaster without reason. His tone changed. It became smooth, silky, in a way that disguised the depth of his own anger. "I understand that you referred to Dave Sommer's death when you confronted Struan."

"No, I didn't."

"I'm told you did."

"You're told wrong."

"I think that your attack on Sommer has given you a taste for violence."

"What attack on Sommer?"

"I think you know what I mean."

"I think you've forgotten that Sommer attacked *me*. And shoved dog shit in my mouth. And *you* did fuck-all about it."

"Dick," said Jim, looking toward the senior master. "I think we have to put this matter into the hands of the police."

"Right," said Dick, standing up.

"Good," said Angus—though for the first time his bravado wavered a little. And Jim saw it.

"Wait one second, Dick," Jim said. Dick sat down again. Jim didn't speak again for a full minute, apparently thinking. "Look, Angus, I recognize that you are carrying some justified anger over Sommer's actions towards you last spring. But I also think you've lost control. I'm going to suggest that you come clean with us and admit that you killed Dave Sommer. We've now seen undeniably, with plenty of witnesses this time, what happens when you lose control. Admit what you've done, and the school will testify—*I* will testify—that what you experienced was very wrong. And I'm sure the courts will be lenient with you, given your age—you're a minor—and given the prior provocation."

Angus leaned forward in his seat. "I. Did. Not. Kill. Dave. Sommer," he said, enunciating each word clearly. "I'm glad as fuck he's dead, but I didn't kill him. And yes, I beat up Struan Lynch, but he had it coming. And *you* helped create the environment where he felt comfortable saying what he said. That's what I think. And that's what my parents think, too."

Dick began warming up to say something, but Jim held up a hand to quiet him. "Luke," he said, "please take Angus back to his residence and help him pack his bags. I will call his parents to pick him up. Angus, I regret that your St. Cuthbert's career had to end this way, but I cannot accept this kind of violence and arrogance. Go."

Luke stood up. Angus stood up. But Angus had one more shot to fire. "My parents are going to sue you. They're going to sue the school for not doing the right thing when I was assaulted."

"Angus, come," said Luke, putting his hand on the boy's shoulder. "This isn't helpful. This isn't doing any good."

Angus shrugged Luke's hand off, but he turned and followed him out the door. Jim and Dick looked at each other. "I'll tell you what hurts the most this moment," said Jim. "I'm angry with the boy, but there's some justice in what he said."

"No," Dick began, "you shouldn't take this on your—"

But Jim shut him down again. "It's okay, Dick. I'm a big boy. I must think this one through."

Luke and Angus didn't speak when they left the headmaster's office. They cut across the anteroom, Luke giving a quick nod to Debbie, then out past the reception area, with Carol at her desk. Another nod. They strode along the foyer and out the school's main doors to the path that led to the driveway, then round the chapel and through the grove of oak trees toward one of the playing fields. Angus was walking quickly, but Luke had no difficulty keeping up: he matched him stride for stride. In this way they crossed the playing field together.

"Do you believe I killed Sommer?" asked Angus suddenly.

Luke didn't hesitate. "No. I don't. I don't know who did, but I'm pretty confident you didn't."

"Thank you for that."

"You're welcome. I'm sorry it's come to this."

Angus shrugged. "Maybe it just had to be. I figure TCS or Lakefield will expel someone this fall, and I'll get in there. Or Ashbury. It won't be so bad."

"Can I ask you a question?" Luke said.

"Sure."

"Where were you Sunday evening? And why wouldn't you tell Mr. Waters?"

Angus thought for a moment. They were approaching Ingram House, but no one else was in sight. "I don't suppose it matters if I tell you. It might even keep someone from getting killed."

Luke jerked his head towards him. "Getting killed!" he blurted.

Angus laughed mirthlessly. "Not what you're thinking. I was up on the roof." He gestured with his head. "Smoking. A group of us go up nearly every night. We can't be arsed to go into the woods, so we just go up there."

"Okay," said Luke. "Wouldn't it have been simpler to just tell Mr. Waters that?" They came up to the entrance to the residence, and Angus fished out his key.

"Maybe," said Angus, "but I'd have been sent home for smoking, and it would have made me pretty unpopular with the other guys for telling where we were—even though I wouldn't have given Waters any names."

"It was a high price to pay, Angus," Luke said, following him into the residence.

DICK CARGILL HAD just left his office, and Jim stared at his phone. His next challenges were to call Struan's parents—and Angus's. Of the two calls, he dreaded the one to Angus's parents more. Jim was not afraid to make decisions, and over the course of his career in administration he'd made a lot of difficult ones that many people had deemed wise, and about which he himself felt confident. He was usually a good judge of character. He saw defending the integrity of the school he led, and promoting its growth, as his dual missions—missions to which he was prepared to sacrifice sleep, popularity, and the feelings of people who got in the way. He was not, broadly speaking, an introspective man. He didn't brood, didn't ruminate. But every now and then he made a decision that he deeply regretted, and he saw, now, that allowing Dave Sommer to return to St. Cuthbert's had been a serious mistake. His parents' gift to the school didn't begin to undo the wrongness of that one.

Debbie drummed her fingernails lightly on the open door to catch his attention, then came towards the desk with five small slips of pink paper. "Parents requesting a call, Jim," she said. Even without looking at them, Jim knew what they were about: withdrawing their children from the school. He was presiding over a crisis in the life of St. Cuthbert's.

DETECTIVE-SERGEANTS BREZICKI and Stewart met at the fold-up table on the soccer field. Callum handed her the evidence bag with the knife inside. "Fairbairn-Sykes. British SAS."

Diane looked at the knife through the clear plastic. She pursed her lips in a near whistle. "1940," she said. "A collector's item now."

"Not the sort of thing you'd expect to find on a private-school campus in Canada," said Callum.

"No. But many of these kids are wealthy, and some of them come from fairly cosmopolitan backgrounds." Diane looked at Callum. "This seems to me to make it less likely we're dealing with someone from outside the school."

"Why?"

"Because an outsider would probably have left via the highway rather than striking out into the woods. For outsiders, the woods are *terra incognita*. For the kids, an extension of home— their backyard."

Callum considered this. "Maybe. In which case, it would be worth checking to see if any of them are the children of British military officers."

"Or high-ranking Canadian officers who served with NATO in Britain," said Diane. "Or, for that matter, anyone at the school with military connections." She handed the bag back to Callum. "Do you want to take this to the lab? Or shall I?"

"I'll take it. You've had more dealings with people here. Have a word with your helpful priest."

"I'll start with Luke," said Diane. "But I suspect that the admissions office will have more information." She pulled out her cell phone.

DR. O'BRIEN ARRIVED at the school's health centre at half past three, some hours later than his scheduled rounds. This wasn't altogether unusual: he had a busy practice in the village, and an emergency there would often mean a long wait for students at the school. A handsome young man with a trim physique and sandy blonde hair, he was popular with his patients. At least a couple of girls at St. Cuthbert's had worked out that he was the Tuesday doctor-on-call, often developing mild fevers or period pain on that day. He breezed into the building, flirted briefly with Jill, then headed towards the first examining room, only to be intercepted by head nurse Martha, who was immune to his charms.

"Just a couple for you today, Dr. O'Brien," she said. "There's Struan Lynch in room one. He's been banged up badly: a broken nose, black eyes, fractured jaw—but the thing I'm most concerned about is concussion. You may want to have him X-rayed, though we can certainly keep an eye on him here if you think I'm overreacting. We've been checking up on him every twenty minutes."

"Not the sort of injuries I'm used to seeing here," said Dr. O'Brien. "Rugby?"

"No. He lost a fight," said Martha laconically. "And there's another boy in room two, Marcus Bolduc. He had an anxiety attack at lunch. I'd usually just give a student a lie-down and a cup of camomile tea, but this fellow was with the boy who was murdered Sunday night, so I thought you might like to have a little chat with him."

"Ah, okay. Sometimes these kinds of things are more complicated than physical damage," said Dr. O'Brien, suddenly serious. "Any history of mental illness?"

"No," said Martha. "But I'd say he's very troubled at the moment."

The doctor emerged from the first of his two sessions ten minutes later in a very different mood than the one he came in with. "I want to have Lynch X-rayed," he said. "He's not in good shape."

"I'll have Jill order him a taxi," said Martha.

"No, I'm going to suggest an ambulance," said Dr. O'Brien. "I want a qualified paramedic on hand just in case he starts seizing on the journey."

"It's that bad?"

"Maybe. I'm not sure," Dr. O'Brien said. "Best sit with him until the ambulance arrives. I'll see the other boy now."

Alexis Wardle had a locker in the tech wing of Bath Secondary School. In grades nine through eleven, the tech wing would have been a dangerous place for a young man who liked to wear a little eye shadow, dress in a trench coat, and sport gold in his ears and around his neck. But being at the top of the school's age pyramid brought certain protections, and Alexis's size, his Doc Martens, and his reputation—carefully cultivated—for edgy weirdness, meant he could now walk down these corridors, and go into the bathrooms, with relative safety. He was surprised when, at the end of the school day, he saw his Kingston friend, Trevor, standing in the middle of the hallway, looking lost.

"Hey, Trev," said Alexis, coming up behind him. "Whatcha doing here?"

"I came to see you," said Trevor, turning around quickly at the sound of Alexis's voice. "Lotta weird-looking people at this school."

"Yeah." Alexis laughed. "Good to see you, man. How you doing?"

"Not so good. I'm feeling low."

"You wanna go outside for a smoke?"

"Yeah."

"I just need to ditch my books." Alexis spun the dial of his combination lock.

With buses arriving to take kids home, the smoking area was crowded, so Alexis and Trevor headed to a place on the other side of the parking lot that, though not an official extension of the smoking area, was sometimes used in that way by senior students. There was no one else there, and they lit up and sat down at a picnic table.

"So, wassup?" said Alexis.

"I did a dumb thing Sunday night," said Trevor.

Alexis stared at him. "Oh, Jesus. Did you fuck up Sommer?"

"No. No, man," said Trevor, waving off the question. "I mean, I was going up to talk to him, but I sort of got waylaid."

"Waylaid by what?"

"I met Caroline on the bus," said Trevor.

"Caroline, your ex?"

"Yeah. My girl before Peggy. We went out for like eight months."

"Of course, I remember her. So?"

"Well, we got to talking, and laughing, and shit, and one thing led to another."

"Oh-oh, I can see what's coming."

"Yeah. We got off at the park, and we fooled around a bit on one of the benches, and then we went behind the public bathrooms, you know, on the side away from the road."

"Uh-huh."

"And we had ourselves a little fun up against the wall."

"A trembler!"

"Yup."

"You horn-dog. You dirty dog, you."

"I know."

Alexis took a deep draw on his cigarette. "So now what?"

"It was fun, but I kinda love Peggy."

"Peggy's good. Peggy's great."

"So do I tell her?"

"Are you going to do it again with Caroline?"

"I don't plan to."

"You haven't made plans to hook up again?"

"No. It was a one-off. Just something that got outta hand."

Alexis shrugged. "Then don't tell Peggy."

"You wouldn't if you cheated on Joanie?"

"Hell, no."

"What if it gets out?"

"Who's gonna tell?"

"Yeah, I guess nobody."

"So, relax. Nice memory. Move on. Buy Peggy something nice, maybe, without telling her why."

"Okay. Okay." He took a deep draw on his cigarette, then threw it away. "Thanks, man."

"What for?"

"The advice."

"Hey, vamps before tramps, yeah?" Alexis laughed. "Let's see if we can find our ladies."

By 3:30, every girl in Wilcox who played a team sport was either on her way to practice or had already left for a game. Jiao knew that Krista, Bonita's roommate, had field hockey practice. She also knew that Bonita had a term off sports, and that if she hadn't gone for a walk into the village, or wasn't visiting a friend on campus, she'd likely be in her room. Jiao knocked on her door.

"Come in," Bonita called from inside, and Jiao entered, closing the door behind her.

"Hi, Bonita. Got a few minutes?"

Bonita was sitting on her bed, wearing headphones and listening to music. She removed the headphones and eyed Jiao warily. "Yes."

Jiao sat down on the bed, looked at Bonita kindly, then took the note she had retrieved from Bonita's wastebasket, unfolded it, and put it down between them: *Meet me in the chapel tonight at 9:40. Make sure you smell good. Take a shower. LOL*

Bonita burst into tears. "It is not good! It is a *wick* thing! I never want to see it again!"

Jiao picked up the piece of paper, refolded it, and put it back in her pocket. "Talk to me," she said. "Tell me everything. Let's find a solution."

And so the story tumbled out. "In the first week of school," Bonita said, "Sommer came to me, and he said he want to do sex with me. And I say *no*. I tell him I am a wirgin. And he say that he don't care, that he likes wirgins, that he wants to do it with me even more. He say that he have lots of money, and he can buy me beautiful things and take me places, but I have to suck his cock, or do other things he want, three times every week, and he will look after me. And I tell him I don't want to suck his cock, and I don't want to be look after, but he say that I have no choice."

"Oh my God," said Jiao. "That bastard."

"So I tell Krista. Krista is my good friend, and she get very angry, and she tell me to keep saying no, and I keep saying no, but then he give me this note at brunch on Sunday. And Krista say she have an idea—that I should tell him at dinner that I *will* meet him in the chapel at 9:40 that night. That she have a plan."

"Did you write *him* a note?"

"No! Krista told me just to speak to him very quiet, with no one else there, so that is what I do." Bonita paused.

"Go on," said Jiao.

"So Krista and I go to the chapel at 9:30, before Sommer comes, and Krista brings a knife to scare him—just to scare him. And she hides behind the altar. And when Sommer comes, he is all please to see me and tells me he will fuck me behind the altar, and then Krista comes out and she tells him, she says, 'I will cut your dick off if you keep *hassing* Bonita."

Bonita had stopped crying, but she needed to blow her nose—and did so. Jiao waited.

"And he no believe her, and he laugh, and he say girls not know how to use knife, and he try to take it away from Krista, and Krista is really strong and she, she push the knife into him— push, he bend over, then stab in the neck! And he bleeds! He bleeds so much!"

"Oh my God."

"And we leave and we run back here, and I go in to make sure that no one is in the hall, and no one is, and I go and get Krista and say *Come in*, and she comes in, and she takes off her clothes with the blood, and I put the clothes in the laundry basket with things over them, and the knife too, and I take the clothes to the washing machine, and put in lots of bleach, and I wash the knife with bleach in the laundry tub, and she takes a shower in the bathroom. And then when she comes out of the shower, she puts the knife in her gym bag and she takes it into the forest and throw it away."

"Where did the knife come from?"

"It was the knife of her granddad," said Bonita. "He was with the British in the war, and he gave it to her, not to her dad, because her dad don't like knives. And she kept it in her drawer and I never saw it before. She never show anyone."

"Okay," said Jiao. "Oh, God, Bonita, this is difficult."

"And we say that we will never, never tell anyone anything," said Bonita, beginning to cry again, "but I am so stupid and did not burn the note and now you know, too, because you snooped! You cannot say anything, Jiao! You cannot tell on us! Sommer was a *wick* boy! He was not a good person. Krista did not mean to kill him."

"I've got to think, Sweetheart," said Jiao. "Give me time to think. Okay? I'll come back later tonight and talk to both of you. There may be a way out of this. I don't know."

"Please don't tell anyone!" said Bonita, her eyes streaming.

"I'm not going to say anything now. I just need to think. I need to think things through. I'll see you tonight." And Jiao got up and left.

Dennis Murdoch knew he had a problem a few seconds after he came through the door from coaching the cross-country running team. Julie had a grim look on her face, and their children, Audrey (seven) and Chelsea (five) weren't playing in the living room as they usually were: he could hear the television in the family room, and the volume was turned up loud. "Hey," he said. "What's wrong?"

His wife pointed to a chair at the kitchen table. "We need to talk," she said.

"Can I have a shower first?"

"No." There was a tension in Julie's posture that Dennis had never seen before, and it hit him suddenly that she knew. She knew of his affair with Barbara. His only option was to lie, lie, lie, and pray that she would believe him. He took a seat.

"I hear that Leslie Ng walked in on you and Barbara Meeks *fucking*," Julie said—spitting out the final word.

"We weren't *fucking*," said Dennis. "Not even close. Not even remotely."

"Do you want to explain what you *were* doing?"

"Sure. I'd knocked on her door to talk about how the girls were doing with the news about Dave Sommer, and she'd just come out of the shower, and she was reaching for something on her desk and I guess her towel slipped." Even as he delivered this speech, he felt its hollowness.

"So you're saying that Barbara invited you in wearing just a towel, and you closed the door *even after you saw she was nearly naked*?"

"Yeah. It probably wasn't a good idea to, to close the door, but I guess she thought the towel was secure, and I trusted, trusted her judgment—"

"Do you think I'm a fool?"

"No, no—"

"Do you think I'm stupid? Do you really think I'd believe that you closed the door and *innocently* closeted yourself with a naked girl who's just a little older than a teenager? Are you out of your mind?"

"No, I really, I really don't think you're being fair—"

"Because I'm not stupid, Dennis! I'm not stupid when it comes to male fantasies. I've been wondering why you were so eager to do such regular rounds of the house this year"—she put air quotes around *rounds*—"and here's my answer: you've been having it off with my residential don. You've been fucking the little bitch gymnast who's supposed to make *my* life easier!"

"I have not—" Dennis began, but at that moment Audrey, their older daughter, came into the room. "Mommy, why are you shouting?" she asked, looking from parent to parent with a vulnerability that suddenly made Dennis's heart bleed. *How could I have done this? How could I have jeopardised my family life?*

"Mommy's angry with your dad," said Julie. "Now, I want you to go back into the family room and close the door. Everything will be all right, but Mommy and Dad need to settle some things and we can't do it with you here."

Chelsea, their five-year-old, was behind her sister. "Mommy, please don't be angry. Please don't shout at Daddy."

"I'll try not to shout, my darlings," said Julie, "but I'm very angry and I need to get some things off my chest. So please go back into the family room and close the door. Go on. Dennis, support me here!"

"Yes, girls, please go back—" Dennis began, but at that moment Audrey began to cry, hard, and an instant later Chelsea was crying, too.

Julie looked at him with loathing. "I'll deal with them," she said. "Go pack a suitcase. You're not staying here. Get a hotel room or stay with your parents. And you can take your little whore with you, for all I care."

"You can't just order me out!" said Dennis.

"Yes, I can," said Julie. "I'm the head of house, and I say that your presence is disruptive to the health and safety of the residence. You need to go. Now. Pack your bags!"

★

Outside, in the hall, several girls heard the raised voices, and could make out enough to know what was happening. In a matter of moments, everyone knew.

Angus's parents, Arthur and Jane, arrived at Ingram House from Ottawa exactly on time. Angus had remained at the residence waiting for them, though Luke had come over at 5:20 p.m. and offered to escort him to and from dinner in the dining hall. "No, I'd better make sure I'm here when they show up," Angus had said. "We'll get something to eat in Kingston." The head of house, David Waters, had been looking out his study window every few minutes to see whether there were any cars in the circular driveway next to the residence; when he saw the Graveses pull in, he made his way through his apartment and out through his study to meet them.

"Hi, Mom. Hi, Dad," said Angus, hugging his parents as they came into his room. His belongings were all packed, and most of his gear was already standing by the residence's front door so that it could be loaded easily into the car. Chaplain Luke stood awkwardly by the desk, waiting to lend a hand in moving the two remaining items: the computer and a small stereo. Pablo, Angus's roommate, had already said his good-byes—and there had been several other farewells in the previous half-hour. Angus was not wildly popular, but he had a few close friends, and two had skipped their practices to spend some time with him. It was by his request that they had left, fearful that he would weep when his parents arrived and he left the campus for the last time.

"Hello, son," said his dad, hugging him close. "I am so angry about this. So sad for you." Angus's mother could not speak.

David Waters spoke up from the door. "We're sad too," he said. "Your son is a fine young man."

"If you really thought that," said Arthur Graves, rounding on David, "you'd have defended him like a father, instead of joining the inquisition! We trusted you, Mr. Waters. We trusted you to look after our son. And you betrayed our trust!"

"Dad—" Angus began.

"No, I'm really angry," said Arthur. "*Really* angry. I don't want to see or hear anyone who treated my son like dirt." At that instant, Paul Makepeace showed up at the door, just behind David. "I don't want to see you either, Paul," Arthur said. "You were great last spring, but your behaviour in the past couple of days just disgusts me. It nauseates me. We sent our son here in good faith, and you have let us down in every way possible!"

"Mr. Graves," Luke said, "we understand—"

"No, you don't, chaplain," said Arthur. "And maybe I should be most angry with you. You call yourself a man of God, and yet you've done the Devil's work here, making my son's life unbearable—accusing him of things he hasn't done and would never do."

Luke, Paul and David saw there was no way of assuaging Arthur Graves's anger. Luke briefly laid his hand on Angus's shoulder, squeezed it, nodded to Mrs. Graves, and left, pausing to allow David and Paul to precede him. "Please join me in my apartment," David said quietly, so Luke and Paul changed course and followed him, leaving the Graveses alone to take their leave of the room and the residence.

"Can I offer either of you a whiskey?" said David, as he closed the door of his study on the residence. His hand was shaking a little.

IT WAS A four-minute minute drive from St. Cuthbert's to the Bath Tim Hortons. Jiao would sometimes walk there, but this evening she had to be back at the house by 7:20 P.M. to start settling the girls down so they would be ready for study period. Driving gave her time to whip into the restaurant, line up, place her order, and get back comfortably by 7:15. She didn't believe in using the drive-through: too much unnecessary exhaust pumped into the air.

Jiao and her family had come to Canada from Hong Kong when she was just a few months old. They had never returned, not even for a holiday. Her father had been a police officer, and he'd run afoul of one of the gangs that dominated the drug business on the island. A package containing a cardboard triangle covered in red paint had arrived at the family home, and Jiao's dad had decided that Toronto would be a safer place to raise his children. He and his wife, Nuo, had taught Jiao and her brother a robust respect for the law, and as a teenager Jiao had briefly considered a career in policing.

The Timmies' parking lot was almost full, but Jiao found a spot, parked her Honda fluidly, and made her way inside, holding the door open for an elderly gentleman exiting with a coffee in each hand. There were several Bath teenagers in the line ahead of her, joshing and kibbitzing with each other, and Jiao found herself grateful that there weren't any St. Cuthbert's kids there, too. She loved her young charges, but it was good to be somewhere she wasn't immediately recognized and greeted. Anonymity was welcome sometimes—especially when she had something important to think through. Her Timmies' order required little thought: green tea and a bran muffin.

But if Jiao had been raised to respect the law, she'd also had an experience that lent another dimension to her perspective. At the age of sixteen she'd attended a party at the home of another grade eleven student, and she'd had too much to drink. Gauging her condition, the hostess had taken her upstairs to her own bedroom and told her to sleep it off while the party went on downstairs. Jiao had fallen asleep quickly, but she'd woken up some time later to find that two older boys were in the process of undressing her.

She had tried to resist, but she was drunk and they were older and much stronger. They'd both interfered with her, and one of them had eventually penetrated her. He'd put his hand over her mouth to prevent her from screaming. The other boy had wanted to rape her too, but he couldn't sustain an erection. They'd left her only after she threw up on herself and on the bed-clothes.

Jiao had wanted to take action: she'd been clear in her own mind that she was not at fault; but the lawyer she'd consulted courtesy of the Kingston Rape Crisis Centre told her, with sympathy and regret, that she faced a number of challenges. First, she'd showered and douched when she'd got home, so the physical evidence of the assault had been washed away. Secondly, she'd been drunk, and this tended to complicate things if the trial went to a jury. And third, and most seriously, she couldn't confidently identify the two young men who had assaulted her. Getting a conviction, the lawyer said, would be very difficult.

Jiao placed her order, paid with her debit card, collected her green tea and bran muffin, and headed back to her car. There was a slight chill in the air.

MARCUS'S MOTHER SIMONE Bolduc parked in the lot next to the health centre. It had been a long drive from Quebec's Eastern Townships, and she felt tired and grungy from the road. Her husband was in New York on business and hadn't been able to get away, and this summons from the school was ill-timed for her. It had kept her from attending her dancercise class that evening, and if Marcus's illness—if he really was ill—proved to be prolonged, it might prevent her from going on a spa weekend in Montreal with her girlfriends (some of whom had to work during the week). Surely Marcus could have taken the bus? It's not as though he'd broken his leg or was in traction.

The head nurse, Martha Ellis, greeted her: she, too, looked tired, but that didn't impress Simone. School staff were paid to look after students. Anxiety attacks were easy to deal with: you gave them an Ativan or whatever, and everything was much better ten minutes later.

"Could we have a little talk before I take you in to see Marcus?" asked Martha. Not waiting for an answer, she turned and walked into her tiny office, clearly expecting that Simone would follow her. So rude.

"I have a question before you begin," said Simone, taking charge of the situation. "Why couldn't you treat this little problem here? Panic attacks have been around since the beginning of time."

Martha looked at her strangely. "I'm not known for coddling students," she replied. "Some of my patients call me the Dragon Lady, and I take pride in the nickname."

"Oh, well," Simone began, prepared with a comeback that showed she couldn't give two hoots what nicknames students gave this woman—

"But your son has had a traumatic experience," said Martha. "He feels some sense of responsibility for the death of his friend. He feels he should have done something. I don't think that's a rational response, but it's a real one. He needs the kind of TLC that only a mother can provide, at least for a few days." If there was any irony in her tone, it was not easily detectable.

"Oh," said Simone, briefly derailed.

"He's been crying, off and on, through the day," Martha added. "And he's shaking. And I haven't been able to get any solid food in him, so I've been giving him Ensure milkshakes. Are you able to buy them in Quebec?"

"I don't know."

"They're probably available in your drugstores, but just in case not, I'll send a half-dozen along with you. He needs to be anywhere other than here."

"Hasn't this murder been solved yet? It can't possibly take that long with modern forensics and things."

"I don't know," said Martha. "That's not my business. My business is to deal with the sick. And your son is sick. I'll take you to Marcus now." She got up and bustled out of her office.

Simone followed, realizing, in some part of herself, that she'd just been handled and out-manoeuvred by a high school nurse. *So* irritating.

Marcus was sleeping when his mother and the nurse entered the room. In the moment before he woke, his face looking like the young boy he had been before he first went off to boarding school years before, Simone felt a small movement in her chest. It was, perhaps, a metaphorical movement, but it was enough that she took a real step forward, leaned down, and kissed her son's forehead, eliciting a grunt of approval from the Dragon Lady who had stepped off to the side.

Marcus's eyes fluttered open at the touch: "Mom!" he said.

Barbara had not attended lunch or dinner. She had gone straight from Ben's home to her room in Scott House. There had been plenty of activity in the halls, but no one had knocked on her door, and she'd locked it to keep the cleaner out. The head-master's secretary had called her twice, and the chaplain three times, but she hadn't answered. She'd cried into her pillow, slept fitfully, even tried meditating in an effort to derail her thoughts. Nothing had helped. Her situation looked bad from every angle.

What she dreaded most, of course, was an altercation with Julie Murdoch. She liked Julie. She respected her. *What the hell was I thinking, fooling around with Dennis? Sure, it was fun... but I've had more dynamic lovers before. Perhaps the first time it was simply the challenge, landing a married man... but then his* gratitude. *God, he had been so grateful.* She had felt worshipped—as though he hadn't seen a naked woman for years, let alone been allowed to touch one. *What happens in a marriage that a wife just stops making love with her husband? Is it a power-play? Resentment? Fatigue? Couldn't she orgasm with him? Did Julie have someone on the side?*

She was lying on her bed, brooding over these things, when she heard a small noise from the direction of the door. She propped herself up, looked behind her, and spotted an envelope on the floor. She got up, picked it up, saw that there was no name on the front, opened it. *Pack your bags and leave tonight,* it read in Julie's handwriting. *Send your resignation by email. You betrayed my trust. I don't want to see you again.*

Barbara flinched, closed her eyes for a moment, then pulled out her suitcase from under the bed.

As Jiao headed down the hall toward Bonita and Krista's room, she felt a weight on her shoulders she could not shrug off. These were *her* girls: it's not that she knew the two of them very well, but she felt like a big sister toward them even so. And they were *good* girls. Bonita was a sweetheart—warm, innocent, vulnerable. Krista was strong—strong physically, yes, but, more importantly, strong morally. A young woman you could trust. A young woman who would stand by you. A young woman who would *defend* you. And Dave Sommer? He was a malicious psychopath: cruel, violent, rapacious. But. But. She had a duty before the law, did she not? Murder was murder. She could not allow herself to become an accessory to that. She knocked on the door, and entered without waiting for a reply.

Krista was sitting in her desk chair, but it was spun around so she faced the door. Bonita was sitting on her bed, but she too faced the door. They were waiting for her, and *their* dread, Jiao reckoned, was far greater than hers. She hesitated briefly, then went and sat on Bonita's desk chair, facing the two of them. "Talk to me, Krista," she said.

"I don't know what to say," said Krista. "I simply meant to threaten him. I didn't mean to kill him. But I'm not sorry he's dead, Jiao: he was an awful person. He treated Bonita like shit. He treated any girl like shit. He literally made Angus Graves *eat* shit. I can't feel sorry about the fact that he's dead."

"I know that," said Jiao. "But…"

"There was *no-thing* good in him," said Bonita. "He wanted to *use* me like an old sock."

Jiao took this in, paused. "Have you told anyone else—either one of you?"

"Of course not," said Krista.

"Krista is angry with me for telling you," Bonita said.

"I'm not *angry*, Bonita. I just wish you had flushed the note away," said Krista. She sounded tired.

"Who knows about the knife?" Jiao asked.

"I think they found it this afternoon," said Krista.

"I washed it with bleach!" Bonita said.

"Yeah, they won't find any fingerprints on it," said Krista. "But they'll know it was the weapon that killed him."

"Can it be traced to you?" Jiao asked.

"No," said Krista firmly. "Even Bonita had never seen it before. I kept it wrapped up in a scarf in my bottom drawer.

"But your parents?"

"No," Krista said—again firmly. "It was a gift from my grandfather a few months before he died. My parents turned Quaker years ago, and they hate any kind of weapon. I've kept it hidden since he gave it to me."

There was a bottle of water between Bonita and Krista's beds. Jiao found herself staring at it.

"Krista," Jiao said. "I'm going to ask you one last time. Does anyone else—*anyone*—know that you owned that knife?"

"No one," said Krista. "No one in the world. My grandmother died years ago. My granddad and I were really close. He was in the British army. I want to join the Canadian army. He would have wanted that."

"Krista love her grandfather," said Bonita solemnly. "She talk about him all the time."

Jiao stared at her hands for a full minute, then stood up, and walked over to the bottle of water. "Does either one of you have a glass?"

Krista reached back to her desk and pulled one from the corner. "It's not clean," she said. "You're probably better off drinking out of the bottle."

"I'm not going to drink," Jiao said. She took the glass from Krista, put it on the bedside table, unscrewed the water bottle, and filled the glass to roughly three-quarters of its capacity. She then took Sommer's note from her pocket, unfolded it, held it up so both girls could see it—then dipped it into the glass. She swirled it around a few times, pulled it out a little, dipped it in again. The ink began to dissolve. She repeated the process several more times. The ink leached away, and the water became a little discoloured. She removed the paper, now very soggy, and scrunched it into a ball, wringing the water out into the glass. She handed the soggy paper to Bonita. "Flush it," she said.

"Now?" said Bonita.

"Now," said Jiao. "Stay and make sure it goes down. Flush twice to make absolutely sure."

Bonita got off the bed, took the soggy ball from Jiao, and scuttled out the door. Jiao and Krista sat in silence until she returned. "It's gone," Bonita said. "Thank you. Thank you so much. *Gracias, gracias.*"

"Yes, thank you," said Krista. "I don't know what else to say."

"Listen to me," said Jiao. "We take this secret to our graves—do you understand? I'm now in this just as deeply as you are. None of us can say anything."

"You can count on me," said Krista. "I want to be an officer."

"I will never tell!" said Bonita. "It would be a disgrace to me."

Jiao stood up, put her hand in front of her, palm down. After a moment's hesitation, Krista scrambled to her feet, moved forward, and put her hand on top of Jiao's. They both looked at Bonita. Bonita suddenly understood what they were doing. "It is a team thing!" she said. She joined them, placing her hand on top of Krista's. They then clasped hands.

"Yes," said Jiao. "It's a team thing. Now do your homework. And make sure you get to bed on time tonight."

"We will be good little *wirgins* all year!" said Bonita. Krista gave a startled laugh.

Luke arrived at the headmaster's office to find Dick and Jim already there. It was just two hours before the 3:00 p.m. funeral for Dave Sommer. The whole school, theoretically, would be attending. "Close the door and have a seat, Luke," said Jim.

"We've just had a meeting with Detective Stewart," said Dick. "She made all sorts of encouraging noises, but essentially they're no further ahead with their investigation. There were no prints on the knife."

"No prints," confirmed Jim, "and none of our parents has any connection with the British military. None. It's been several years since there was anyone here with that kind of background. And a police search of collectors' databases has found no trace of this particular weapon."

"So we've decided it was an outside job," said Dick. "Someone who came in off the highway."

"Is that what Diane says?" asked Luke, startled.

There was a pause. "No," said Jim. "That's what *we've* decided."

"I'm not sure I understand."

"We have a problem," Jim continued. "We're losing students. We're losing applicants. We are bleeding. We need to say something definitive—something that will staunch the flow."

"Okay," said Luke. "I get that."

"So we're going to say that the killer wasn't a member of the community and that the threat has gone. That the murder was arbitrary—it could have happened anywhere," said Jim. "We're going to hire a night watchman and put up some security cams. With time, with *time*, the memory of it will recede."

Dick leaned forward. "Even *if* it was someone in this community who did it, we figure that it was an action specific to

Sommer. We don't think there's some crazy person wandering the campus planning to kill people randomly." He leaned back again and made a fluttering upward movement with his arms to encompass a large geographic area.

"That certainly seems unlikely," said Luke cautiously.

"Exactly," said Jim. "No one else here is at risk. That's the message we'll be putting out."

"And Diane has agreed not to contradict that message," said Dick. "She's not going to announce that. She's not going to say that's the conclusion *she* has reached. But she won't say anything to challenge it."

"Okay," said Luke again. "And has this some bearing on the funeral?"

Dick shrugged. "Just a little," he said. "At some point, during your remarks, we'd like you to say something reassuring, something that resonates with that, with that *perspective*."

"We're not looking for an explicit statement," said Jim. "That's for me to worry about. But something that prepares the way. Something that lowers the temperature."

"We know that your voice is respected, Luke," said Dick. "We need you to help start a..." He fumbled for the right words.

"A healing process," said Jim.

"Yes, a healing process," said Dick.

DAVE SOMMER'S OAK casket was wheeled into the flower-filled chapel at 2:40, the Silvers, Steven and Ernie, presiding over the process. Six boys from Roper House, including Stephen Bradley, had been selected to serve as pall bearers, but the absence of steps meant they didn't have to carry the casket once they'd placed it on the church truck—a folding set of wheels. They fell in behind it, profoundly self-conscious in their movements. "Straight ahead, gentlemen, step smartly," said the senior Mr. Silver over his shoulder, as they all headed up the aisle to the casket's destination at the front.

The organist arrived a moment after the pallbearers were seated in the second row and began to play almost immediately. Students, and a few dons and teachers, started filing into the chapel five minutes later. The students were dressed in their "number ones," their dress uniforms; dons and teachers were dressed in their equivalents: dark suits for the men and subdued dresses for the women. For this rare ritual occasion, Luke had recruited a male grade twelve student to serve as crucifer and two female grade eleven students to serve as choristers. The days were long gone when the school could field a team of servers or a choir of singers well versed in Christian hymns: Nick, Elise, and Rachael had all been active in their home churches before coming to St. Cuthbert's. Their expertise, such as it was, had been learned elsewhere.

Mr. and Mrs. Sommer came into the narthex at 3:00 P.M., accompanied by a couple they'd identified to Luke as their son's honorary aunt and uncle. The four of them were met at the inner chapel door by Jim and Glenda Harvey, and the six went in together and headed for the front pew. As soon as they came in, the whole school rose as a mark of respect. Mr. and Mrs. Sommer both touched the casket, which remained closed, before sitting down. Jim Harvey was the last of the party to sit; once he was seated, the rest of the congregation sat also.

Of course, neither Marcus Bolduc nor Angus Graves was present, but Krista and Bonita had, at Jiao's urging, decided to attend. ("We shouldn't draw attention to ourselves in any way," Jiao had advised.) They sat near the back, with the rest of Wilcox House. Krista gave Bonita's hand a discreet squeeze just before the service began. Detective-Sergeant Diane Stewart was also there, though her colleague, Callum Brezicki, was not.

The crucifer, followed by Luke and the choristers, advanced to the front of the chapel a moment after everyone sat down. This was a reversal of the usual order of things, but it was what the Sommers had requested. While uneasy about the symbolism, Luke had acquiesced.

Luke briefly welcomed the congregation and expressed the school's sorrow to the deceased's parents. The choristers sang "Great Is Thy Faithfulness," and then Leopold Sommer rose to speak.

He was not a particularly big man, Mr. Sommer, and he did-n't have a big voice, but he, like his son, was wiry and fluid in his movements, and the physical similarities between them com-manded the attention of everyone sitting in the pews. "My son," he began, "was a good boy. He was true to the values we taught him. I'm confident that he would have had a great career in busi-ness or the law."

"My wife and I taught him to work hard and respect his elders. One of the teachers at his previous school told us that he was the most chivalrous—"

At that moment, unfortunately, a grade nine student, Daphne Morrows, cried out, bent over, and vomited extrava-gantly against the back of the pew in front of her. For a few moments, while the head nurse and another nurse ministered to her, then spirited her out of the chapel and back to the health centre, Mr. Sommer felt compelled to cease speaking and take his seat. When he resumed, it was as though a kind of spell had been broken: people still listened, quietly enough, to what he had to say, but the silence was no longer as respectful as it had been before. One could sense, Paul Makepeace said later, a "certain cynicism." One could feel the eyes roll.

Another hymn by the choristers followed Mr. Sommer's remarks, then Luke stepped forward to speak. He was keenly aware of the changed mood in the congregation, and keenly aware of the pungent smell of vomit that now permeated the chapel. "I will be brief," he said.

"Dave Sommer made some good friends at this school: friends who appreciated his sense of adventure, his athletic prowess, and his interest in engaging with the wider community. I'm sure his parents will forgive me for saying that he was not without flaws—because we are *all* flawed—but he was, and is, a child of God, and it is sad beyond words that he will not have the chance to become the man he aspired to be."

There was more of this kind, and Luke managed to work in a couple of brief anecdotes he had gleaned from the boys in Roper House—thin things in themselves, but, properly massaged and embellished, hinting that Dave Sommer could, at times, be reasonably convivial. Luke felt that the vows he had made as a priest constrained him from lying, but that his pastoral obligations compelled him to put the best possible spin on Sommer's life. It was a balancing act.

He approached the final part of his eulogy with some apprehension. He knew it would not fully satisfy Jim Harvey and Dick Cargill, but he could not bring himself to go as far as they clearly wished him to go.

"We cannot be absolutely sure who is responsible for Dave's death," he said. "There are some signs, certainly, that the perpetrator could be from outside our own community. We just don't know. I can, with confidence, say two things: first, that the police never give up on a murder case, and I have great faith in the investigative powers of Detective-Sergeants Stewart and Brezicki; and second, that I do not myself fear that the killer will strike again in this community. I will not hesitate to take nightly walks around this campus."

"And there is a third thing I can say with equal confidence. Dave Sommer is with God, his heavenly Father. His parents will see him again at the Resurrection. That is the essence of our Lord's teaching: that Love redeems us all."

A little more pomp and ceremony followed: a reading, a final hymn, a procession out of the chapel, the family following the casket which would be lifted back into the hearse and driven out to Cataraqui Cemetery. Luke's work was not quite done: there would be a small gathering graveside, and then Glenda Harvey would host a quiet reception in her home.

Detective-Sergeant Stewart had slipped out before the final hymn, and she stood in the warm autumn sun watching students and staff exit the chapel, some of the kids already talking in loud, excited voices, unable to sustain the false solemnity that had been required of them during the service. She herself felt sure that the perpetrator was among those she was watching now—some of whom looked at her with curiosity, but most of whom were as oblivious of her as they were, in this instant, of their own mortality. She took in the swagger of some of the older boys, the strength in their limbs, the potential for violence coiled in their muscles.

Her eyes alighted briefly on three attractive young women walking close together; one in a black dress, the others in student uniforms. The two younger ones were talking quietly with each other; the one in the black dress met her glance and gave her a wan smile. Diane felt a tiny shiver of desire: she was faithful to her partner, but her fidelity did not keep her from admiring another beautiful woman. Her eyes moved on swiftly, however. She was looking for a leer of psychopathic satisfaction—or, more likely perhaps, someone who could not look at *her*, who refused to meet her gaze. She mentally paged through a brief chapter in one of her police college texts: "Signs of acute stress."

She was aware, suddenly, that a slight middle-aged woman was standing at her elbow also watching the students streaming out of the chapel. "You're a police officer, aren't you?" she said.

"Yes, I am," said Diane. "Are you on staff here?"

"Well, not one of the teachers," said the woman. "I'm just a cleaning lady." She laughed. "I look after two of the girls' houses. Clean them both, top to bottom, every weekday."

"I imagine that keeps you busy," said Diane, still carefully monitoring the young people exiting the chapel.

"Oh, yes, it does. It certainly does," said the woman. "My name is Doris."

"Nice to meet you, Doris," said Diane. "I'm Diane."

"Yes, I clean Wilcox House in the morning, and Gallagher House in the afternoon."

"Those are big houses to clean every day," said Diane politely.

"Oh, yes, they are. Big houses. Lots of girls. But you get to know them. You really do," said Doris. "And some of them tell you things they don't even tell their own parents."

"Do they?" said Diane. "Actually, that doesn't surprise me when I think about it. After all, they spend more time here than they do at home." She glanced down at Doris, who was a good six inches shorter than she was, and smiled.

"Oh, yes," said Doris. "We cleaning ladies hear things. We hear a lot of things. You'd be surprised."

Diane glanced down at Doris again, then looked back at the students. Then looked at Doris again, more intently. "Could I buy you a cup of coffee?"

ACKNOWLEDGEMENTS & THANKS

I am indebted to the following people who read an early draft of the manuscript, and who gave me some formidably helpful notes: Leona Dobbie, Anna Heffernan, Drew Gilmour, Grant Tucker, Dan Taylor, Charlotte Jacklein, Peter Gould, Jane Beharriell, Sylvia Sutherland and Steven Silver.

It's worth noting that five of these are former students of mine: their willingness to help was a very special gift to their old teacher. I am equally grateful to the other five, however, who brought their own special expertise to the table.

I am also grateful to an even larger group of former students (and a few colleagues) whose emails and messages provided me with insight into private school rituals and relationships:

Jennifer Tough, Michelle Tremblay, Kathleen Killen, Brigid McGrath, Dave Clark, Janine Steyn, Lindsay Rebecca, Ashley Eaton, Hayden Curtin, Rachael Larose, Tess Kelsey, Corby Peterson, Iain Hill, Kylie Clark, Todd Pinckard, Jacqueline Johnson-Coughlin, Stephanie Rentel, Stephane Gervais-Harreman, Evan Hadfield, Isaac Bryan Brown, Matt Switocz, Luke O'Regan, Troy Shootah, Lynn Arsenault, Andrew Sparling, Max Binnie, Graham Angus, Pete Grose, Meaghan Brown, Patricia Gab, Pat Doran, Nick Pullen, Eric Malcolmson, Carolyn Marrelli-Dill, Rob Mitchell, Brett Leach, Henry Cundill and Rachael Mason.

Some of the things these people told me brought me to tears; some astonished me; some made me laugh. A few of their stories are reflected in this novel, but all added colour and texture to the narrative and have provided me with enough material for the next six books in the series.

I salute my publisher, Chris Needham, for his faith in another Mason novel, and my wise and diligent editor, Heather Sangster.